The New World
A New Life

Clothed in deer skin,
Skinner Benet was a figure of awe and fear—
a man carved and chiseled from
the flesh and stone of Canada.

Chained within the iron of indentured servitude
to Skinner Benet, Abbott was a boyish wisp
of hope and strength. He was savagely
tutored and mastered by Benet,
yet, while other men died, Abbott,
by the hand and wisdom of Benet, survived.

Eagle Fur

is a magnificent novel—
rugged and big as Canada, and intimate
as the bond between a boy and a man.
They met as master and servant, lived and fought
as warriors, and said good-bye as
father and son.

EAGLE FUR

ROBERT NEWTON PECK

AVON
PUBLISHERS OF BARD, CAMELOT AND DISCUS BOOKS

AVON BOOKS
a division of
The Hearst Corporation
959 Eighth Avenue
New York, New York 10019

First Avon Printing, July, 1979

AVON TRADEMARK REG. U.S. PAT. OFF. AND IN
OTHER COUNTRIES, MARCA REGISTRADA,
HECHO EN U.S.A.

Printed in the U.S.A.

to Sweedoo

HER BELLY, *torn and scarred, lay in icy water; her nose grinding into gravel, her ribs snapped in the hurdling of fallen timbers, her hide ripped by rocks and rapids . . . yet laden with her cargo of song and fur and fortitude, she dared to conquer a northern empire from sea to sea, centuries before the iron horse or a covered wagon.*

A toast, to the bark canoe.

ONE BRAVE MAN.

He is all I need, I told myself, for a trek in a birchbark canoe through Canada. A man as tough as a *voyageur*, who can paddle into a billion insects that sting with fury, endure backbreaking portages along with days and nights of being wet and cold, and not drown in icy water so swift and so angry that it can smash his bones on logs and stone.

Then I found my partner, Austin Bentley.

He is neither husky nor heighty. Fair enough, as courage is not measured in muscle or pounds but rather in bowels and brains. Austin is a schoolteacher with a soft voice and a beard. His students respect him and so do I. His leatherwork is artistic and sturdy. This man, I then decided, could patch a torn canoe.

Together we mapped this book and shaped the curve of her hull and whittled her paddle.

—R.N.P.

Chapter 1

"BULL HIM DOWN."

I kicked, trying to free myself, but my struggling served me little good. The two other men were husky. Strong fingers locked into my hair, forcing my spine to knife as my face bent downward, until the deadly cold of the blacksmith's anvil knuckled into my cheek. I could smell the heat of the red iron. One final clanking blow of the smith's hammer and the collar was ready for my throat. This shackle would be mine to wear for five years.

"Best you wet his neck."

A bucket of icy water dumped on my head, without ceremony and with little mirth, as the blacksmith had ordered.

"That's so this here collar don't scorch the hide off that lily-white neck of yours, boy," said the blacksmith.

An angry hiss of hot iron made me flinch as I heard the smith dunk my collar, an open C, into the water of his temper tub. Since my face and head were water-soaked, the three men would take little note of my weeping. As the hot rod of metal slid under my neck, I shuddered out a scream that was half pain and half panic. The stink of the hot iron cut into my nose.

"Easy now, boy."

The deep notes of the blacksmith's voice rang with confidence, as if to say that, with tongs in each hand, he had fused many a collar about the neck of many a bondservant, and to tell me that he'd purpose me little hurt.

"Steady, my lad, while I marry these ends, butt to butt. Don't fret it, boy. Like a woman bearing a baby, this here's a onetime agony and it's soon forgot."

Hot pain screamed about my neck, as again I tried to twist and kick but with no success. More icy water, please . . . please . . . and then my silent wish was granted. The great tongs plunged my iron into the cooling tub as though the collar were naught but an empty ring. Fighting for breath, my face in the foul brown water with the tarty taste and the smell of horses, I was both scalded and frozen in the snap of a finger.

At last their fists yanked up my hair.

"There you be, boy," said the big smith, his moon face burned red from years of forging, "a wee hot around the collar for a day, but you're sound."

Swallowing my pain, I could say nothing. Advancing toward me a step closer, as his two helpers turned me loose, the blacksmith squinted as his massive hand turned the collar about my neck. His ability to read the lettering surprised me.

"A. Coe," the smith read slowly, "property of S. Benet of Hudson's Bay Company."

"Only for five years," I managed to say through my tortured throat.

"And then what?"

"Then I am Abbott Coe, a free citizen to go south to New France or New England, or stay here in Canada . . . wherever I wish to homestead."

"Well spoke." The big fist of the blacksmith thudded down upon my right shoulder as weighty as a thunderclap. His round face gave me a grin. "Don't let this iron be a collar to your spirit. Many a soul's come to Canada sporting iron on his neck. Or *her* neck. And to the south, away down in Virginny and Carolina and like locations, I hear some of them servants is slaves and black as Africa. Best you count your blessings."

One of the men snorted. "Five years with Benet for a master is five lifetimes."

"Who is S. Benet?" I asked, knowing only that my bond stated that I must serve S. Benet of the Hudson's Bay Company to pay for my ocean passage.

"He's the *bourgeois* here at Fort Albany. The big boss man, or so he lets folks think."

"For five years"—I tried to sound older than my sixteen years—"I could oblige even Satan."

12

"Ha!" laughed the smith. "And that's what the *S* of S. Benet stands for. Ha, ha, ha!" Again his fist was heavy upon my shoulder, yet his intent was not to cause me discomfort of body. Only of mind.

"You met the man yet?" asked his helper.

"No, sir. Only today did the ship *Costain* weight anchor and I was brought here by seamen under orders to be collared."

"I know, boy. And we got our fun from the business, like always. Hot iron and cold water is all parts of your welcome. Canada is one big land, with a future just as meaty, and you ain't the first or the last to wear iron and work off your passage. And you sure ain't the first to sweat for S. Benet."

"What does the *S* really stand for?"

"Skinner. That's what we call him."

"How do I address him?"

"*Mister* Benet, seeing as you're British lad. All the *voyageurs* call him *Monsieur* Benet. And what the redhide injun and the stinking eskimo call him would blush a harlot. Ha!"

"Until now," I said, "I thought his name was Bennett."

"No indeed. Benet's a Frenchie, so you say his name like Ben with an *A* after it. Ben *A,* simple as pudding. You don't say the *T.*"

"Thank you, sir." My hand shifted the hot collar around my neck. "Will it leave a scar?"

The blacksmith nodded. "She surely will. You'll tote a black gullet, boy, for all eternal and right to your grave, even if you live to spit at a hundred." His big hand rubbed some water on my neck. "Aye, you'll be as ring-necked as a pheasant."

"I hate it," I said, my fingers foolishly yanking at the warm metal as if they thought to rip it from my throat.

"So do I," said the blacksmith. "I don't cotton to bondserving whites and slaving blacks. But you owe Benet a debt, lad. And a debt's to be honored. You agree?"

"I do agree."

He held out his big hand. "Abbott Coe, my name is John Howland and I welcome you to Canada." His handshake was as hardy as his tongs. The other men were Israel

Stoddard and Pierre Varmette, the latter a Frenchman. We shook hands.

"What language is spoken here, sir?"

The big hand scratched gray hair. "Well, it don't matter a whole lot. Some folks like myself and Israel here are English, so we speak the mother tongue. I can *parlez-vous* a bit of French and Pierre does right well on English and Huron."

"How about Benet?"

"Benet speaks French and English and injun. Some say he can talk Eskimo, too. I don't guess it'd surprise me much if Skinner Benet died and sunk to Hades and taught a few naughty words to Old Harry Lucifer."

John Howland wiped the midday sweat from his round and red face. His hands came for my throat, but only to tug my collar to inspect the welding.

"Will it come off?" I asked, hoping that it would.

"In five years, boy. If you're still alive. Providing you don't freeze to death in winter, or get your person bit to death by summer bugs, or fall through the muskeg and drown. Or die with an eskimo lance hrough your gizzard or a Cree arrow in your craw. Maybe make the mistake of calling some Frenchie a Britisher, or the other way around. Or hang yourself because you went snow crazy."

"I'll be alive, sir."

"Hope so. Where's your folks?"

"Dead. I am orphaned."

"An orphan. Then how do you know they're dead?"

"I don't," I told John Howland.

"You sound like you make the best of things."

"I try to," I said.

"Best you do. Canada's beautiful, yet she can be brutal as sin. Skinner Benet is one tough biscuit, but I wager you can learn more from that man in one voyage than you can sop up from a whole schoolhouse full of books."

"But you dislike Mister Benet."

Howland's eyes narrowed. "Who said?"

"No one. I can tell."

"Life is short in Canada for folks who can't bobbin their own loom, my lad. You set one man against another and you may find thyself 'twixt the twain. Understand?"

"Yes. I am sorry, Mister Howland."

"You can call me John. I ain't fancy."

"Thank you, John."

"I have work to do. Israel, did La Tour ever bring his stallion like he said he would?"

"Yes," said Stoddard. "He's here now."

"Dang that beast. There's only two animals on earth that really gripe me in the bowels, and that be injuns and stallions. Fetch me a twitch."

Pierre located a rod of dark wood, no longer than a man's arm, at one end of which was a small loop of what appeared to be woven root or vine. At the large open door, a man in black finery appeared on foot, leading a gray-dapple stallion. The animal's ears were back, and I also took notice of his mouth, which was grinding to and fro, baring teeth like a pair of sawblades.

"I hate a dang stallion," muttered the smith. "Truth be known, I would sooner try to tack iron on the paws of a panther. You can trust a studhorse about as much as you can trust an injun that's full on rum."

La Tour, the horse's owner, smiled at the blacksmith. "Monsieur, I will tell Seecoya that you say that." His smile seemed to enjoy little humor. I also noticed that La Tour spoke English very well, but with a slight French accent.

"Ha! You do that, Mister La Tour. You do that. And I hope you meet up with Seecoya some dark night out yonder in the wild and thorny."

"I would climb the tree," said La Tour.

"Yes, and old Seecoya would chaw it down like a beaver and gobble you for his supper and that cussed stallion of yours for his breakfast."

"Who is *he?*" La Tour nodded at me.

"Tell the man, Coe," said John Howland.

"I am Abbott Coe, sir."

"Fresh off the boat. Off the *Costain,*" added John.

I saw La Tour's eyes cool as he saw the collar about my neck, his chin slightly lifting as if he had no need to acquaint himself with someone as lowly as a bondservant. Turning to John Howland, La Tour said only one word as he adjusted the lace at his wrists: "Whose?"

"Skinner Benet's."

La Tour muttered a French phrase that I did not comprehend. Only Pierre seemed to understand. La Tour's mouth appeared as though he wished to spit and could locate no land or receptacle worthy of his saliva. Instead, he spoke to his stallion: "Stand still, Charlemagne."

"Slip that noose over his nose and twist the stick," ordered the blacksmith to his English helper, "until this son of a she-bear is drawed up so tight in the face that he can't even wink an eye at a runny mare."

"*Non!*" said La Tour.

John Howland's fists rested on his own hips. "No? Well then, *you* can shod his hunk of sled-dog meat you call a studhorse and get your own little French ass bit . . . all by your sweet lonesome."

"My big Charlemagne is not used to the loop."

"Ain't that nice. And you can tell that plowpuller that my backside still recollects his fangs and my shinbone still smarts from his hoof. You tell him."

"I tell," said La Tour. "Charlemagne, this English smith is afraid of you, *n'est-ce pas?* He is the coward."

Listening to their talk, I wondered how well John Howland and all his mass would take to being called a coward by a Frenchman who was half his size. I had little time to be curious as John's reply was prompt.

"A coward? La Tour, right now I admit to it. By my count, there's a narrow line betwixt cowardice and good sense. A man is a fool to get his nog split open and his brains mashed just to show how tomfool brave he can be around a heavy hoof."

"Aye," said Stoddard.

"Monsieur," said La Tour, "if you were not the *only* blacksmith at Fort Albany, I would take my Charlemagne to the other."

John Howland quietly nodded his gray woolly head. "So be it then. No twitch, no reset of his shoes."

La Tour's face darkened. He held out his hands and shrugged his shoulders to say to no one in particular that he was somehow at the helpless mercy of a situation. Fate had somehow cuffed his cheek with an unjust glove, as though to urge his decision on whether he should submit to superstitious English peasantry.

"I remind you, Howland, that you work for us."

"That I do. I hired on eighteen years back, to smith for the Hudson's Bay Company, and I'm still at it."

"And *I* am an owner."

"Well be. And *I* am still on my feet because I got some sense kicked into me. There is no way that I can work a shoe on that animal unless his velvet snugs a twitch, *and* one of my helpers heft up one of his feet. With two feet lifted, no horse I ever knew will dance too gay a jig."

"Like a master's violin," said La Tour, his soft-looking hand stroking the gray of Charlemagne's nose, "my stallion is highly strung. A thoroughbred, something you Saxons know little about."

The beefy blacksmith was slow to boil. Rightly so, as his size would inflict considerable discomfort upon such a puny adversary as La Tour in his fine clothes and delicate lace. "True enough," said Howland, "but I know studs, and in particular, I intend to swallow no harm from this here ornery son-of-a-bear you call a horse."

"Charlemagne's grandsire was once ridden in the boar-hunt by the King of France. *Le roi!*"

"Aye, and I'd wager his old grandsire took a chunk out of the king's royal rump, which don't mean Charlie Mane here is allowed to nibble at mine."

"*C'est vrai,*" said Pierre Varmette with an agreeable nod of his head, which wore a black and brimless hat. It was plain to see that Varmette's loyalty lay not with his haughty countryman.

With an upward tilt of his chin, La Tour started to lead Charlemagne away, but only executed a narrow circle in the brown dirt outside the smith's open door. Once again he stopped. "I reconsidered."

"How noble of you, Monsieur." Howland bowed.

"But *I* hold the twitch," said La Tour.

"Hell you will. La Tour, the only thing you can hold is your water. Or hold your doggone tongue so's a man can have at his living and warrant his bread. You're worse than some old squaw who never opens up her mouth that a complaint don't pop out. You must of drove them people in Paris all crazy. One of *my* men will handle the twitch."

"You do not *trust* me?"

"Sure I do. My helper, Varmette, being an exception, I trust a Frenchie like you as much as I'd trust an injun barber who's fixing to drag a new razor along my neck."

In spite of the collar around my throat that was still warm, and my flesh feeling as if it were yet afire, I was starting to like Canada. A land that could spawn a man like John Howland was a land with a future merry and fair. My mouth, all on its own as if to answer to the genuine amusement of my ribs, stretched into a smile.

La Tour did not laugh. Instead, he pointed at me, white lace spilling from his black sleeve, and scowled. "I tell Benet," he spat at me, "that I am insulted by a serf."

"My, my, my," sighed Howland, "between your telling Seecoya on me and then to tattle on young freshy to Benet, you're going to be one busy old hen."

"*Assez!*"

"Aye," said Howland. "Enough is enough."

"Do my horse," said La Tour.

"Do . . . my . . . wash," Howland answered.

"Monsieur, if this were France, you would be punished. You would be . . ." La Tour stamped his boot.

"Well, it ain't," said the big blacksmith. "In fact, to my ear, it ain't even to be *New* France. This be Canada, and here on the bonnie shores of Hudson's Bay, you and me and everybody else is about to play a whole different game of skittles."

"I am nobility," said La Tour in nearly a shout. "And what . . . what are *you?*"

"Me? Just the only smith in town."

As his big hand gently rested his fullering iron with a whisper of a clank among the rows of its sister tools, all was quiet, until my hands started to clap, one against the other. I stood at the anvil where my neck had just been banded by a five-year shackle and applauded the man who had fit the iron.

"Fools!" spat La Tour. Throwing the stallion's halter rope to Israel Stoddard, the Frenchman turned abruptly to march away in a brisk and flouncy step.

As he patted the stallion, John Howland smiled.

"Will you be punished?" I asked him.

"Aye," he said as he gently applied the twitch, "I shall be punished, but only when I die and be judged by Jehovah."

"Good," I said.

"And, far as I know, it ain't been established for certain that God is French."

Once again, John Howland ragged his wide wet face. Sliding the wooden lid halfway off a barrel, his hand dropped a gourd and brought it up abrim with water. Raising the yellow dipper to his mouth, he paused, looking down Fort Albany's main street of log structures as though his attention had suddenly abandoned his watery thirst.

"I'll be hogtied," he whispered.

Israel Stoddard, Pierre Varmette, and I rushed to follow the line of his arm as John Howland pointed. What we all then saw were four men on horseback, all holding ropes that led to the neck of a most strange animal. A cow? From its monstrous head sprouted a pair of black horns that curved upward, each in a quarter circle. The front half of its body wore a blanket of heavy blackish-brown fur, its hindquarters lighter and less hairy. It was shedding. Also it was, upon occasion, fighting the four ropes held by the four riders that boxed the beast. The animal appeared exhausted, breathing heavily, seeming to be saving its strength for a sudden lunge that would unseat the quartet of riders and possibly pull down their mounts.

I asked, "What is that animal?"

"My lad," said John Howland, "that's a buffalo."

"A buffalo."

"For sure and certain. Some folks here at Fort Albany call it a bison."

"What do you call it?"

"I'd call him trouble. But if'n I was you, I just might run out into the mud and introduce yourself to that big cuss, on account you and that buffalo has got common interest."

"How so?"

"You and that buffalo both belong to Skinner Benet."

I was curious. "What does Mister Benet plan to do with a buffalo?"

John Howland squinted one eye as he looked at me, as if to announce that his answer was a statement in which he himself held little belief.

"Ride him."

19

Chapter 2

"DOES IT BITE?"

I asked the question half in jest, and the man who stood beside me gave a half grin. Other men laughed, telling me that my question was indeed the sort of inquiry that a greenhorn would make. Several indian women pointed at me and muttered jokes among themselves. I found them to be of excess weight and slightly more attractive than a sow, yet equally as fragrant.

"No, but it's the only virtue a buffalo's got," answered the man on my right.

We were mostly English, I observed. All of us numbered about one hundred as we formed a circle of varied humanity around the high ring of unpainted fence, a circular enclosure that someone called a corral. I wondered if the word was French or English, Huron or Cree, Eskimo or just one more Canadian expression that was a part of this exciting land. John Howland stood nearby, his big hands on the top rail of the unpainted fencing that stacked up four rails high, with a space between. Each rail was sturdy, supported at both ends by thick posts that had been pounded into the soft brown earth that was already greening with new spring grass. Varmette and Stoddard stood behind me.

Men bet tokens. Clinks and clanks of coin exchanged hands as wagers would be offered and accepted, odds dickered on, and neutral persons elected to hold the bets. I saw the wagering of more silver than I believed had ever been minted, despite the fact that their clothing was sewn from a strange material that was light brown in color with fringe on the arms and shoulders.

"What sort of shoes are those?" I asked.

"Mocs."

"And the cloth?"

"Deerskin, or buckskin. Frenchies say *caribou*."

"Is *he* an indian?"

"Not him. That there is Eskimo Elky."

"He looks like a Chinaman I once saw in Newcastle."

A trio of Scots argued over a bet in heated burrs. One of them wore a kilt, a Scottish skirt woven in plaid and worn by both men and women of the Highlands. Oft they paraded in England, their pipes wailing and droning to the warlike pound of their drums. People in Newcastle said the Scots were savages that God had created to make war upon the enemies of King George and upon the foe of all our kings. Scots were uncivilized and Presbyterian.

"Came on the *Costain,* did ye?" asked a man.

"Yes," I said. "This is my first day in Canada."

The man eyed my collar iron. "Benet?"

I nodded my head.

"God rest ye, lad, for surely Benet will nay do it. Then I suppose you learned that early."

"I have not seen my new master, nor has he seen me. My name is Abbott Coe."

"Soon enough, lad. But soft, look you at the deep chest of that devil of a beast."

"You mean that injun woman?" asked another man, and laughter engulfed us.

"No, the bison. Could any man claim his own sanity and still fork his legs *aboot* the spine of such a tribulation with neither saddle nor bit?"

"Only one man."

"Aye, it be Skinner Benet."

"A man of much bark."

"I hate his bowels."

"Only one way to ride a buffalo and live."

"How so?"

"Be meaner than the buffalo."

More laughter followed. I tried to hear all that was said about S. Benet. Too much was offered to remember. The collar at my throat tightened whenever I heard Benet's name.

"The man is a bastard."

"*Non.* Worse, a half-breed."

"*Vous avez raison.* His father was a walrus and his mother was a great white bear."

"Benet was weaned on the milk of a musk ox."

"Say that to his face, brave one."

"I don't have to. Benet said it."

"That man. He brags too much."

"Aye, but never does he talk about the thing that he cannot do."

"Like the season he was a *hivernant,* wintering in the northern camp where the *caribou* fawn. But he did not starve."

"A pity he did not."

"He ate his mocs to survive. And his buckskin clothing."

"*Oui!* That's true."

"Who said?"

"Blanchard told me."

"Ha! Blanchard would tell his dying mother that he was vowing to be a nun."

We all laughed.

"Here he comes!"

"Blanchard?"

"No, you goat. Here comes Benet."

Why, I asked myself, would one hundred human heads turn away from a creature so strange as a buffalo merely to behold a man? Did I see what *they* all saw? Only a mortal. Average size, near to forty years old, certainly neither giant nor deity. So this was S. Benet, the obligee of my contract, who had advanced the price of my passage in the *Costain* from England to Boston and north into Hudson's Bay to Fort Albany. My master-to-be for five years. Around my neck, the cool iron still felt hot and burned like a brand. The ring choked even my empty swallow. I watched a dozen men, all afoot, barely preventing the bolt of a bison, as Benet hooked a leg over the top rail and jumped lightly into the dry dust of the enclosure. As he alighted, his mocs made no sound. Walking, he was more woman than man, his each step stretching forward toe upon toe, as though a French dancing master had introduced him to ambulation. Toward the buffalo he walked, easy in his gait, as though his feet were the only feet that heard some silent minuet.

Benet drew his hip knife.

"Will he stab the thing?" The voice that asked the question did so in a barely audible whisper, as if expecting no one to be so bold as to predict Benet's intent.

Quickly, holding the knife by its blade, Benet flung it suddenly forward, end over end, until its silver tip bit and buried into the thickest of the mushroom-top corral posts. Quivering as if afraid, its brown handle trembled to a rest. Ah! Suddenly I understood. No man rides a buffalo while a knife rides his belt.

Benet wore a blouse and long leggings of a material that looked to be of extreme softness, as though from the hide of a doe. His hair was grayer than smoke. Half-breed hair? Was he part French and part indian? His appearance would seem so. As he walked closer, the brown eyes of that buffalo stared only at Skinner Benet as if no other human shared the ring. Before any of us could ask why, Benet's leg shot forward to kick the animal in its shaggy belly. Yet the animal did not rear or plunge. Men dropped ropes, shaking them free. Only two ropes remained as a pair of loose ends from a halter that bound the great black-brown head. Once again, Benet's leg kicked, but this time his body followed and he sat upon the spine of the beast, holding two ropes.

"Spill me, Billy," yelled Benet.

As though in understanding, the buffalo leaped, all four of its cloven hoofs kicking dust into the midday air, then hammering into the brown earth. Benet's body hunched his own landing, appearing to absorb the battering. Both ropes were gripped in the rider's right fist as the fingers of his left hand locked into the thick furry coat for a handle. Thighs to heels, Benet's lean legs dug in like the twin roots of a back tooth.

"He's still on," said someone.

Plunging forward, twisting into an undisciplined sundance that sought only to toss (and perhaps trample) his rider, Billy's big body charged forward, and sideward, often totally in the air. Benet stuck, as if he'd been painted on the fur, and the man was even smiling.

"All the ducats, or whatever they were, in all of King

Solomon's treasure wouldn't put my butt on that devil," said one of the Scots.

"He won't stick."

"The hell he won't."

"Double the bet?"

"Aye. Double it."

"Or triple."

"God, how I would enjoy being that young bull buffalo for right now. Just so's I could dump Benet's backside into the grit and then gore his guts."

"Ha! Benet's guts are longer than yours or mine."

"True enough. No human would ride a creature like that, and Skinner Benet ain't no exception."

"Which do you hate the more, Hal? Skinner Benet or Seecoya?"

"A damn shame we can't dig a big hole and throw the both in it and let 'em pitdog."

Holding my tongue, I was too frightened to utter a sound. What a land this Canada! A place where a cow is not a peaceful old girl beneath the elmshade of English pasture. Cows in Canada are like Billy, Benet's buffalo. Canada is the only place on earth, said a sailor aboard the *Costain*, where even the does have antlers. Female *caribou*, the sailor swore, have horns. Few aboard ship would believe such a story. Had I not seen such an untamed bull of a beast as Billy, I would have thought the describer to be a liar, one possessed of devils and wild dreams.

"I say," a voice said along the fence, "if Satan had decided to be an animal . . ."

"He'd be a bison," someone finished.

"Or he'd be Benet."

Grunting, snorting, bucking, twisting, kicking, mouth afoam with yellow-green spittle, the bull buffalo tore up clods of earth from inside the corral. Dust frosted us. Yet the rider stayed on the back of his beast. Even when the buffalo rubbed his great flanks on the rough rails, Benet only lifted his sandwiched leg or it would have become broken pulp.

"Hang on, Skinner!"

"Hah! I thought you hated Benet."

"I do. But I just decided that if'n I got me a choice, I don't guess I'd hate me a buffalo any less."

"Toss him off, Billy!"

"Aye! Tip him into the down and dusty where you can carve him proper with them two hooks."

Why, I wondered, was Skinner Benet trying to ride a buffalo? Because so many wanted to see the man's neck break? Did it give Benet his French pleasure to disappoint the hostile English crowd? Was this feat of daring his slap in the face to his fellow citizens at this British fort?

The crowd screamed.

Benet's body rolled in the dust. Hoofs and horns fishtailed around in quick pursuit, intending to gore, to stomp, to kill. Suddenly men who claimed they hated Benet were through the bars, or over, into the ring with waving and yelling whoops, in an effort to divert the charging bison from the fallen rider.

"Yah! Yah! Yah!"

A half-grown boy even charged the buffalo, waving a red hat to attract the brute's attention. The massive head swung from left to right, confused and breathless. Brightly colored sashes were torn from waists to whip at the buffalo and divert his interest, or even invite his attack.

"Moi! Moi!" yelled Varmette, who had knocked me aside in his haste to enter the ring to save Benet. A small man, Pierre Varmette was a mouse charging a great brown cat, a catamount with horns and hoofs and white flame in his eye.

John Howland reached the fallen Benet first, scooping him up as easily as if Skinner had been a kitten in the path of a chariot. Being a large man, John Howland made an excellent target for a charging buffalo, yet Billy remained relatively in one spot, hoofs pawing the loose dirt and breathing in great mist-producing snorts.

"You old fool," Howland said to Benet as the big blacksmith stuffed the *bourgeois* through the bars and to safety.

The bettors who had wagered against Benet, and had given odds, were joyous in their clinking victory. Tokens poured into hats, and were dropped to the dirt. Smiles reached at frowns to grab their winnings. Losers claimed that S. Benet had stayed long enough aboard Billy's brown bear of a back to establish mastery. It was true! No man could have ridden a more valiant ride. John Howland lectured Skinner Benet as a parent nagging a truant child. Next to the crimson visage of the beefy blacksmith, Benet's face appeared pale and childlike and shaken. Much as I found the buffalo an object of curiosity, I could not take my eyes off Skinner Benet, the man who had attempted to ride a bison, the master of my life for the next five years. Was this the time to present myself to my lord?

Like the others, I stumbled forward as if I could not see enough of Benet, who sat in the dust as though his head spun. Several helped him to his feet. Standing just outside the circular corral which still confined big Billy, Benet rested his right hand upon a rail to steady his person, shaking his head in an effort to clear his senses and return his reason. People paid no attention to me. I could have run off. A hasty thought, as I had nowhere to run, except to all of Canada. In half a day, since the docking of H.M.S. *Costain* early in this morning's cold July mist, I had learned more of this new Canada than my mind could hold.

My iron collar, a buffalo, and now my master. Beneath the muscle of my chest, my heart pounded louder than the many sounds beneath the English flag above Fort Albany.

"Aye," said Israel Stoddard, "there is Benet."

"What should I do?"

"Whatever crosses your mind, lad, think not upon escape. Or upon standing up to Skinner Benet like you doubt he's your better. He can be both dog and cat, so best you mind your manners."

"I thank you for the advice, sir."

"Welcome you be to it, boy. I just don't want to see a good English lad like yourself be wasted or cuffed about by a French fist. Don't get yourself bit over a meatless bone."

"Nay," I said, "I will not."

All of us moved with the current of the crowd, one hundred surging forward, heads abob from left to right as if trying to catch a glimpse of Benet in case he happened to fall into a faint. Everyone was talking. Words I had never heard buzzed about my head, strange swarms of

language in tongues too foreign to fathom. Gut sounds
coming from red women, and noise spoken through an
occasional French nose. I was surprised any French were
here at all. Yet some were.

"Long live Benet!" someone shouted.

"And longer may live Billy."

People laughed, still quarreling over amounts of money
wagered and money paid. No one, winner or loser, seemed
disinterested in the vanquished rider, who rubbed his left
hip.

"Pierre, *you* ride next."

"Pas jamais!"

"Never?"

"Not today."

Reaching over the fence, Benet yanked his knife from
its bite into the corral post, hiding its shiny blade once
more in the sheath at his belt. Now that I was closer I
could see the features of his face, as being part of the
crowd allowed me to stare as just one more member of a
curious multitude, affording me relief in that I could
secretly look without myself being likewise looked upon.

"Aye, that was a ride," said a Scot.

"And a tumble *doon.*"

Studying the face of Skinner Benet, I saw features
fine and patrician, an aristocrat's nose, a determined jaw,
a high hairline above a brow of few wrinkles, ears closely
set upon an oval head, and hair so gray that it was akin
to white. But what fascinated me most about him were
the two blue eyes, like twin and tiny skies that were win-
dows to look into a deep and distant land. Soft eyes in a
hard face. Yet fierce eyes! Eyes that seemed to be alone
regardless of all the faces they beheld. I imagind Jesus
of Nazareth to have had eyes not unlike those of my
master, Benet. Despite his smoke-colored gray hair, his
eyebrows were blacker than coal.

"You," he said to me, speaking English.

Everyone turned, and I was in a split moment the center
of all awareness. Had he seen my collar? For some reason,
my feet stumbled forward, advancing to obey an order
that had been unspoken. His voice was soft and compel-
ling, but with an edge on each word that passed from his
thin lips like the slashes of a prince's dagger.

"Are you Coe?" he asked.

"Aye, sir . . . I am Abbott Coe."

"And did you witness the fall of your master?"

My mouth atwitch, I smiled, although not at all amused. "That I did, sir."

"So what think you now, Sirrah Coe, upon watching my spine bounce along the ruts of Canada?"

Swallowing, I felt the iron collar choking my words, as though it had commanded my silence. To my ear, my voice sounded spare and strident as I answered Benet's question.

"Sir . . . I think . . ."

"Yes?"

"I know, sir, that I favor serving Mister Benet rather than serving his buffalo."

Chapter 3

"Come," said Benet, "and we'll walk."

"Very good, sir."

"At least you will walk, Coe. I will limp."

With my bundle, all that I owned in the entire world under my arm, I walked at the side of (and slightly behind) Mister Benet. Together we entered the main gate of the high stockade, the great military wall of vertical logs that stood at the southern side of Fort Albany. For a man with gray hair who had been tossed high from the back of a bull buffalo, Skinner Benet walked with a surprisingly spry gait. Only once did I detect his mouth twist with the discomfort of his stride. As we rounded the corner of what smelled like a smokehouse, a short and stocky man approached us, falling to his knees before Benet, speaking in a begging whine.

"*Monsieur, s'il vous plaît, permettez-moi . . . aller avec vous . . . voyage prochain?*"

"Contois," said Benet without breaking his stride, "I would not take you on my next trip to the privy." Then, with a whipping swing of his leg, Benet turned to plant a solid kick in the belly of the imploring Contois. Grunting, the man spilled backward into pancakes of dried cow manure.

"*Chien!*" said Benet.

We kept walking.

"On my last *voyage* upriver, Contois complained about the work, the water, and the cold. He stole food that was not his share, stole tobacco, and molested indian women to the extent that he nearly stuck arrows in all our backs.

29

And one other shortcoming, for which I cannot forgive him . . . more sour than an early grape does he sing."

"Was he the worst of your crew, sir?"

"No," said Benet, "he is one of my best." His fist slapped my ribs, striking like a snake into my unprotected body, but his laugh healed the hurting so quickly that I found myself joining in until my ribs ached from quite a different cause.

"Sir, why do you speak English instead of French?"

"Coe, you will learn here at Fort Albany, and perhaps one day in all of Canada, this one truth. English is the tongue of the boss, the ruler, the *bourgeois,* and the owners of the Hudson's Bay Company. French is spoken only by peaporkers."

"Is Contois a peaporker, sir?"

"Yes. A paddler, a beast of burden, a river rat who is fit to keep company with the Huron or the Cree. Remember that, Coe."

"I will, sir."

"And as far as you are concerned, you will also obey my orders to the letter, and without question. Fur trading and Canada are both new to you, but to me they are mother and father. All that we do here in Fort Albany has but one purpose, that being to earn a profit from the eagle's fur for the Hudson's Bay Company."

"Very good, sir."

The tart smell of a tannery hit my nose, and I heard the scraping of hides. With faces like leather, two old indian women stood at the stretched hide of a large four-footed animal and drew their knife blades to and fro. As they saw Skinner Benet, their knives worked faster and their tongues less.

"We are not in Canada," continued Benet, "to engage in politics or military vanity or to convert some red heathen into becoming a Christian by telling him he will burn in Hell if he continues to eat the flesh of his fellow humans. We are not here to salute flags or humble ourselves before the ambitions of an English Crown or a French one. Is that clear?"

"It is clear, sir."

"You are to follow no orders but mine. Shareholders, the bigwigs from London and Europe who invested in the

Hudson's Bay Company, arrive here often by boat to audit
our ledgers and flood us with advice fit only for fools.
They usually depart as soon as the ship is ready to ride
the tide. If they stay, and make themselves into obstacles
of commerce, we take on an expedition of inspection, upriver in a bark canoe, and feed them to the Cree."

My stomach heaved, only slightly, at the mention of the
thought of being captured by hungry red savages. I wondered if my face turned sudden pallid. Benet was not idle.

"Ferguson," he yelled to a Scot, "run this bale through
the press again. I want as little air and as little moisture
as possible between the hides."

"Aye, Mister Benet."

"Coe," said Benet, as he sat without ceremony upon a
stack of loose pelts, "I'll have a look at your bond." He
held out his hand with a snap of his fingers.

"It's inside my shirt, sir."

"Fetch it here."

Unfolding the tan and crackly paper that bore a seal
of red wax and a gold-colored ribbon, Benet read the contract aloud, as though his purpose were to insure my
absolute understanding of our agreement and its legal
duration:

BOND

So be it writ *upon this parchment and upon this
date, being the 3rd day of December of the year 1754,
that one orphan by the name of Abbott Coe (age 16)
certifies that he is sound of mind and fit of body, and
willing to assume all duties assigned to him by his
master for a term of five (5) years, during which he
shall fully undertake without wages other than bed
and board.*

*In exchange for this bonded servitude, one Abbott
Coe (hereafter known as the obligor) is to receive
free passage embarking from Southampton in England
aboard His Majesty's Ship the* Costain, *stopping at
Boston town in the colony of Massachusetts, disem-
barking only at Hudson's Bay.*

Obligor will obey and respect the obligee, one S.

*Benet (the latter having paid in advance the ship's
passage plus found befitting a passenger of bondservant status), serving generally as an apprentice in fur
trade and specifically for the fuller enrichment and
prosperity of the Hudson's Bay Company, that being
the legal entity that doth sponsor this document of
bond and seal.*

*Be it known by all persons in both England and
her colonies that should this obligor, A. Coe, refuse
to serve or become a Fugitive from his bond master,
he is to have legally and lawfully an F branded on
his face with a hot iron. And should the obligor take
up weapon against his master obligee, or lift either
fist or foot to strike, the penalty has been hitherto
established that one hand of the offender shall be
lashed to a wooden block to be then chopped off and
apart from his body at the wrist by one blow of an
axe.*

*It is the right of the obligee to fetter about the neck
of his serf an iron band that directs the return of such
property to his master by all who read and perceive
its message. Removal of this shackle by any person
other than the obligee amounts to a wanton crime and
tort, punishable by fine or confinement in His Majesty's prison.*

*And then, after five years from this date, that be-
coming the 3rd day of December of 1759, and after
the obligor has willingly discharged all tasks assigned
to him by his obligee, owning no debt either criminal
or civil, this bondservant ceases to be obliged property
and is then a free citizen and a loyal subject of King
George.*

W. A. Appleby
HAND AND SEAL.

"I have read it many times, sir. So oft that I near know
it by heart."

"And you find the conditions unjust?" Benet asked.

"I do not, sir. If I may, please, I would like to thank
you, sir, for my passage to Canada."

"By damn, Coe! You are the first bondservant who has
ever said as much. Now if you will forgive me when I

boot your tail from Hell to breakfast for disobedience or insubordination, we'll get along. I have too much responsibility here for one man. Over a hundred *voyageurs* report to me, directly or through a lesser *bourgeois*. And worse, when the dignitaries come in their brocaded coats and carry lace to wipe their noses, they demand my time with their trivia. So I get the guff from underlings and shareholders alike. From below and from above."

"My duties, sir?"

"You will relieve me of some responsibility, the details of which I shall soon determine when I find if you are cut from a sturdy bolt. You are English, yes?"

"Truly I am, sir. I be as British as you are French."

"Soft. My father was French, but my mother, God rest her, was an Englishwoman who committed the error of unity with a Frenchman without wedlock. My father never gave her his name, nor me. I took it. As freely as I later took Benet. I told everyone in the slums of Paris that my name was Guy Trudell, for that was the name of the man who shared my mother's bed."

"Was he an outlaw, a libertine?"

"Worse. My sire was a *scholar,* a composer of verse and lyric and a critic of art and music and even of the clothes my mother took in as laundry. Coe, are you a Catholic by any chance?"

"No, sir, I am Protestant."

"My father was a Huguenot, a French Protestant, who was clubbed to death by three Catholics in the name of righteousness and religion. Do you attend church?"

Before responding, I wondered what answer Mister Benet wanted to hear. And as he waited for my reply, his tongue seemed to shift an article from one jaw to another, creating a slight bulge in his opposite cheek. I decided then to always tell Benet the truth and so I fired my answer.

"Sir, I attend only one hour a week."

"Good, I can't abide overly religious people. Our preacher died last winter. Now we have only an old priest to keep tabs on births and baptisms, and *beds,* seeing as Father Joseph is primarily interested in marrying every *voyageur* to every indian damsel that tickles his fancy."

"You dislike Father Joseph?"

"Not really. Once a winter we play chess together. I always win."

"I would have guessed, sir."

"He disapproves of my game, my reckless style of play, as much as he disapproves of the patterns of my life. When I first told him that I am a Huguenot, his mouth dropped open and he crossed himself. But he serves a purpose."

"What purpose, sir?"

"You will see. Father Joseph's duties do not concern you. *Your* duties will. We who sleep by the frozen sea of Hudson's Bay have many chores to perform. Yet it isn't the work that weighs me, but rather the constant parade of bigwigs, military officers, and clergy that constantly land here at Fort Albany to *assist* me. Each hauls a sack of worthless suggestions and insists that each folly be pursued to the letter. Damn!"

"I beg your pardon, sir?"

"Nothing! Except why do I tell you all this, but to rid my chest of its burdens? I have to talk to someone or go crazy, and yours is the first intelligent face that I have seen here in a fist of seasons. Coe, can you look at a man or a horse or a sled dog and judge quality? Well, I can. Oh, on occasion I'll be wrong, but not oft. *You* are quality, Coe. And 'tis my guess that you may have been born from a commoner dam, yet you may be the son of a noble."

"Thank you, sir."

"And that's why I sent to an English workhouse for someone much like you. A man young enough to be trained as a boy who is still supple enough to bend under my orders and not shatter. Can you do that?"

"I can, sir."

"You're an orphan."

"Yes, sir."

"Excellent. Compared to a British orphanage, even the wilderness of upriver Canada will seem heavenly. Coe, how do you think I got all my Frenchies, my peaporking *voyageurs*, to endure trip after trip into a hinterland that is rife with insects, drowning, and arrows?"

His black eyebrows frowned for an instant as though he were impatient that I did not answer. So I let him wait, to test his impulses, to see whether or not I could remain silent to allow him to continue in monologue. I was correct. His words flew at me like nesting doves before a dog.

"I will tell you why these French canoemen paddle for me. Because back home in France they had nothing and never would have a *sou*. Nothing. *Rien du tout*. Except to be beaten by a master or noble or farmer. Here they are free. And if they survive the next *voyage*, then they will have a few gold pieces in the folds of their purses, until they squander their last penny on a comb for an indian girlfriend."

"Sir, I don't understand why you need Frenchmen to attend your vessels."

"Ha! Because mules are too intelligent to ride a canoe. That's why God created the French."

I started to laugh.

"Even you, Coe, will look down on them, and what are *you?* Nothing! My chattel. For five years you are property and not one notch higher. But if you always remember that and know your place, you will learn much about the eagle fur and your master who makes it sing. Tell me, Coe, what does the word *bourgeois* mean to you?"

"Sir, it means you are the boss."

"Right and wrong. In France *bourgeois* means middle class. A foreman of limited success. But here in Fort Albany, it does mean boss, so here I am a king. I live and laugh and love better than any monarch in Paris or London. And at my own whim I allow lesser men to call me Skinner. But you will call me *sir,* as is already your habit, or you may use Mister Benet."

"Very good, sir."

He held up a pelt. "What is this?"

"A piece of fur, sir."

"It is beaver. Our stock-in-trade. And we take more beaver than any other animal. Why?"

"Because there are more of them?"

"Not quite, though the beaver is plentiful. Yet his hair is a mass of barbs, almost like the quills of a porcupine, which strengthens the weave of any felt. Locks it in, forms a stronger bond for a hat that some European fop will stroll about under. Sickening, isn't it?"

I said nothing, not fully sure I understood the cause of my master's ire, and Benet continued his tirade.

"Pity," he said, "that we cannot trap a thousand European nobles and from their pelts fashion hats for our beaver. Coe, there are times when I loathe the fur trade, as I prefer the company of one beaver to all the aristocrats that have ever invested in, and infested, the Hudson's Bay Company. One beaver," he repeated in a quiet voice, holding up the pelt of rich brown fur with his left hand, and with his right, stroking its shiny softness as though caressing a woman, "has more dignity and more nobility."

I saw a softening in the blue eyes of S. Benet that caused me to believe his care was genuine. His teeth bit down on whatever was lodged between his jaws. Deeply he sighed. And then, as I studied his eyes, they became darker and harder, widening to look beyond me to the main gate.

"Look you quickly," he pointed.

Turning, I saw a British officer in a tunic of bright red astride a snowy-white horse as he rode through the main gate of Fort Albany and to the spacious compound within. With a light hand he held the brown reins, his other fist resting casually on the handle of his saber. Everyone turned to look, and even the two indian women paused in their scraping of what I now guess was the hide of a buck *caribou*. The British officer was young, very young, with apple cheeks beneath a wig as white as his mount. White breeches, black boots that could outsparkle coal; but what caught my eye was the shine of the British officer's silver breastplate. His token armor gleamed as haughtily as any halo, almost to claim that the soldier who wore it was a deity.

Benet spat. "Coe," he said, "look well and mark what you see. Is it any wonder that the British so easily usurp near all of the New World? The British come as *gods!* His hip wears that saber with the grace of Thor brandishing a bolt of lightning."

The white horse walked slowly by a small Frenchman, who crossed himself without, it seemed to me, questioning why. His hand just blessed his own humble body as though confronting Jehovah. No one spoke. The white mare snorted.

"Now you know," said Benet, "why England will one day rule land and sea and earth and stars. Because to the squinting eyes of the dazzled peasant, be he Chinaman or

African or eskimo, the British officer appears holier than Heaven."

Benet spoke truly.

I had seen the red tunics of British officers back in England. The hoofs of their horses clattering down the cobblestones of a Newcastle street always caused our citizens to hold breath in the awe of appreciation. And even the eyes of Skinner Benet were transfixed by just one British officer in full dress and saddle.

"How?" I heard Benet's whisper. "How could a lad from Spain or Holland or France or Moorish dunes ever pretend to face such an adversary and combat him?"

"Your mother was English, sir, you say."

"Indeed she was. When I was a wee lad, she would spin me a bedtime tale of the London parades that escorted the King from court to castle. So vivid were her descriptions that my young ears heard the pipes and my toes even wiggled to march with British drums."

"I recognize that officer."

"Of course. No Englishman arrives here at Fort Albany this day except on the *Costain*. Did he come with you from England?"

"Nay," I said. "I saw him board us, horse and all, at the town called Boston in Massachusetts Bay."

"I wonder what brings him to Fort Albany."

"Do not soldiers come and go here?"

"Truly," said Benet, "but this man is no ordinary soldier. And mark me, boy, he is not in Canada in quest of the eagle fur."

Chapter 4

"How well do you cipher?"

"I manage, sir."

"Then," said Benet, "manage yourself back to the water-front and keep a sharp eye out for when they start loading the hold of the *Costain*. You will outfit your hand with paper, and you will feather down an accurate count of every bale that is hoisted aboard her."

"Very good, sir."

"Coe, if you don't know the particular substance that they lower into her hold, then ask. And if you suspect the answer is less than the straight of it, ask a second soul, as a check."

"Aye, Mister Benet."

"Trust no one, as this merry old world is abrim with scoundrels, especially around places where a wharf bites the sea. I will join you presently if I can, and later if I be netted by the snarls of commerce."

I tossed him a salute and scampered at a trot across the infield of the stockade and out through the main gate. People were trading. I saw cows, chickens, pigs, geese, and an indian canoe. At my feet I found a perfectly ripened apple which my stomach claimed in five bites. Then, still hungry, I ate the core and the pips. The seeds were bitter, but I chewed them to pulp.

"Hello," I called to John Howland, and the big black-smith waved his hammer.

Already I felt as though I belonged to Canada and she to me. Life was strange here, but in the land where red savages eat people and where the boss rides a buffalo, I felt part of a new chance, a rebirth into an exciting and adventurous existence. I wanted to sing. Being an orphan in England was comparable, someone had told me, to being a criminal or a bastard. But here, at Fort Albany, little would matter as to a man's history. Or a woman's. Naught surprises me in this place, I thought; and were I to learn that a disorderly woman, a prostitute, were elected to be the lord mayor, my shoulders would shrug it all off as though to say . . . of course, as this is Canada.

"Canada!"

My lips spoke the word aloud without my command, as though my ears thirsted to dance with the tune. A sailor aboard the *Costain* had been to Fort Albany before, and had described Canada more vast than any ocean. More distant, he had said, than sky or sea. Yet more to see, to conquer, and to become. In less than five years, I will be Mister Abbott Coe, a citizen of the colony of Canada. I will own land and cattle and also indulge in fur trade. My heart felt as if already it held a treasure.

His Majesty's Ship *Costain* settled into the sea, her belly laden with cargo, skins, and stuffs bound for England. For two days, not even a straw or a seed or even a curious indian went aboard the *Costain* that I did not log. The ship's master, Captain Smith, even asked me if Mister Benet's buffalo were for sale, as he so longed to bring such a bison home to Scotland.

"You will have to ask Mister Benet," I said.

"Alas, I speak no French."

"For a crown, I will inquire for you." I told him, taking a quick advantage of the man's misinformation.

"Do you speak French, boy?"

"Very little, Captain. But I will ask for you."

"A bargain."

I asked Mister Benet if his buffalo were merchandise. "No," said Benet to me, as he had taken much pains in getting Billy to Fort Albany by canoe (as a calf) and the bison was not for sale. The gold crown found its way to my dark and empty purse.

When the *Costain* hoisted her sails and bound herself for England, many of the Fort Albany folk turned out to wave farewell, yet fewer than the number who had, days earlier, witnessed our docking. As northward she departed, I said goodbye to all that was my orphaned youth, more willing to be free of England than she was no doubt eager to be rid of one more kinless pauper. Even though my neck now wore iron, no thoughts of stowing away aboard the *Costain* entered my mind.

I belong here, I said to myself, arm raised in a farewell to her full canvas. I belong to Canada.

With a flourish, I handed my sums of shipment over to Mister Benet, who promptly spotted an error in my arithmetic in the column of fox fur. Before I could duck, the flat of his hand cracked the side of my head and sent me sprawling. Though I was more surprised than hurt, I was a bit slow to regain my standing, seeing Benet above me with his feet widely spread as if he stored for me another clout.

"Coe," he said, "when you err in the sums of shipment, at least make the error in *our* favor and not theirs. To state that we sent one hogshead more is sweeter than being so coy that we claim one hog less. Is that understood?"

"Aye, sir, it is."

"I look upon your mistakes as weakness. Only fools make constant errors. And fools pay dearly for them, so get yourself in the habit of perfection, which is just as simple . . . no, in fact, simpler . . . to form than the habit of fault."

"I understand, sir."

"Best you do. A wee mixup in supplies here at Fort Albany can snowball into a critical mess when such a slip is realized five hundred miles upriver. A dot of ink here, a bucket of blood up yonder where only eagles go. And nitwits, like me."

I felt my face frowning. Not because Benet had knocked me down but because he was right and I had been, in my haste to report, a dolt. As he looked at me, wondering perhaps if his sermon had soaked in, his two black eyebrows knitted toward the bridge of his thin nose. His eyes were blue as truth.

We faced each other, both of us standing in Benet's small but orderly office within the stockade. Though a hot afternoon, Benet did not seem to sweat, while I was near drenched with the wetness of my work. The office was composed of two rooms, a larger one in front with desk and files and even an extra chair to offer a visitor; the back room contained supplies of paper, business forms and bills of account, and also the bunk upon which I slept. One of my duties was to see that his office remained unmolested and that the metal chest containing Benet's records of receipt and shipment (for the Hudson's Bay Company) was seen by no eyes except his own. Not even by a shareholder.

"Lock up," he said to me.

"It is early, sir."

"So it is, but I am already tired of enriching the lords of London. For the rest of this day, their purses and paunches must swell with no further effort of mine . . . or yours."

"I have to sweep up, sir, and burn the trash."

"Do it come the morrow."

"As you say, sir."

"Coe, do you play chess?"

"No, sir," I blurted out, suddenly feeling the heart inside my shirt when I realized that my answer was off-target and I would possibly be rewarded with a cuff for my bluntness. Quickly I recovered. "But I could soon learn."

A bondservant to Mister Benet must allow such a master the answer that he wishes to hear. Provided, of course, such a promise be within the realm of performance. The sudden tempering of his blue eyes informed me that my recovery was made in time to patch what could have been a rent in his expectations.

"Tell me, Coe . . . if you were playing chess and matched against your master, would you try to defeat me? Let us say you craftily saw a move, one pivotal play, that would swing the advantage over to you. Your hand reaches out to lift your bishop, and then you hold yourself within propriety. What then? Do you play to defeat your boss?"

Without answering, my hand slowly reached for an inkbottle that sat on his desk. Carefully I lifted it and placed it down atop his hand so that he could not budge without toppling the well.

"Good move, Coe."

"I would play to win, sir. To defeat you, and to credit your ability as the chessmaster who had taught me such strategy."

"You speak well, young man." Lightly he shifted the

well of ink to free his hand. His fingers were thin and curved like a cutlass. Everything about him was spare and honed. His buckskins fitted him with more precision than any tailor had ever outfitted a monarch with lace and linen. "Who educated you?"

"Sister Elizabeth, at Saint Mark's Orphanage, sir. She read to us by the hour. We were her only family. Sister told us to read good books and we would willy-nilly educate ourselves. Thus I became a reader."

"You come from Newcastle."

"Yes, sir, I do."

"Coe? Perchance your name be short for coal?"

"I do not allow myself to dream, sir."

"Ah, but what is a man without a fantasy or two to spin about in his slumber. I wager your kin were colliers, miners . . . the way a family of Pitt or Pick or Pict reveals that they be as black as lung as they are of face."

"Perhaps, sir."

"And your mother I envision as a young miner's daughter, fair and innocent, until she extends her favors to a landed gentleman who forsakes her with child. Afraid of her father's fists, she runs away, bears her babe, and forfeits him to an orphanage, where he will—"

"No," I said.

"You cut me off, Coe."

"Aye, so I did."

"Best you apologize to me. At once."

"I agree, and I apologize, sir."

"And were I to again pursue your lineage?"

"Again, sir, I would cut you off." Holding my breath, I knew that I had gone too far and had put myself in jeopardy.

"Some matters are personal, eh?" he asked. There was no keen edge in his voice, as if he too remembered the shortcomings of his childhood.

"Yes, sir, some are."

"I was testing you, Coe. That's all."

"Like a game of chess?"

"Somewhat."

"But you *knew* your mother and your father. I knew only the good Sisters of the Church of England and the walls of Saint Mark's."

"Good move, Coe. You tie tags to my tail and you put me to the run. No man can ever imagine the Hell of not knowing one's mother and father. I do well imagine it haunts you."

Constantly, I wanted to tell him. Every day and every night I scream into the wind to ask who they be, and where. Who am I? And am I really Abbott Coe, or is that an early charity from the Sisters at Saint Mark's? Assign a name, as a sack of flour is assigned a number? As the thoughts reared in my brain, I was more than thankful that such musings were private matters. Then I spoke.

"I try not to think about it."

"Curiosity is a normal thing. A sign of intelligence. How well I recall all the questions I asked of the stars as I made my boat trip from France to Canada. After my father was beaten to death, my mother went insane. She hanged herself. When I came in the door, her feet touched my face, slowly twisting and cold stiff. I couldn't even scream."

"How old were you, sir?"

"I was ten. And now I am nearing forty and a *bourgeois* in Canada for the Hudson's Bay Company, harvesters of the eagle's fur."

"When will you teach me chess, sir?"

"Perhaps this evening."

"I'd like that."

"Very well. I will take you to my house on the edge of town and you will be served an excellent meal. Bring a lantern, as it will be dark when you return."

"Aye, sir."

Benet and I secured his office, making sure the crossbar rested in its hooks so that the shutters of the window would not be pushed inward to allow entering. My eyes blinked as we stepped out into the bright afternoon of a July in Fort Albany. I carried the lantern in my outside hand, where it would not bump between our knees. Skinner Benet was half a hand taller than I, an observation that caused me to walk in an upright posture, even though Sister Elizabeth would never witness my improved carriage. We slipped out the west gate.

The late sun was a red ball, big and hot, a welcome sight for this country of cold nights and misty mornings.

The delta of the Albany River opened wide, the lazy current busily etching swirls in the infinity of pebbles and sand. We could see far in every direction. Scattered shacks were sprinkled here and there. "Teepee cones" were what Skinner Benet called the few indian dwellings that appeared to be roofed with *caribou* hides. Threads of smoke, slim and gray and soft as loose yarn, stretched upward until scattered into unseen fibers by a high breeze. Shattered fragments of upcountry ice still came downriver, grinding on the delta grit with a scraping sound, to die on the sand like beached whales. Cooking smells abounded. Somewhere inside a cabin a hand tapped a wooden spoon upon the edge of a bubbling kettle.

This was always the time of day when I felt empty of soul, and longed to be filled by belonging to someplace or to someone. My hand wanted to reach and touch Skinner Benet, not because he was my master, but only as he happened to be my company. I wanted one day to be able to say to my fellow workers at day's end, "I am going home to supper."

Benet looked at the western sky, where the sun had already dunked its orange belly into a black and jagged horizon of evergreen. He walked slowly, an act he rarely performed, appearing to be as lazy as a fed cat, yet with the ability to pounce on a sudden situation and claw it to death with one rake of its paw.

"Sundown," said Benet.

"It is, sir."

"Lonely, is is not?" He spoke as if he had somehow read my mind.

"Aye, to be sure."

"As if the sun is a tired old man who seeks his rest in a cold bed with no woman to comfort him or to pull a quilt over his shoulder."

" 'Tis all of that, sir."

"Did you court yourself a sweetheart in Newcastle?"

"Nay, I did not."

"For shame! A strapping lad like yourself should have kissed a lass or two. And here in Fort Albany, pretty girls are rare as tits on a boarhog."

"Not every man has a wife?"

"Nay, only one in ten. Some have squaws that they keep

upriver. And some of the French *voyageurs* have each other. What I want most of all is a female buffalo."

I burst out laughing.

Skinner Benet shook his head. "No, not for myself, but as a mate for Billy. To the west, the trappers tell me that the plains indians eat the buffalo at almost every meal, as do the eskimo live on *caribou* deer."

A meat business as well as a fur business? More than a fur trader is this man Benet. More than just a middle-class *bourgeois* in charge of a crew of oarsmen, I was thinking, listening to his plans. The two of us left the stockade and its outbuildings behind, crossing the flatland of delta pebbles, continuing to walk to the west until I spotted a house of logs that somehow just had to belong to Skinner Benet. Larger than the other cabins, the structure was neatly formed and sturdy, chinked with active moss that garnished the cabin with stripes of green as though to dress it for a Sunday.

"Yours?" I asked.

"Yes, and I built her myself."

Smoke curled from its only chimney, a fact that caused me to wonder who was inside the cabin. Benet's wife? Not once, in the short time that I had served him, had he ever made mention of a woman. During the day he was totally the businessman, except for the one minute that he had taken to ride Billy. On the back of a bison, I would guess, a minute is an impossibility . . . even for a man like Benet who seemed accustomed to victory. A man who would canoe to a place far upriver, for fur.

On either side of the plank door, yellow flowers grew in earthenware tubs. We entered, Benet going in first, even though I was his guest. Soft, I warned myself. You are not his guest but his bondservant, so remember your rank and place. At the hearth, her broad back to us, stood an indian woman, who turned to give us a toothless smile as I closed the door. The cabin smelled of food.

Was this old woman Benet's wife?

"Tobacco," he said to her, causing the old woman to scurry away from the fire to fetch a pipe for Benet. As she filled the bowl, her old fingers dropped two tiny shreds of tobacco, which she carefully reclaimed for the bowl of the pipe. Bringing a scarlet and glowing twig from the fire, she held the flame to allow Benet to puff. Thus the pipe was lit, and the old woman scurried back to her cookery.

Benet smoked, offering me neither tobacco nor pipe, allowing me to sit and watch him puff his pleasure. It mattered little to me since I found the smoking of tobacco to be a foul habit and a clay pipestem merely a fount of brown and unsavory juices. Yet I could see that Benet enjoyed his first pipe of the evening.

"That"—he nodded to indicate the old woman—"is Kapeeka. I killed her husband with this knife"—his hand touched his hip—"and so by Cree law his widow becomes my ward. That, to me, is only just. Kapeeka is an excellent cook, and the only time she scowls at me is when I insist that she use soap to wash her hands. You will take supper with me, Coe."

"Thank you, sir."

Leaning back in his chair, Benet slowly puffed his pipe, permitting wisps of smoke to escape from his thin lips to billow up toward the dark rafters. Softly, in a low and charming voice, he began to sing. Not one word did I understand. And yet his song, which I guessed to be in Cree or Huron, floated about the room in wee moths of music.

'Twas then I saw her.

The door opened, and she entered the cabin, and my soul, with one creamy gesture of her legs and body. A tiny woman, smaller than I, and younger. Her face was child-like in its purity, but her coppery body was as complete, as ripe, as mature and beckoning as a body could ever become. I supposed her age at fourteen or fifteen. Her deerskin dress was identical in hue to the buckskin worn by Benet. Almost white, trimmed with designs and emblems of tiny blue beads. Each bead was the color of Benet's eyes. As if her robe could see.

A sweet agony suddenly burst deep inside my belly, because I saw how she looked at Benet, with the same hunger with which I looked at her.

"Benet," she said, her mouth forming the word as though the saying of it were a woman's craft, a work of art, or a privilege granted only to her, an act which she performed with the ritual that only his name could warrant. As he looked at her, he continued to sing her the song, but now much more softly and with a deepening baritone that could have been intended only to summon a mate.

Yet his mate was a child. She appeared to be an indian doll that had been artistically fashioned as a Christmas gift for a princess. Her hair was blacker than a crow. Her hands were delicate petals like the feathery tips on the wing of a wren. As she again spoke his name in a whisper, she made the name part of a melody. A missing note that fluttered to its rightful nest. His song ended, and he held out his arms, then gently held her. Benet's eyes closed.

"Doe," he said.

Chapter 5

"WELL," SAID JOHN HOWLAND, his hammy hand clubbing my shoulder as if to honor my ability to take such a hearty, yet friendly blow, "how do you find Canada?"

We sat together in the July sunshine, on the log steps that lay before the open door of the Hudson's Bay Company store. The big blacksmith and I had both paused in the workday to partake of a noon meal, bread and dried moose meat, and a half jug of apple cider from last autumn's orchard to wash it all down.

"I like Canada."

"And how does Benet treat you?"

As well as any eskimo treats his dog. That was what I wanted to say. But it would be unwise to degrade Mister Benet as Fort Albany was indeed a small place, where mouths seemed to find ears.

"Well enough," I told John. "I am to learn to play the game of chess as soon as Mister Benet finds a spare hour to teach me."

"Did you see his cabin?"

"Yes, sir. We stopped there a few days ago."

"So I suppose you met his old cooky and his little missy."

The "little missy" sounded innocent enough the way John Howland said it. His voice was basso deep, and it seemed to bathe clean whatever it chose to discuss. "His little missy," however, tightened my fists until my knuckles were white, and inside my mouth, the bread tasted like candlewax.

"Yes, I met the brace of them."

"Mother and daughter, so everyone hereabouts seems to

48

say they be. Benet brung 'em back from upriver. Can't say as I blame him none."

Stop it! My brain was hollering, as I wished to hear no more of Benet's being with Doe. Since first seeing her, I think of little else. Doe! I say her name upon awakening in my shabby cot, and I go to sleep whispering her name over and over again, hour upon darkened hour until sleep finally comes. If I dream happily, Doe is with me and the two of us share our world with no other. Until Benet enters my dream and my heart turns bitter and empty. In my daylight imagination I see Benet and Doe, strolling together toward some hidden glade, closing the curtain of some green bower of boughs where meadow fragrances abound.

"Doe," said John Howland. "That's her name and well does it fit her. Like a weeborn deer she be, all soft and wild of eye. Legs all atremble."

Inside my mouth, the bread rested in the pocket of my cheek, an unchewed cud of inedible pulp. About my neck, the iron shrank as was its custom, whenever I was disturbed by my thrashing thoughts. Up crept my fingers in a futile gesture to loosen the ring of irons so that I could flood my chest with air and my gut with food. And my soul with liberty.

"Why do you fight your collar, boy?"

"For no reason."

"Tell me the straight of it. Your young throat is tight over some pesky thing, I can tell."

"No, it is not," I lied, fearing he would guess my discomfort concerning the indian girl who shared Benet's cabin and his life. Doe . . . whenever I spoke her name, even silently which I did often, the hunger to be with her clawed at my belly in fury.

"How soon you heading upriver?" asked John.

"Soon. Benet is recruiting *voyageurs* for two canoes, and he has placed me in charge of all the trade goods that we will stow in our Yorkboats. I do not understand why the indians trap fur in exchange for such worthless trinkets."

"Best you let old Skinner worry that."

"Aye, best I do. I have seen both a Yorkboat and a canoe here on the bay. The first is slow and heavy while the canoe is light and swift. Why must we use Yorkboats from Fort Albany to Henley House?"

"Boy, I ain't no riverman. So whatever I say ain't worth a rat's rump in a rainstorm. But if I was to take a guess . . ."

"Go ahead and guess then."

"Well, I'd say there's precious little birch around here to patch a canoe. None, in fact. But you go upriver far as the forks, then you'll see birchbark aplenty . . . along with hickory and spruce and a few folks up yonder who know the stem of a canoe from the stern."

"Is that the reason for Yorkboats?"

"Appears to me it is. I went upriver once and I swore to the Almighty that if I ever come back to Hudson's Bay, I'd stay myself put. All them big trees and wilderness and redskins give me the all-overs. I'd hear a loon hoot at sundown and my mind would see a dozen injuns with paint on their faces and screaming worse than a fiddle in Perdition."

"Tell me about upriver."

"Ain't much to tell, boy. Most times I was so scairt that I never opened my eyes to see boo."

"Did you run into Seecoya?"

"Him?" John Howland's big hand grabbed his own hair and shook it. "Not if'n I still got hair."

"Mister Benet said that Seecoya's father came to Fort Albany."

"Before my time, thank the good saints."

"He said that he knows Seecoya. Even talks to him."

"That wouldn't dismay me a mite. No indeedy. If you want my judgment of the matter, Skinner Benet probably talks to the Devil and then buys the Old Boy's fur at half its worth."

"Are you and Mister Benet friends?"

"Boy, that man don't have any friends. Around here at Fort Albany, seeing as we're located in the dark desolation, we all sort of brother along, if you catch my meaning."

"Brother along?"

"Sure. I figure we all could die together real peaceful, so best we at least take a stab at peaceable *living*."

"That makes reason."

"Don't ask me what I'm doing here at Fort Albany, except pounding hot iron, the way a blacksmith ought. There was no future for me in England. Here, well, I'm sort of my own boss. And if I harken to nap at noonmeal, I nap, and there's not a count or a commoner who'll poke me awake and order me to hop to. I'm my own man."

"I will be *my* own man."

"Less than five years."

"Sooner perhaps."

"You got fine and fancy ideas for a bondservant. Maybe old Skinner's uppity nature rubbed off on you some."

"Maybe so."

John Howland said nothing. He only stuffed his big mouth with cold meat and raked his gray shirtsleeve across the shine of his chin, squinting one eye as if to tell me that he was looking at somebody (me) that he couldn't figure. His pumpkin face slowly chewed.

"Abbott," he finally mumbled through his meat, "if I be you, I'd glean all your notions of liberty and put-by for winter."

"What do you mean?"

"Don't stand up to Old Skin. If he tells you there's a cow behind the moon that wants milking, go fetch a bucket. Benet's a strange one. Nobody gets close to him. But if I was to go upriver, even as far as the forks, rather than take a regiment of British redcoats . . . I'd take Benet."

"So would I."

"I got work to do. Come on and walk with me back to the smithy. You're fair company."

"And you, John."

John Howland stood up thick as a stump, a rock of a man. Arms stouter than most men's legs, lungs big as bellows, boots that sunk into the brown dirt much deeper than did mine. John looked as if he'd outweigh half a mule. Side by side we walked back toward his shop, as people waved to John, everyone at Fort Albany seeming to know him. Rounding a corner, we both saw the white horse in one glance, and the man who softly held the halter.

"Hmm," said the big smith.

"I know who he is," I said.

"Ain't he the one who come on the *Costain?*"

"Yes, he boarded at Boston."

"What's his name?"

"I overheard it spoke aboard ship and I beieve it to be McKee or McGee."

We walked faster. I guessed that John Howland could size up whether or not a customer was cash or cuff. As we got to the smithy, the British officer smiled, and I liked his open face. He wore a less formal uniform, but the red tunic burned redder the closer we came. His wig was white, tied behind in a small black bow. The horse was so white that she seemed to be a confection, a statue of a white horse made of sugar in a fairy tale.

"Good day," said the officer.

"Aye, 'tis that," said Howland.

"Please allow me to present myself. I am Owen McKee, or rather Ensign Owen McKee of His Majesty's Coldstream Guards, at your service, sir."

Manners! This young man, I thought, had been drilled and buffed and polished since the first day of his infancy. Nothing, I once concluded for myself, denotes one's rank in the English social order more than the way one speaks. Sir Walter Raleigh could not have bowed to Queen Elizabeth with more grace than Ensign Owen McKee addressing a Fort Albany blacksmith. Every word, every gesture, every thread of his uniform bespoke a quiet quality. McKee would not ever raise his voice, and yet whenever he spoke, all others would lean to hear . . . and obey. He was cream and he knew it.

"Ensign McKee, I am John Howland. And to put the business straight, sir, I am at *your* service."

"Excellent." McKee smiled. "And if you can serve the left front hoof of my mount, all the better. I shall not pester you with my own assessment of her fault, as with one heft of her hoof your practiced eye will discern far more."

My mouth must have been open as I listened to the young ensign speak. Compared to the thick throat of the blacksmith, the words of Owen McKee flew more lightly than a flock of doves. He turned to welcome me to the conversation, extending his hand, as if he would deny not even a bondservant the pleasure of meeting him. He smiled gently.

"I am Owen McKee." Out shot his hand to clasp mine with fingers lean and strong.

"My name is Abbott Coe."

"A fine British name, young sir. There are Coes aplenty in the dale called Thistleton that abuts the lands of my uncle and aunt. And good farmers all."

"No kin of mine, sir."

"You are not a farmer, then. And surely not one in Canada, for I see little or no tilling."

"I am a bondservant."

"Yes, so I observe. Then may I wish that your term of obligation passes quickly and that your master is one of kindly nature."

John Howland snorted.

Whirling with grace and quickness, the ensign knelt to observe the hoofs of his white mare, a hoof now cupped in heavy hands.

"What think you?" he asked the smith.

"Does she limp, sir?" asked Howland.

"Aye, she does, yet ever so slightly that I believe the disorder to be a petty one. Do you agree?"

John Howland nodded his massive head. "Her hoof has been a hair overcut, and too much of her frog's exposed. Does her hoof favor a bit when she walks . . . like your hand pulls back when you touch a hot oven?"

"Yes," said Ensign McKee, "and precisely so."

"I can doctor that, sir."

"Can you really?"

"Indeed and sudden. All your merry miss needs is a thicker shoe, to soak more of the step. And the added heft will stem her pace from getting so flighty."

"Excellent, good sir," said Owen McKee.

"John," I said, pointing at the man, "is the best smith in town."

"True," said Howland, "and the only!"

We all laughed.

"A fine white mare, this lass," said the smith as he gently began to pry the iron shoe loose from the hoof. "You boated her all the way from England, eh, through the ice and to Fort Albany."

"Nay," said McKee, "I did not. My bonnie nag was a gift from a Virginian."

"A friend of long standing, I wager."

"Hardly not. 'Twas only recent that I did meet my Virginia friend, during February last, at which time my first ship landed at Hampton Roads. I was fortunate enough to attend a party at his home and be an overnight guest."

John looked up from the mare's hoof. "And he gave you this mare?"

"So he did. He and I are the same age, and we sort of fell into a fair friendship. Never would I believe to meet such a man in Virginia who knows horses so well and, may I add, gallops them even faster."

Hands upon his hips, Owen McKee stared up into the clouds, a wide smile on his pleasant face. Suddenly his hand cracked his own thigh as though his mind were struck by inspiration. "Jove! I shall have to write to George and tell him the wonders of Canada."

With a clank, the loosened shoe fell from hoof to floor. I noticed that when the smith released the mare's foot, she rested it upon its edge, reluctant to burden it with a quarter of her weight. John Howland selected a thicker shoe and, with the bellowing of charcoal, reddened and hammered and shaped it to his liking, cooled its hissing anger in the water of his temper tub.

"Do you always shoe hot, John?"

"Aye, I do."

"A bonnie practice," said McKee. "Were I my mare, I might welcome the warmth of fresh iron to prance upon. Like cozy slippers on a wintry night, eh?"

John Howland nodded. "She's a sweet girl, your white mare, and it be a pleasure to manicure such an animal."

"Ah, but the pleasure is ours, sir. Or rather hers."

"Has she a name?"

"That she has. Her name is Virtue."

Hearing the ensign pronounce the name caused me to smile, as Virtue so befitted his mare. A perfect name for what appeared to my eye to be a perfect mount. I studied the face of the young ensign, guessing his age to be about twenty-one. Twenty-two at the most. No older. 'Twould be hard to decide which was the more patrician: the ensign, or his white Virginian mount.

"Steady, my lady."

John Howland's deep voice softened to almost a whisper

54

as he married the iron to hoof. The first nail pounded home while he held the others in his lips, one by one to pierce the iron and the hoof, whiskering up to be then twisted off by tongs and then filed smooth.

"A Virginia mare," said John.

"That she be. Virginian Virtue."

"And truly a beauty of a beast. I daresay some Arabian stallion made his presence known in her lineage. Look you at the sculpture of her face, the thin nostrils, and mark the trim of her ears."

"Her foal will be a prize," said Owen McKee.

Lifting his eyebrows, John asked, "True, she's to be a mother?"

"Very true, according to Washington."

"Who is he? Some midwife for mares?"

"George Washington is the name of my newfound friend in Virginia. A very large fellow."

"Never heard of the man," said John.

"No, I presume not, as Virginia and Hudson's Bay are hardly neighbor and neighbor. Yet he is a man worth knowing, and perhaps his name will be well remembered among the green farmlands of Virginia, even if he is famous nowhere else."

"What does he do, this Washington?"

"Everything. He hunts and shoots and rides with facility. And he doth survey, cutting land as easily as you and I could slice bread, uphill or down. He showed his instruments of topography to me in a most scholarly fashion. George is cultured and refined, yet his lore of stream and field is second to none I have previously met. He is a superb pistol shot. George is gifted in all manner and modesty, save one."

"And what might that be?"

"I noticed," said Ensign McKee, "that my gentlemanly friend is a bit shy among the ladies."

"Is that so?" John laughed.

"True enough. Oh, his eye is sharp when he admires a ripe raspberry from a distance. Yet as she approaches him, his fingers drop glasses of punch, his tongue ties in knots . . . and he becomes a more ungifted dancer than any draft horse before a wagon. My dear friend George Washington trips as well as a lame goose."

"Fine way to talk of a chap who has given you such a steed as Virtue."

"I agree, sir, and I bow my head in shame." Owen McKee laughed. "And were he only here, he would indeed laugh with us all, for my Virginia friend is one who happens to know exactly what he is."

"And what is he, sir?"

"George Washington is and will be many things. A planter, a slaveholder, a surveyor . . . and perhaps one more thing."

Ensign Owen McKee again looked at the sky, as if remembering the frolic and friendship that he had found in the company of his friend.

"He may soon be a soldier."

Chapter 6

"WHY?"

John Howland spoke a one-word question as we both watched Ensign McKee lead his mare away from the smithy, heading for the livery of one Peter Clure.

"Why," repeated the big blacksmith, "does a soldier such as Owen McKee arrive at Fort Albany?"

"Soldiers make war."

"Aye, they do. Yet not with one lone officer. He's a Coldstreamer, and that makes him the finest of the fine, a regiment less touched by politics, I hear."

"How do you read that?"

"Well, my lad, I think that the mighty commanders of His Majesty's finest would ne'er send an Owen McKee to Hudson's Bay without cause."

I saw John Howland's face knot into a frown, so I asked, "You distrust him?"

"Nay, I do not. Owen McKee is open and forthright. Much like yourself. Had I a son, perhaps I'd wish him to be like you as a lad, and like our proud ensign as a man."

"I be a stranger to you."

"That you are. But we need new blood here in Canada. Skinner Benet and the rest of us are gray and groaning with arthritis. Youth has an endearing property."

"I understand little of what you say."

"By that I mean we all look with favor upon a pup, a yellow chick still wet from its shell, a dropped calf that wobbles to nurse his ma, a new green sprout that whiskers up from winter's barren mud . . . the older we grow, the greater our joy in beholding the weeborn."

"John, you should write down your words."

Heavily, he sat on a keg, elbows to his knees. Eyes squinting, he watched the British officer and the mare. "I am weary," he said.

So am I, I thought.

"Coe!"

Before I could sit, my head turned to see Benet standing within the easy cast of a stone from the smithy. Slowly he walked to where I stood and where John sat. And then I noticed that even though Benet weighed far less than the other man, the big blacksmith rose to his feet as Benet approached us. I never saw Benet's hand. The back of his knuckles exploded against my cheek, twisting me about, sending my body sprawling to the straw-colored ground as my arms and legs thrashed aimlessly. Not a punch. Nay, just a backhand slap that nearly broke my jaw with its force, or so I thought.

"Get up, Coe."

This was not the first slap I had received from Skinner Benet. Nor would it be the last. Secretly I counted every knock and knee and kick that I owed the man, storing such a tally away in my memory, along with a personal vow that each and every blow delivered would be repaid. In my dreams, my fist crashed into his face, and then I would knock him to the earth, again and again . . . while Doe silently saw me do it. Doe and all of Fort Albany.

My eyes narrowed as I stood up to face Benet.

"Ease yourself, Coe. You are not hurt. And I daresay you suffer little more than a smarting cheek. To match a smarting pride. So remember this, Abbot Coe. When I bond a servant, pay his passage, and agree to give him found, I expect him to be a worker and not a social biddy."

"The man's right," said Howland.

Over his eyes, Benet's brows seemed to dart toward each other like a pair of blacksnakes, as his frown faced them off, one against the other. Benet turned to John Howland.

"John, I'll not need your help."

Howland snorted.

Turning his back to the blacksmith, Benet faced me, as if to betray that he had more to fear from a bondservant who was less than a full-grown man. For some reason, I hoped that John Howland would intervene, but the smith did not move. Was he afraid of Benet? It was apparent that Benet had no fear of the big man, absolutely none, even though there could be no question as to which man possessed the greater strength. John Howland had timbers for arms and a hogbarrel for a chest.

"I apologize, sir."

"Ha! For your laziness or for your thoughts?"

"My thoughts, sir?"

"Yes, your thoughts. Your eyes betray you, Coe, as oft they do when your butt stings from my boot or your cheek from my cuffing. How your eyes burn with revenge."

"I am not vengeful, Mister Benet."

"Time will prove you right or wrong."

"Aye, it will."

"Were our roles reversed, and had you spilled my back-side to the ground, I can promise you that my secret thoughts would be hotter than yours are at this moment. I understand you, Coe. Yet that is not what matters in our relation. What matters is that *you* understand *me*."

"I do, sir."

"Get back to work. You are unhurt. So be thankful that your cruel and heartless master taught you such a quick lesson without fracturing your baby bones."

"Right away, sir."

Damn it, but Benet was right. The more I watched Skinner Benet with others, the more I realized that he whacked everyone around, yet he inflicted little damage. My body was never bruised. Only, as Benet had said, my pride. Would he have dared to strike John Howland? Smiting such an oak of a man would be tantamount to self-destruction, like lowering one's own head and charging a bull. Or a buffalo. What would our beefy blacksmith do if Benet put a fist to his face? No, Benet would not do it.

Two indians in dirty blankets stood at the door of Benet's office as I returned.

"Benet," one of them grunted.

"Not here." I pointed at the smithy.

Even after they trudged away, kicking dust with their torn mocs, I could still sense the reek of their breath and their bodies, a smell that hollered inside my nostrils as though trapped and cornered. I took three deep breaths to flush my nose free of Huron.

I smiled.

Having been here at Fort Albany long enough to discern a Huron from a Cree now pleased me. I would trust neither, no more than anyone at the post would trust Eskimo Elky. And yet every manjack would, for some reason, trust Skinner Benet. Inside, I took a seat high up on the stool behind my ledger and began to cipher my accounts. Although my eyes looked at figures, I only saw the large frame of John Howland, and how the big blacksmith appeared to be slightly smaller when Benet was there.

Curse that man!

"You fascinate me, Benet."

Why I spoke aloud to my own ear was a mystery. My action caused my mouth to slip into a grin. Alas, I do not lose the facility to laugh at myself, nor am I so bereft of wit that I will commit the impatient act against my master. Benet reads me as easily as he reads others, and to him, Abbott Coe is an open book. Do I hide from this? Do I scamper? Nay, not so. Instead of lurking my thoughts in stealth and shadow, *I* will learn to read Benet.

"You have a fine mind, dear Abbott."

The words I heard were not my own, but Sister's, back in the orphanage in England. She believed in my brain. It was she who fed books to my starving curiosity. She tamed me, as one would tame a windowsill sparrow . . . until I gently munched seeds of wisdom from the palm of her hand.

"Be you poet or soldier," Sister Elizabeth had spoken to me, "I so know, my dear Abbott, that you shall ever do yourself proud."

God, I shall weep in remembering her. For she had been father and mother and angel to all her boys. And should any fool dare to ask Abbott Coe if 'tis true that angels have golden hair, I will answer nay, for angel hair is white like Sister's.

I worked hard.

Not only did I complete all my paperwork, but I cleaned the office, straightened my personal quarters, rubbed soap into my dirty linen and hung it out back to dry. And I also ran down to the stockpens and took my daily look at

Billy, the bison. And to check if there be adequate hay in his manger.

What a brute! And to think that Benet actually swung his leg atop such a beast and tried to ride it like a horse. With no saddle. Few men at Hudson's Bay would have the bowels to turn such a trick. I knew I could never try. I may be a coward, but I am no fool. I would not even extend my hand between the bars in order to pet this buffalo. A week ago I saw Benet stroking his animal as though Billy were no more than a house cat.

Slowly I walked back to the office.

Benet returned.

"I am leaving to go inland, to find someone."

"Very good, sir."

"Look for me back by dawn."

"Aye, that I will."

"Allow no one in this office. And if someone asks you of my whereabouts, play dumb. You don't know. I'm trusting you, Coe."

"Thank you, Mister Benet."

"Don't thank me. All you owe me this day is a smack across the chops."

I smiled. *"Yes, sir, I do."*

"See that you continue to owe me. Those two Huron that were here know where Allard is holed up, with some squaw, and I need him. So I'm going to fetch the cur."

"Allard's the one who throws the axe?"

"Yes. And if he hits me with it, I hereby charge you to tend the busines for five years at a profit and then turn yourself loose. Agreed?"

"Agreed."

"How much did you get done?"

"All of it, sir. Every lick."

"See how you can hustle? All you needed was a jolt of fatherly persuasion, so that you employ the top half of your head instead of the bottom."

My hand touched my jaw. The pain I felt was not from his earlier blow but rather from his posing as my father. He saw my face cloud. His own eyes showed that he understood and yet allowed that he didn't care. His hands were busy shoving a shirt and some extra mocs into a sack. Then a red blanket and a few lanyards of deergut.

"Those two Huron," he said, "are going to paddle faster and farther this night than they bloody well imagined they could. We'll take a canoe. If the wind is too strong, we'll take a Yorkboat."

"You'll be back at dawn?"

Benet shrugged. "We're going upriver for a few miles and then south into the muskeg. If our friend Allard is sober, we'll be back at firstlight. If not, look for us around midday."

"I will, sir."

"Who cleaned up our mess? My mess."

I nodded that I had.

"Place looks civilized. See you at sunup. It'll be a pleasure to kick the *derrière* of that *chien* from backwood to breakfast." Benet laughed a hearty laugh. "Be a good lad."

"You'll need food," I said.

I'll roast one of the Huron."

Benet's remark made me chuckle. Even though there was little doubt in my mind that, were he hungry enough, Skinner Benet would eat both Huron and the canoe. Hopefully, before they ate him. As he threw the buckskin sack over his shoulder, his blue eyes looked at me strangely, as though they wanted to speak my name in farewell.

"By the way, Coe, I am a bit regretful about the clout I gave your jaw, so Kapeeka is bringing you a supper fit for King George."

"Thank you, sir."

"Enjoy it, for my sake if not your own. I'll be upriver with two Huron, and we'll eat raw turtle's eggs and cold mud. And afterward I can listen to a sparkling discourse of one grunting to the other."

He turned his back and left.

But then I spotted a can of Red Lion tea on an office shelf. For some reason, I ran after him and stood dumbly while he shoved the tiny tin into his sack, not slowing his stride as he did so.

"Why did you bring me tea?"

"For your supper," I said.

"You are thoughtful."

Then, before I could bask in his gratitude, his hand

flicked forward again to strike my face in a solid slap. He smiled at me.

"Never trust anyone, Coe."

"No, sir, I shall not."

Why, I asked myself, would a man of forty forsake his bed and his meal and go upriver after someone named Allard who throws axes? For the same reason he attempts to ride a buffalo? He is insane. Either that or a fascinating study of sanity and a symbol of order in a brutal wilderness. How would the Hudson's Bay Company fare without Skinner Benet? I watched him greet the two Huron as he approached them, fully expecting him to punch one and pummel the other, but he was quite civil. He spoke something to them, in Huron, words too distant and too foreign for my ear to catch, and the two hopped toward their duties. Both pointed upriver. I saw no canoe, only three men heading southwest at a dogtrot, packs bouncing, until I could no longer hear the crunch their mocs made on the pebbles.

"Goodbye, old man," I said.

Stupidly, I wanted Benet to come back. Canada, I decided was a territory where logic be fickle as weather and about as reliable as the word of a Huron. Walking back toward Benet's office, I kicked a stone, wondering about the man whom I must serve for five years. Well, serve him I shall, though he be a curious concoction of mind and muscle. I can learn from Benet. He knows Canada, he knows the eagle fur, and he somehow knows all the breeds of humanity that melt into this cold caldron called Fort Albany. He understands them all, as a cook masters her row of kitchen spices, each one possessing its own tart and tang and flavor.

Benet the cook.

Stirring up trouble, I wager. But soft, I warned myself, for were trouble to come, we all might well flee to Benet to fight at his hip. He wears the face of a fox at times, rife with animal cunning and survival instinct. His nostrils would sniff the wind and his nose detect the scent of an oncoming threat. And whether the trouble stem from French soldiers to the south, from Cree or Huron or the Innuit and their snapping sled dogs, we all would trot under Benet's wing like peeping chicks to their hen. Perhaps even John Howland would ask Benet what to do and then do it. Aye, we would all seek his shelter. All of us, save one.

All except McKee.

Behind that British smile there dwells a warrior. Ensign Owen McKee would never cut and run. Not from one painted Huron or from a score. Retreat? 'Twould hardly be considered good form at Oxford or Cambridge or Harrow or Eton or wherever Owen McKee had been schooled. Astride his white Virginia mare, his saber swinging great circles of flashing silver, this ensign would attack a horde. And what is so ironic is that he might well turn them back. I oft wonder at the count of heathen savages on our planet that have stood in terror at the sound of one Scottish bagpipe. And thus, in their red tunics, like gods, they come to charge and astound and conquer.

Tired, I felt the ache of a servant's work gnaw at my bones as I lay on my cot. Do not perish, Benet. Else I will die here in Canada by the hand of a harder master. Boredom. You clout me, Skinner, and you fascinate me so . . . but, by damn, sir, you do not bore me. Where is Kapeeka? Old woman, please bring me my board. I fell asleep, to be awakened by the knock of a fist upon the door. Supper! I had eaten Kapeeka's food on three occasions, and the fat old sow could cook. Hurriedly, hungrily, I opened the door. But I saw no Kapeeka.

I saw Doe.

Chapter 7

THOUGHTS OF FOOD LEFT ME.

The hole of hunger that had bored into my body now vanished, replaced by another emptiness. I could not keep myself from staring at her face. The color of her skin made her possibly a half-breed. The flesh of her hands and face was a delicate blend of copper and cream. Dark eyes, brown as buckeyes or horse chestnuts, each eye containing a wee star. Twinkling twins of some inner sky intended to be seen only by a Cree.

"Come . . . come in."

Doe remained standing. Slowly she lifted up a stewpan of what appeared to be steaming deermeat and baked apples, a wisp of juniper, a succulent fragrance that was spiced with red currant berries and mint. My hands touched her as I took the cookpot. Yow! The pot was very warm, and I wondered how Doe had carried it so far without burning her fingers. She entered Benet's office as though she had been there before, and no doubt had. Wildly, I tried to set down the pot before its heat melted the palms of my hands. Finally, I did so, resting my supper heavily on one end of a pine bench, which allowed me to shake my fingers free of the momentary, but intense, discomfort.

"Hot," I said.

Doe watched me as though amused, perhaps wondering why her hands bore the hot pan for a mile, while mine could stand the pain for little longer than a deep breath. As she smiled, I saw that her teeth were very white and very young. Cree skin, yet not a Cree face. European? British? Scottish? French?

65

I pointed at a chair. "Please . . . sit . . ."

Wedged into the crimson strip of flannel that tightly belted her waist was a wooden spoon, which she slowly withdrew, passing the tool to my hand. As I took it, her fingers were then free to pull the crimson belt more snugly about her body, thrusting forward her breasts. Doe's dress was as white as Owen McKee's mare. Not shiny, but rather a soft white and not a hard one. I saw that her dress displayed trim about the neck and cuffs, composed of colored beads in a neat row, and also a line of tiny pink seashells.

Nothing about her was even average in size. Her hands were more delicate than sprigs of April leaves. Doe was not an indian. She was an indian doll.

"Thank you . . . for bringing it."

How perfect, I was thinking, a woman's eyes and nose and mouth must be, in order to twist her long black hair so severely into one braid. Black as the tail of Satan's mare. Will she stay? Or will she silently glide out of the door and melt into the Canada night? If she does, I will pursue her, to overtake her in some secret darkness where there will be only Doe and I.

Say something, please!

I felt like such a fool when my hand dropped the spoon. Clattering, it came to an awkward rest at an incline, its bowl across my shoe buckle.

"Doe," I said. "Doe . . . you are *here*."

She nodded as though she understood what I was trying so hard, and so pathetically failing, to say.

Oh, please talk. Say anything! Tell me what a clumsy clod of a boy I am, so I can tell you that I am surely no longer a boy. No boy on earth could look upon a female in the manner in which I now behold you. And you, my sweet Doe, are no longer a maiden. Your eyes reveal that already you command a fuller measure of wisdom about men than I shall ever begin to presume about women. How can I ever hope to hold you when I cannot even handle a spoon of wood? Oh, thank Heaven I am bigger than she! Taller and more husky. Am I older? Yes, I am certain of that. Yet only in years.

"It's good," I said, the venison porridge dribbling down my chin as I spooned mouthful upon mouthful. And it was. Never had my gullet been so hotly rewarded for a day's work. As I ate, Doe continued to watch me, climbing slowly onto the stool upon which I usually sat behind the clerk's desk. Her knees curled up, as the heels of her white mocs rested on the stool's top rung, and her arms encircled her thighs. Doe rested her chin on her right knee. She was a graceful serpent who had mounted a rock to sun herself. High up, from where she could look down upon her prey, or her nest.

I straddled the bench as if it were a horse, lowering the level inside the stewpot, tasting wisps of wintergreen and wild honey. Her mocs were not low cut, like slippers, but rather like high white boots that ended with a fringed cuff below her smooth coppery knees. Her upper legs lay naked in the shadow of her skirt, yellowy, warmer than two fresh loaves of cornbread. She noticed that I had observed her body.

"Benet will kill you," said Doe.

Those were her first words to me. On the evening of my first visit away from the stockade to Skinner Benet's cabin, I had heard her voice only in whispers, and she spoke only to Benet or to the old woman. Only in Cree. For days, and for many nights, I had longed to hear Doe's voice speak words that were intended only for me. Her lips to brush my ear lightly. And now she had spoken, of death, warning me as I looked at her that Benet would kill me because my eyes sought his woman.

"He will try," I said. My voice said the three words in a deeper tone than I usually spoke. My throat was steady and confident, and suddenly never had I felt myself to be so much of a man.

"Take care, Abbott."

"I serve him, Doe, as I am legally bound to do for five years. Yet I am not obliged to fear him. There must be one man at Fort Albany who fears not Benet. I am he."

"You are British."

I nodded.

"Benet says that the British are fighting fools."

"Does he?"

"Benet has seen the British officer who rides a mare of milk. He comes to Canada to rile the French, who will rile the Huron to canoe north and attack Fort Albany."

"He says much, your Benet."

"He is not *my* Benet."

"Are you his?"

Before speaking, she stared at my throat. "I wear no collar about my neck that says I am property."

About my neck, the iron ring was shrinking, as did it always whenever my spirit fought to outgrow it. Swallowing the stew became an effort. Without intention, my left hand darted upward to claw at the metal with my fingers.

"Olo," she said softly.

"What is Olo?"

"A sled dog that belonged to Eskimo Elky. He was so very handsome."

"Handsome? Eskimo Elky?"

Quickly her face bloomed with hilarity, becoming a creamy garden of happiness, and I was even merrier that I had given her laughter. So I decided to further my cause.

"Well," I said, "there is surely no explaining what a woman thinks of as comely. So," I sighed, "I guess if you think Eskimo Elky is another Sir Walter, that's surely your right."

Doe's face was a pansy of joy; my spirit was kindled to share our humor, and I was momentarily free of my iron collar. In the hearth, a log rolled and fell, and the room filled with a new light that was fresh and orange.

"Even the fire can laugh," she said.

"Do you like to watch the wood crackle?"

"Very much. Every little flame is like a man or a woman or a child. And the one that roars brightly and growls and dies is Olo."

"A dog?"

"Aye."

Hearing her use the Scottish expression made me smile. I held back my mirth, wishing her to continue telling me about the dog.

"What of Olo?"

"Like you, he fought his collar. Often he would try to wedge his head in a crack between rocks."

"To shed his bondage."

"Yes. And doing so, he hanged himself."

"And I am another Olo."

"Please don't be."

"Would it matter if I were to hang?"

"To me, perhaps. And think, if you hang, how greatly it would matter to you."

"At least it would not matter to Benet." I let her reflect upon this, spooning up the delicious dregs of Kapeeka's chowder, waiting for her to agree.

"Much matters to Benet," she said softly.

"Ha! What matters to Skinner Benet are the chattels owned by him. His precious eagle fur."

"You do not know this man."

"But I do. Well enough."

"No, you do not know him, Abbott. Do you know where Benet is this night?"

"To fetch Allard."

"Yes, to fetch Allard. But why?"

"He wants him to work."

"True. But soon Benet goes on a fur run, upriver for days and days and nights and nights and nights. He wants Allard to come along. Yet you will never guess the reason."

"No, I shall never."

"Allard has a wife and eight children. Benet forces Allard to work to feed his woman and his young. Benet makes Allard be a man."

"He likes Allard?"

"Hardly at all. But he is generous to Allard's children. And because of them, Benet would drive Allard to Quebec and back as a goatherd drives a goat, so that the children do not starve. And more, so that they have a papa to respect."

I could think of little to say. Doe's loyalty to Skinner Benet, I then decided, had been tested by others, and to witness such allegiance spurred my wondering if the day would come when I would be equally pledged to Benet. Without the iron encircling my throat how faithful would be Abbott Coe?

"Your supper is finished," she noticed.

"Yes, and please tell Kapeeka how good it is. Or was."

"I shall." She smiled. "Even though I cooked it."

"You? Was it venison?"

"No," she said, "it was possum."

We both laughed.

"I enjoy the laughter of a man," she said.

"Why is that?"

"Because," she said, "men seem always to release a downhill laugh, like a runaway barrel that no one can ever pursue and catch."

"You speak English so well. Who taught you? Or could I easily guess?"

"Quite easily."

"But your language is *better* than Benet's."

"Hardly so. Part of the credit belong perhaps to Father Joseph."

"The old Jesuit?"

"He speaks both English and French better than I speak Cree."

"I could hear you speak all night."

Her eyes widened.

"But . . . I did not mean it like that."

"No, you did not."

"Then why do you blush?"

"Because I am a woman, and I have a great many ideas from my own belly, none of which originate from the loins of a male. I, too, am an animal."

"You excite me."

"As you do also excite me, Abbott Coe."

"You are *his*."

"Benet does not own me. He is very old and I am very young, in years. Before he dies, it is my wish to bear him a child."

"Why?"

"Because he loves children."

Doe's response was so pure and so honest that I was disarmed by it. She was a miniature of Canada, clean and open and unspoiled by the complications of society, of civilization. And even, perhaps, a miniature Benet. She seemed as strong as a sprig of ivy, to live and to thrive and to entwine, yet never to halter a man with her womanhood. The purpose of a child in her womb would not be to contain Benet by containing his son or daughter. The child would be a gift to be shared.

"His seed," she said quietly, "is too worthy not to be planted. He must flower before he dies."

"I understand."

"Honestly do you?"

"Yes, and I hate myself for understanding."

"You and Benet are . . . brothers."

"Why do you say that?"

"Because," she said, "you pray to the same god."

"By that, do you mean the one God in Heaven, or the many and diverse gods of Canada and Fort Albany and the Hudson's Bay Company?"

"The many gods," she said.

"Do you believe there is a god of love?"

"Perhaps. But more, I believe that there is a stockade between you and me, and it is a fence that grows weaker with each moment that we spend together."

"Does it frighten you, Doe?"

Her hands covered her ears. "We say things to each other that are not easily heard. And worse, we say what Benet will hear. He could be far away and still hear with his heart, and that is one of his fears . . . that I will leave him for someone my own age."

"Would he do you harm?"

"Benet might do himself harm. I wish to hurt no one's heart. Neither his nor yours. Whatever I do, I wish Benet to know of it. To bless me or curse me for my action, but by all means to *know* what I do, so that he is never wounded by his wondering."

"Each night I think of you."

"And I of you, Abbott. Your cheek lies upon my pillow, your lips touch my face, and your body . . ."

Her eyes became suddenly wet.

I stood up from the bench. As my arms opened toward her, she came to me, and I was stunned by the determination of her small body. Doe was no longer a child. Nor a doll. A woman, small and strong and sweet. I felt her fingers about my neck, as though she had the power to discern its secret, its ring's end.

"There is no end, Doe. No door and no window. The end that you search for is an ending that be five years distant."

"You must never hate him," she said.

"But I have his collar around my neck."

"And my arms."

As my own arms tightened about her tiny body, the iron seemed to do likewise at my throat, warning me of the laws of property. John Howland's iron ring was roaring at me, a clanging in my ears, telling me to beware . . . that both Doe and I belonged to Skinner Benet.

I was choking.

Suddenly I knew why Olo, the sled dog once belonging to Eskimo Elky, had hanged himself. To die rather than to serve. Can a dog take his own life? Olo, wherever you are, and wherever your spirit is now at liberty to bark at an Arctic moon, I envy your independence. Olo, you have more soul than I.

"I know little about girls," I told her.

"And we," she said, "who have never had hot iron ringing our necks know little of being a bondservant."

I tore the bag of ticking from off my cot, to provide softness for Doe and me to lie upon, close to the hearth. Beneath our bodies, the fragrance of crushed muskeg moss was pungent and alive and made us a part of Canada. I did not enter her body, but the night would soon come when Doe and I would be man and woman together, as I wanted *my* child to grow inside her belly . . . not Benet's. Yet when I kissed her mouth, he saw me. If I touched her breasts, it was Benet and not Doe who pulled away my hand. And it was Benet's fingers around my neck and not a bondservant's iron.

Doe's fingers touched me lightly, seeking and finding and caressing me, filling me to overflowing with more pleasure than my body and my heart could hold.

Chapter 8

SKINNER BENET RETURNED.

Allard was with him, a muss of a man who walked unevenly, looking exhausted and somewhat frightened of Benet. The two Huron did not return, nor did I ask of their fate. We stood outside the office.

"Go home to your children," Benet said rather calmly as his moc thudded into Allard's backside. "Bid your wife a fond farewell, tell your children that their Uncle Benet loves them, and be ready to leave for upriver day after tomorrow or I will feed you to Billy, my buffalo."

"*Oui*, Monsieur Benet."

Skinner kicked him once more. "*Assez?*"

"*Assez! Assez!*"

"Be ready to travel, *chien*."

Whiskers and dirt and fatigue stained Benet's face. His body slumped, starved for rest, and his eyes fought to stay open. He looked older.

"Well, did Kapeeka bring you a supper?" He tossed me the tin of tea as he unloaded the sack to air out his wet gear.

"No, sir."

"Someone else did."

I hesitated. "Yes."

"And you found everything delicious." As he spoke, I saw red flecks in his eyes, as though some devil inside his head had smashed two goblets of red glass that had been filled with red wine, throwing the goblets at Benet's pride.

Would he draw his knife?

"Doe knows better," he snarled, "than to come to the

73

fort after sundown . . . just to bring table scraps to a tramp dog."

I let his remark slip by.

"Kapeeka! I should rip her red throat for allowing it."

"Mister Benet, I walked home with Doe, so that she would be in no danger."

"Ha! What protection would *you* be?"

"Enough to protect her from myself."

There! I said the words, and saw them sting his ears as though each word had slapped his face. Above his eyes, the black brows moved closer together, a sure indication of his rage. At his hip, I saw his hand swing closer to the knife handle.

"I'll cut you, boy. If you as much as ponder about her, or even speak her name once more, your belly gets slashed like I'd gut a deer. Do . . . you . . . understand?"

"Sir, I understand."

"She deserves a beating for this."

Coward! I yelled the word at my own bowels, or lack of them, as I stood silent . . . not daring to defend Doe. Yet somehow I knew he mentioned the beating in order to give *me* discomfort. I had seen him with her. His hand was too loving, too adoring, to yank and uproot even one ebon hair. Hurting her was not for him, and if the moment came for his wanting to give her pain, he would be impotent.

"You young whelp."

"Sir, my age is not a fault."

"I don't blame you. And I will not punish you for this matter, as the fault lies with her."

His ill choice of phrase staggered his own awareness, and for a moment the features of his face seemed to be at odds. He looked tired and betrayed, confused, not knowing what had happened or whom to blame. He stood there, seeming to hate his age as he hated mine. And hers.

"I must sleep." Inside his mouth, I saw the small object shift from the pocket of one cheek to the other, and back again.

"All is prepared for your voyage, sir. Everything you told me to do is done. Food, a carrot of tobacco for every *voyageur*, trinkets for Cree, powder and ball . . ."

"Don't recite to me, Coe."

"I'll not, sir."

Breathing in deeply, he sighed. "I am going to my cabin."

A man coughed. "Monsieur Benet?"

Both of us turned our heads to see Ensign McKee, his white wig and his red tunic; a tubular case that was long and black was tucked casually under his left arm. His right hand smartly saluted.

"Sir, may I present myself please? I am Ensign Owen McKee of His Majesty's Coldstream Guards."

"I know who you are," said Benet.

"You flatter me, sir. My orders are, with your permission, of course, to call upon you in order that I might solicit your advice in certain social and geographical matters."

"Ensign McKee, do you ask us all to believe that you in your red tunic come to Canada as a geographer?"

Owen McKee smiled. "Sir, I do not. As one can see, I come as a soldier."

"You come as a uniform, McKee, and whether or nay there be a warrior within is yet to contest."

"Correct, good sir." McKee laughed. "Be there a battler behind my buttons or merely empty brass? A good question and a fair one."

"I'm tired. What do you want?"

"To wish you a good morning, sir," said Owen, "and a good morning to young Abbott Coe, your loyal and faithful attender."

"Good morning to you, Ensign McKee," I said.

"What bring you?" Benet nodded his head at the black tube of leather under Owen's arm.

"Maps," said McKee.

"Of what and where?"

"Canada."

"Who drew them?"

"I daresay," said McKee, "the most learned cartographers of London, which, I imagine, renders them worthless if they be compared to only idle remnants of your recollection of land and stream."

"Well spoke, lad. Only an idiot believes in a map that other idiots draw."

"I request your help, sir."

"Do you now? You want me to point you in a southerly direction so that you can charge through half a thousand miles of wilderness, and Huron, to smite the French soldiers a stunner or two. And then, with some poor Frenchie's ear to skewer on your saber, you'll about-face and strut back to Fort Albany to medal your chest."

McKee laughed. "How rich, sir, is your jest. And your wit is far from lost on me."

Skinner Benet frowned. "My, oh, my, a British officer of the Coldstreamers who can laugh at himself? You are indeed a rarity, Ensign."

"And you, sir, a rare gamesman."

"Do you play chess?" Benet's voice sounded hopeful. "I have tried my best to teach this whoreson how to wage the game, and I'd sooner teach my buffalo. I swear, big Billy will master the game before Coe here even learns the slash of a bishop's path."

"Pity," said McKee.

"You don't play."

"Ah, but I do. More's the pity, Mister Benet, that whether I deploy an army of black or white, I will mate your king and humiliate you."

"Coe!"

"Sir?"

"You have one quarter of an hour to fetch chessboard and men from my cabin. One minute more and I will notch your ear."

I ran.

Kapeeka was chopping firewood when I arrived. She said nothing, only eyed me with a mother's suspicion. And to think that this big thornbush had actually sprouted such a beauty of a bud. Inside the cabin, I grabbed the checkerboard and a deerskin sack of chessmen, kissed Doe quickly upon her cheek before she could ask why I was here and where was Benet, slapped her modest but fault-less buttocks a playful slap, and bolted like a rabbit.

I returned in fourteen minutes.

A pawn hidden in each fist, one black and one white, Benet gave McKee a blind choice. Owen cuffed Benet's left and won white.

"May I watch?" I asked.

"No," said Benet without thinking.

"Then I will never learn, sir, and you'll oppose only Father Joseph."

"Watch then, and be silent. And bring us each a tankard of rum to sharpen our wee bayonets."

McKee started it: king's pawn, and king's pawn; bishop, knight; queen, knight; pawn, pawn . . . The game lasted less than an hour. Ensign Owen McKee played brilliantly. He always attacked while Benet, using black, constantly defended. Act and react. Cornered and helpless and mated, Benet extended the finger of his right hand, tipping over his king. His tiny black face fell downward on a red square.

"I surrender."

"Surrender? Sir, you are defeated."

"Again," demanded Benet. "And this time you play with black. I am much better with white."

"You would have to be." McKee yawned.

Benet looked offended, until the smile of Ensign Owen McKee caused Skinner to throw back his head and roar, nearly tipping the board. McKee and Benet both sat on the bench upon which I had feasted last evening, the board of red and black checks between them. Each man straddled the bench, toe to toe on both floors, a polished English boot facing a worn and mud-spattered moc that was soaking and torn, and as tired as the aging foot it cradled.

"One more game," croaked Benet.

"At your service," said McKee, "right after we examine the maps and charts. Duty demands I execute the obligations of my office. After all, I must serve His Majesty as well as you manage the Hudson's Bay Company, mustn't I?"

Benet feigned anger. "You arrogant prig, I'll kick the pomp out of you in the next game."

"Time," said McKee, "will tell."

"Coe! Run around back and draw us two more tankards of my best rum. And hurry, lad, else you may miss seeing your old master finish off this . . . this . . ."

"Arrogant prig." Owen McKee smiled.

With a resounding clank, again their two pewter tankards collided in a toast, sloshing rum upon bishop and knight and queen with little respect for rank. They played and they drank. Rum did not improve the quality of Benet's moves, nor did it hone his caution.

Once more I filled the tankards and yet again. Observing, I concluded that Ensign Owen McKee of the Coldstream Guards could play better chess roaring drunk than Skinner Benet could sober. Each time one of McKee's black knights would capture Benet's white bishop, as each white castle and white knight and white pawn would fall, Benet downed his dram until the stink of stale rum filled the chamber.

"Again," said Benet, caught with his king down.

"One more game." Owen McKee burped.

"This time I'll birch your breeches."

"I beg pardon, old dear, but you will like Hell."

"A wager!" said Skinner Benet.

"Done," said McKee. "Shake on it."

"We haven't made it yet."

"Oh? Sorry . . ." McKee giggled.

"I bet a barrel of rum," said Benet.

"Worthy! But I have nothing to bet."

"Your sword?"

"No, not that."

"Well, your wig then," hollered Benet. "I always had me a hanker for a wig."

"Do you wish to don it?"

"Dang right." Benet placed the white wig upon his own mop of gray hair. "Well, how's it look?"

"Fine. But the tail doesn't go over your nose. It's supposed to hang in back."

"Who said?"

"General Braddock." McKee saluted the ceiling.

"Who's he?"

"My commanding general."

"Can he play chess?" asked Benet.

"Braddock does everything."

"How well does he do it?"

"Superbly."

"Let's play. I move black this game."

"You play better with white," said McKee.

"Hey! Am I good with white?"

"No. You stench with either."

"Name your bet, soldier boy."

"My white mare against your indian girl."

Benet was silent. His head bobbed as if the muscles of his neck were a bit weak to bear the weight of wisdom. I wondered about his temper.

"Coe! Dang your eyes, my good old tankard is dry, and so is good old Skinner. Get your arse cranked up and fill up McKee here, else he'll quit playing before I can profess to him the finer points of experience."

More rum, more chess; Benet fell off the bench and near into the fire. He captured a white queen by moving a white castle until McKee pointed out the error. Benet hunched lower and lower as though trying to hide behind his own king. He still wore Owen's wig, the tail of which (tied with a neat bow of black) hung down over his right ear. It had been Benet's move for several minutes.

"Your move, Skinny," said McKee.

"Who's skinny?"

"Not you. You're just tipsy."

"Am not."

"I always heard it said that men in the colonies could hold neither their rum nor their women."

"That's a lie," said Benet.

"Move then. Waiting for victory bores me as much as tasting it."

"Only thing you can rightfully taste is a tank of my rum. Coe! Fill us up, sirrah, before I . . ."

"We are quite filled already. And you will lose the wager."

"What wager? I forgot it."

"Mister Benet, you made a wager that if I won every game, I would be allowed to company you upriver on your forthcoming *voyage*."

"The eagle fur," said Benet.

"Eagles have no fur."

"Back into the hills, upriver, to the southwest toward the five great lakes, that is where only the eagle can fly and where only Benet goes to claim the eagle's fur."

"That is a place I must go," said McKee.

"Only if you win. So play!"

"It is your move, Mister Benet."

"No, it's yours."

"Nay to that. Yet does it matter whether you advance a

knight or retreat a rook when your cause is lost? Your little king will totter and tumble."

Benet carelessly moved a pawn.

"And now," said the ensign, "before I presume to humble your sovereign, I will first violate your proud little queen." His bishop struck.

"Dang it all," said Skinner, causing the tail of the white wig he so clownishly wore to flop against his ear like the irate tail of an ass.

"Do you concede, sir?"

"Never!"

"Do you surrender your sword?"

"I have no sword, you popinjay. *You're* the one with the sword. All I have is a little cutter."

As Benet drew his knife, its blade silvery orange in the firelight, he raised it and stabbed the wood of the bench. The handle trembled and was still.

"No one violates my queen," said Benet.

Chapter 9

"HERE," SAID MCKEE, "IS FORT ALBANY."

Ensign Owen McKee had unrolled the largest of his maps upon the floor of the office, allowing Benet and me to crowd in and examine the buff-colored paper. Its edges were neatly cut, its words precisely lettered by what I envisioned as a military hand, complete with rivers, swamps, and names such as Huron and Cree and Iroquois.

"Hogpiss," said Benet.

"I beg your pardon, sir?"

"This map. Worthless."

"But generally is it correct?"

Skinner squinted at the floored map, the four corners held down by three tankards of pewter and one of Red Lion tea. "Yes," he said, "as much as I hate to confess, your map is generally exact. But rife with errors."

"Good," said McKee. "Let's improve it."

"To begin with, Fort Albany is not on Hudson's Bay. Well, it is and it isn't."

"Where then?"

"We're on James Bay. Think of a cow's udder as Hudson's Bay, with one swollen tit that hangs southly down, and that's James. Here we are, where the Albany River flows from the southwest, up from near the greatest of the five lakes. Upriver, we call it not the Albany, but the Kenogami."

"How far," asked McKee, "is Fort Albany from the greatest of the great lakes?"

"Ha! Not even the Cree know that. By canoe, allowing for the twists of the Kenogami, my guess is at least five hundred miles. Less, as the eagle flies."

"Five hundred miles!" McKee burped.

"Why do you wish to go to the great lakes?"

"I don't, sir. Not I."

"Who then?"

"Braddock."

The eyes of Ensign Owen McKee began to look as ill as Benet's. Half open and half closed. I had no idea of the hour. All three of us had put more than a dent into Mister Benet's keg of rum. I felt foggy between my ears.

Benet said, "I don't know any Braddock."

"Ah, but I do. He's my commanding general."

"Back in England?"

"No. Braddock's in Virginia," said McKee, unrolling a second map atop the first. "My father, Brigadier McKee, and General Braddock were, as lads, ensigned together in the Coldstream. Father and he are both originally from Perthshire in Scotland. As a lad I called him Uncle Edward. But now, of course, I call him General Braddock."

"What kind of soldier is he?" asked Benet.

"The best. Braddock is Mars."

"Lenient and beloved?"

"He is tougher than a whalebone. Very strict. Yet if you perform well and your lads are loyal to you, no one is more appreciative than General Braddock. I like him."

"Why is he in Virginia?"

"Look," said McKee, "and try not to spill any rum on these charts."

"You just spilled *your* rum," said Benet indignantly.

"I know." Owen McKee giggled. "Now be serious, Skinny. Look you where these two rivers join, one from Pennsylvania and one from western New York."

"So what?"

"There, in the crotch, Fort Duquesne."

"What river do they form?"

"Washington calls it Ohio."

"Who the Hell is Washington?"

"Oh," I said, "he's Owen's friend. Mister George Washington gave him Virtue."

Benet fell laughing on the Ohio fork, his hands holding his sides, sloshing his tank of rum. McKee also laughed. And I, too.

"Let's sing," said Owen McKee. He giggled.

"After I look at your fool map. Tell me again where Braddock is?"

"He's in Virginia," said Owen. "He and Washington and all the troops are marching soon."

"Marching where?"

"To the Ohio."

"You mean against that French fort?"

"Aye," said McKee, "to take Duquesne."

"Well, I'll be."

"Here it is in a nutshell. We British control the far north, from Hudson's Bay west to the mountains, and beyond. Correct?"

"Correct." Benet nodded.

"And," continued McKee, "we control New York and New Hampshire and all colonies to the south. But betwixt lie the French, from Quebec and Montreal up the Saint Lawrence River and to the five great lakes."

"Aye," said Benet, "and that fur should be ours."

Ensign McKee nodded. "Exactly, sir. So we shall free this territory from France, according to General Braddock, pinching the French from north and south as a lobster would encircle a smelt."

"What?" Benet squinted.

"Braddock moves west from Virginia and northwest into this lake, the Erie, then past the great falls, and against the Huron and the French, an attack from the south. Or west and around to the north lake of Winnipeg."

"And you, Ensign McKee, attack from here?"

"Aye, that I do."

"You have no troops. Only a score or so here at Fort Albany."

"Troops will come."

"Regulars?"

"Better than that. Highlanders."

"Black Watch?"

"Aye, and with drums and pipes."

"Why are you telling me this, McKee?"

"We need your help, sir. 'Tis no secret that, despite your French surname, you hold no affection for French or Huron."

"True enough," said Benet, his cheek resting on the map

over the floor as though it were a pillow. He appeared on the brink of slumber.

"Father will join us here, at Fort Albany, in less than eight weeks."

"He's a Coldstreamer, too?" I asked.

"Quite," said Owen.

"I find it very exciting, sir," I said.

"Oh, so do I. It's a master of a plan to squeeze the French from Canada. I'm here to scout from the north, and by gimcrack, I shall do just that. Make new maps, from here to the far southwest, where roams the eagle fur."

"Aye," I said.

"Skinny is asleep," said Owen. He held up a finger so that Benet not be awakened.

"Ensign McKee, sir, please teach me something."

"Of course. What is it?"

"Chess."

"Ahhh!!!" screamed McKee in fun, falling forward on the map as though the thought of one more chess game would surely turn him into a green illness.

"I want to learn."

"So do I," said Owen, "and that is why I have come to Hudson's Bay. Like you, I'm here to seek my fortune."

"For myself, a fortune in fur."

"Aye. You're a bright lad and you'll do it."

"Thank you, sir."

"Too bright to be a bondservant."

"By the time I am your age, I shall be a free man, and I shall make my way in Canada, you'll see."

"You shall, Abbott."

"And you?"

"Father and I are soldiers. He will die in his red tunic and I in mine. God knows where. His father, my grandfather, was also a soldier. We Scots are warriors, lad. It's our profession, and we know no other. Once I ached so much to be a painter. Or a poet."

"And why not?"

"Father would not hear of it. Mother is dead. I am an only child, no brothers or sisters, so my papa and I are quite close. Needless to say, when Uncle Edward . . . that being General Braddock . . . heard 'twas my want to study painting, he nearly reared up and threw a shoe. So I reluctantly left the verses and hues to other lads and lasses, and became a Coldstreamer."

"Are you glad?"

"Yes, I'm a stout soldier."

I nodded. "You look it, sir."

His hand clapped my shoulder. "Ah, but I am going to fool them all. You see, I am not just a Guardsman. I am a specialist now."

"In what field?"

"Cartography."

"Was this your idea, sir?"

"No, it was General Braddock's. He says no army can win a battle unless it knows where the Hell it's going. I shall surely give Braddock this . . . he knows where he's going."

"Ah, to Fort Duquesne."

"Right as rain. And how I wish I were en route there, with Braddock and Washington. I'm going to miss the parade."

"Will he win?"

Ensign McKee was silent for a moment. Turning suddenly to look at me, he said, "Only if he harkens to Washington."

"But, sir . . . Washington is your age."

"Aye, and even so, Edward Braddock best give the big boy an ear, or else."

"As you will listen to Benet."

"Abbott Coe, you are no fool. Not that I ever thought you one. You are perceptive, civil, and fun-loving. How I wish you were a private in my personal detachment."

"Would I get to be a Coldstreamer?"

"Well, at the least a corporal."

"Sir, what's it like to be in the Coldstream?"

"It is like being one of the Chosen, as if His Majesty has sounded a golden trumpet to which only a few may harken, and gallop to. When I was made an ensign, I wept. Father admitted that he wept also. And even General Braddock as the two stood side by side."

"Your father and the general are close friends, eh?"

"More than friends. Comrades. Do you know, dear Abbott, what it is to be someone's comrade?"

"No, sir, not quite."

"It is a silent vow that one soldier takes for the sake and safety of another. There is no formality, no ritual, but rather a pledge of the heart. To be a comrade is to be thankful that there is life beyond one's self and to honor the preservation of that life. Even, if necessary, with one's own."

"Like a religion."

"Yes, but unspoken and far sweeter. General Braddock would die defending my father, and my dad for Uncle Edward. Neither, if the end came, would hesitate or falter for even one breath."

" 'Tis a loyalty of lovers, of sorts."

"Truly."

"Have you a comrade in Canada, sir?"

"Pity"—his face mocked very serious—"but I do not."

"I would be your comrade, Owen."

"And I yours, Abbott."

"You do me great honor, sir."

"Friendship is a noble thing, lad. I formed an alliance in Virginia that oft occupies my thoughts."

"George Washington."

"Aye. And back home in Scotland, I have a bonnie sweetheart to whom I am betrothed. Would you like to see her picture?"

"Yes, sir, I would."

"Very well." From an inside pocket of his tunic, Owen produced a thin wallet of leather, opening it carefully as though it were a book. First he awarded himself a glance, smiled at the portrait, and handed it around in a half-circle to me.

"She is beautiful," I said.

"What you see is a mere painting. Were you to see her alive, and in song, truly your young heart would handspring as does mine."

"What be her name, sir?"

"Miss Heatherlee Doon MacDonald."

"A comely name for a comely lass."

"Thank you, Abbott. Have you a sweetheart?"

Doe, I wanted to say. Yet I was silent as I looked at the sleeping Benet, who at that moment let out a drunkard's snore. McKee laughed as I pulled the white wig over

Benet's face to muffle further noises that sounded like those of a sawyer.

"No sweetheart?" McKee asked again.

"Yes, I have one, sweeter than a sunset as it kisses the purple clover. And I shall soon wed her and we shall parent a half score of children."

"Aye! That's the lad! Show me her picture."

You have already seen her, Ensign McKee, I wanted to tell him but was afeared to cause more trouble than already created. Doe is her name, and she is half white and half Cree. If she has a surname, I know it not, except that her dam is called Kapeeka. Her mother is as large and wide as Doe is modestly, yet artistically sculptured.

"I cannot. I have none."

"A pity. Her name then."

"I forgot."

"Ha! What a Romeo you are to forget such a fair Juliet. Have you no soul, Coe? No spirit? How could a young swain beg to unthink the name of his true beloved? What a cad! Venus, do you hear? Eve, forsake not your garden nor your fruit, for here is an Adam nay worthy of your limbs and bowers, so beneath . . ." On he ranted, invoking all the tribes of Rome and Egypt and Israel to curse me for such a shallow lapse of memory as to forget my lover's name.

"Ensign McKee," I said, "perhaps we could tote Mister Benet to the back room cot, where his sleep could better restore him. What think you, sir?"

"Aye, let's pack him then. But where shall you sleep?"

"On the floor, sir?"

"For him you sacrifice your own bed? A noble gesture and you be a loyal server, Coe. Never in Padua was there such a Tranio such as you."

"*Taming of the Shrew,*" I said happily.

"Aye, take his shoulders as you are more sober than I."

With little ceremony, we half carried and half dragged poor old Skinner to my waiting cot. He groaned. McKee retook his white wig. Beneath it, Benet's real hair was white in the dark room.

"Grief, I am hungry!" said McKee.

"Let's go and find food, sir."

"A superb idea. I have found the Fort Albany kitchen

to be more than able to fill my growling paunch. Brother Coe, will thou be my guest?"

"Honored, Brother McKee."

He lifted up the tankards, rolled up his maps and cased them, and sighed. "War," he said, "is such a bore and a discomfort. Pity."

"What be a pity?"

"A pity 'tis the only trade I know." He clanked together two of the pewter tankards. "What say, my dear Coe, we avail ourselves and draw off one more measure of Mister Benet's exquisite rum?"

"Done, sir, and done."

We did. Singing, we stumbled down the infield of Fort Albany, in search of food, or song, and to empty two tankards. We toasted the Coldstream Guards and General Braddock; we toasted Canada, the Huron, and the Cree. Last of all, we toasted one Skinner Benet.

And his buffalo.

Chapter 10

"IN THE NAME OF THE FATHER, and the Son, and the Holy Ghost, I bless this voyage . . ."

The voice of old Father Joseph droned on and on, repeating in English what he had just said in French. All of the men who held oars listened intently, as French was their tongue. Several times Father Joseph would cross himself, and the *voyageurs* would do likewise. He obviously enjoyed his momentary importance and being the center of the ceremony.

"The old coot," said Benet.

I said nothing, as Father Joseph and I were still strangers. He had stopped by the office to question me about my past, my religion, and to poke into details concerning the Hudson's Bay Company, not to mention a variety of areas which were hardly his concern. He was even so bold as to comment about the relationship of Skinner Benet and Kapeeka's daughter.

"Indeed," said Benet again, "an old ferret. Yet we all treasure his blessing."

"Why?" I asked.

Benet's fist gently pounded my shoulder. "Because only fools can talk to God, my lad. Wise men are too vain."

We took no canoes. Only a pair of sturdy Yorkboats, flat of bottom. In the well of each, amidships, I noticed a square boot of wood with a hole centered, no doubt to house the lower tip of a mast. Wind permitting, we could sail around the tip of land prior to heading up the Albany River.

"Is our gear packed?" Benet asked me.

"Yes it is, sir."

I knew he would check everything, as one glance of his practiced eye would sum up more than all my accounts and columns, and he would leave little to chance. Benet wore a deerskin suit, atrim with fringe along its sleeves and legs, the color of a dark fawn. Almost a molasses. On his feet were mocs of a like shade. Moving quickly, he examined each boat from prow to stern, tightening ropes of rawhide, smelling containers of food for a telltale sniff of spoiling. If ever we took a blessing with us into a wilderness, it was Benet, and not a prayer. I did believe in God, I told myself, a spirit of vengeance and wrath. And a Giver. Yet, to be honest with my own thoughts, I must confess that I also believed in Skinner Benet.

We all believed.

Father Joseph mercifully stopped praying and crossing himself, and was now smiling. He patted a back here, a shoulder there, trying his best to lift spirits and boost souls. But there was no need for that. All the oarsmen seemed to me to be at the peak of their own excitement, impatient to exchange our two Yorkboats for our two giant canoes, both of which awaited us at Henley House, more than a week upriver.

"Peas and pork," spat Benet.

La Fleur, a *voyageur* in a bright green sash, overheard and smiled in anticipation. *"Mangez bien,"* he said to Benet and me.

"You will eat well, La Fleur, only after you produce a day's labor," said Benet. He pretended to strike the man a blow; La Fleur, in a like clownish manner, pretended to duck.

Eskimo Elky appeared, selling good-luck charms for each *voyageur* to hang about his neck, or attach as an extra rider to neck chains that bore religious medals. Elky sold every one, while Father Joseph glowered his disapproval at the competition.

"These *voyageurs*," said Benet, "are worshipers of spooks and spirits. Name any bugaboo you like and I'll point out a Frenchie who has purchased a bane against it. Every geegaw and trinket that Elky can dream is snatched up by these canoe-mules. And they will even attribute powers to their potions that the eskimo never considered."

"Here comes Ensign McKee," I said.

Benet and I viewed his approach. Owen McKee was not on his white horse, but afoot, in what I imagined was battle dress. His uniform consisted of a white wig, a tunic of searing red, white breeches, and black boots. A sword and pistol made up his weaponry. Under his arm was the long black tube containing his precious maps, the ones he hoped to correct.

"Why," asked Benet of Ensign McKee, "did I ever agree to take you upriver?" Benet sighed a resigned breath.

"For the eagle fur." Owen smiled, giving me a friendly cuff as if to say I was included in his conversation.

"Ensign," said Benet, "you will frighten away every bear, deer, panther, beaver, Cree, or Huron that we may hope to encounter."

"Am I not properly attired?"

"Yes! For an officer's ball."

"Ha! A jolly jest." McKee laughed.

"Do you, Ensign, have any idea where we plan to go, for how long, and for what purpose?"

"I do indeed, sir."

"Where's your gear?"

McKee pointed to the stem of the first Yorkboat. "Stowed away, since early this morning. A change of linen and stocking, my bedding, and even a spare uniform if this one becomes soiled."

"British," sighed Benet.

"And," added Owen McKee, "an extra supply of good English tea to stave off a chill, while we sit around the campfire . . ."

"Exchanging little stories," Benet finished the sentence, shifting the object in his mouth from one cheek to the other. It was a gesture he used when poking sport at what appeared to him as an absurdity.

"Singing merry tunes." McKee laughed.

"Trading tidbits of woodlore," I added.

As his hand twisted my shoulder about, in one gesture, Benet's moc thudded into my rump, as if to inform me that one British buffoon on a trip upriver was quite enough. So hustle I did, going over my list of each and every item, a list that Benet himself had compiled.

We shoved off.

Benet sat in comfort on a highback seat in the stern of

91

the first Yorkboat. Owen and I were in the second boat.
Everyone else was French. Pulling my opposite oar was
La Fleur, who winked at me, a fellow of good spirits, and
he oversaw my rowing with both help and humor. I
wanted to row, to help move the boat, even though Skinner Benet had said that it was beneath the dignity of an
Englishman to work an oar.

Benet had said, "If you are ever to become a boss, a
bourgeois, such status is attained by imploring others to
work, the peaporkers. This is why God made Frenchmen."

The oarsmen suddenly sang.

La Fleur was first to chant out a lyric, in French, which
I did not understand. All I could grasp of the song was
that it was about a pretty young girl who awaited a handsome *voyageur.*

"Le bateau, le bateau . . ." the chorus would echo after
every verse. La Fleur sang only the first one, Allard sang
the second, Normand the third. The song went on and on,
mile after chorus, and stroke upon stroke of our oars. My
hands stiffened on the oar's handle, as though this shaft
of wood were part of me, bone of my bone. And as Owen
sat in the rear seat, beside the tillerman, I watched his
face sing along, doing as I did, picking up a few phrases
of the chorus in order to mix with the music.

The water was not deep. So shallow that I could almost
count the pebbles as they appeared to swim by, passing
between the blade of my oar and the hull. Mud flats.
Several times we splashed ourselves out of the boat in
order to pull her across a sandbar. The water was liquid
ice. My shoes were soaked at once, aching my feet.

On we went, and on went the song, more resolute than
a bagpipe. With each creak of oars inside the oarlocks,
the beat of the song danced in like time, the squeaks add-
ing music of their own. The wind was brutal. A sea wind.
Upon my last day aboard the *Costain,* I had decided early
on that Hudson's Bay and James Bay were little better than
frozen inland oceans. Partly salt, brackish, yet constantly
fed by the host of rivers and brooks of fresh water, flow-
ing gently into the main body from the surrounding flat-
lands. I saw no rapids, no white water.

"Pipe," yelled Benet.

Upon his shout, every French oarsman and one English also hailed out in favor of the first welcomed rest. The *voyageurs* raised their oars, pulling them into the boat, wood clumping upon wood, sounding much like a drumroll. Boats were beached, prows grinding into the grainy shoreline of the mouth of the Albany River. Hardly a breath later, all pipes were lit, each man breaking his carrot of tobacco. We sat in two circles, almost as though the two boat crews were enemy camps. Except for Benet, who sat alone. As he hunkered himself down on a rock, his back was to all of us; he sat quietly looking up the river.

I wondered what his thoughts were. Then I brushed Skinner Benet from my mind as I squatted on a log, choosing to sit near Ensign Owen McKee of the Coldstream Guards, my comrade.

"Well, my young boatsman, and how pulls thy oar?"

"Heavily, sir."

"That I wager. How long do we stop?"

"I do not know, sir. Knowing my master as I do, 'twill not be long before we all return to enrich the Hudson's Bay Company as best we can."

"Rightly spoke, Abbott. Perhaps you have observed, as have I, that our leader in deerskin is a loyal son of such enterprise."

"Aye, or a devoted mother."

"He be that, too. Watching over his only child and heir, the Hudson's Bay Company, as though 'twere a babe in cradle." Owen's fingers drummed on the long black tube which carried his maps. I wondered why he had not left such in the boat. We all watch over something, I mused. Who, I asked myself, will one day watch over Doe?

"Pipes out!"

Upriver we rowed, against little current, as the river was wide here, and thus in no rush. Were these banks to narrow, and compress the stream, I imagined there would be rapids aplenty.

The oarsmen were quiet, reflecting perhaps upon the joys of the last pipe, dreams wafted away with their smoke. Fantasies of men always on the move, yet going nowhere, except to go where only an eagle could fly and fetch home the eagle fur. I rowed, carefully keeping apace with La

Fleur, making sure that the blade of my oar would spin a puddle at its tip that equaled Contois's, the man who rowed with his back to me. About his waist a bright blue sash caught the sun with each doubling of his spine. Tirelessly they pulled their oars, laughing on occasion at a jest in French that I did not understand. I wondered whether upon hearing such a joke in English I would be man enough to appreciate it.

I thought about Benet, and how he had delayed his call of "Pipes out!" until he saw the first man knock the spent ashes from the bowl. Benet, you are as fascinating as Canada herself. And each time that I predict your course, off you go asunder, on a fresh heading and into a foreign wind, fickle as frost. When astride the burly back of a bison, how doth a rider predict as to which direction his steed will leap? And how high? Will the hindfeet kick up, or will the fore?

Such is Benet.

Again they sang, beginning the song as though by some uncanny signal, throats responding in chorus to an unseen baton. I also sang, even though all words were in French, because what mattered most to me was the meter and not the meaning. Pushing away the handle of my oar, I pulled in time to the chant of the music, a cruel cadence that rested neither lungs nor hands. Oar after oar, stroke upon stroke, pipes lit and pipes exhausted, we fought our way slowly and yet evenly up the Albany River. Trees grew taller. Hills that looked as if we would pass them prior to the next pipe turned out to be distant by a day's rowing. Forty feet upward on the trunks of trees I saw scars that were slashed into the bark as if the forest had been lashed by the cats of God.

I asked La Fleur.

"*La glace.*" He nodded at the scars.

"Ice?"

"*Ah, oui, ah, oui.* Ice."

What a sight that would be, I told myself, to see hunks of ice so broken by a spring thaw that they would pile up, layers of white brittle-candy, gashing at treetops.

"Moose," shouted Benet.

We stopped rowing. Ahead of us, not more than twenty lengths of a Yorkboat, stood an animal with great horns,

taller by far than a buffalo. The moose stood ankle deep
in water. As there was no current where we paused, slowly we drifted toward the animal, until I thought the bow
of Benet's Yorkboat would ram the beast. With a great
trumpeting roar, the moose reared high on his hindlegs,
high enough for the two closest oarsmen to raise their
oars like the lances of warriors. None of us could blame
them, as the animal was awesome and could have trampled
us badly. I held my breath.

"By Our Lady," sighed Owen.

"Hyah! Hyah! Fie! Fie! Fie!"

Oarsmen of the lead boat were shouting, waving their
arms. Some reached into the icy water to grab at pebbles
the size of fists, to throw them with force at the moose.
The animal backed a few steps, antlers down, appearing
as though he intended to charge us. His massive horns
would span a man's body, pate to toe, and could no doubt
hack a human to bits. Or mash him. Stabbing my hand
into the river, I hefted up a goodly-sized rock. Too heavy.
Never could I have hurled it far enough and might have
succeeded only in smashing a hole into our lead boat's
flooring.

Brandishing his antlers, the moose tossed his head at the
stem of Benet's boat, whacking it, causing his great rack
of horns to ring.

"What a vibration," said Owen.

"Please," I said, "draw your pistol, sir. Or your sword,
I beg of you."

"Or both," I heard him say.

Benet sat quietly, the only man in the lead boat who
had not gotten to his feet. But now, across his knees lay
a musket, ready at the cock, I well presumed. Compared
to the splashing moose, Benet looked rather modest in size.
Silver drops flew among the oarsmen of the advanced
crew, making me grateful that I was in the trail boat and
not in the lead.

"I say," said Owen, "is no one going to fire?"

"Hold," said Benet, turning a bit to throw his command to us all. "There be no need to cut down such a
king as he."

"But what a trophy," sighed McKee.

"Christ," said Benet, "can't you British look at anything without wanting to kill it?"

Again the moose rushed to the front boat, causing Frenchmen to spill over the side. Some bolted to shore. Others held their oars on high, waving and shouting. It was apparent that Skinner Benet bore the only musket among us.

"What a gift for His Majesty," said Owen.

"Very well, sir," hollered Benet. "But no pistol. Use your sword and slay him if you can."

"Sir," said Owen, "sooner would I attempt to ride your buffalo at my next foxhunt."

I smiled, knowing how disappointed I would feel to see either Benet or McKee draw down on the moose. Just as Benet had said, this beast was a king, and like the Lion of England stands the Moose of Canada. A mighty warrior with an arsenal of antlers. Suddenly standing, Benet raised his musket and fired, pointing its muzzle only at the clouds. The moose bolted. First crossing the stream, or looking as though he wanted to, then wheeling about sharply to charge between our boats, showering us with a volley of water beads as he splashed by. Off he crashed, over the hilly bank and into the trees beyond.

Benet reloaded his musket.

"Jehovah!" sighed Owen. "What a beast. What an animal to confront." Throwing back his head, he howled to the heavens as though hearing some silent bit of wit.

"Abbott . . ."

"Yes, sir," I said.

"I tell you, my lad, that if a moose ever turned into a man, he would become General Braddock."

Chapter 11

"OSPREY," SAID BENET.

As we beached our boats to make camp, I had pointed at the bird, wondering what it was as I watched it dive into the Albany River to emerge with a small trout.

"What is our evening meal?" McKee asked.

As I did not yet know what it would be, Benet was the only man capable of answering Owen's question. "Pork and peas, and we'll split open our rum keg and wet our throats."

"Pity we bring no chessboard," sighed McKee.

"Pity for you if we had," Benet snorted.

Even though my arms were leaden from a day at the oars, I helped Contois gather dry wood for a fire. Contois continued to hum, speaking to me only in nasal French phrases, or nodding to one twig or another.

Brochet was our cook.

In minutes, he had his small fire crackling. Other fires roared, but Brochet kept his small, in order not to burn his cookery. Wads of beef jerky were speared by willow sticks, as the meat was wet and sodden, unappealing to the eye as well, I guessed, as the throat.

Bark pots were filled with river water to boil for tea. Not all of the men poured rum. Brochet himself preferred a hot swallow of tea with his meal, and told me so, in gestures that I could understand. He waved his arms at the keg of rum, while Skinner Benet broke a slat in its moon with one downward punch, using the butt end of his knife.

La Fleur had no cup. He drank from his moc.

We ate Brochet's supper in one tenth of the time that it had taken to prepare it. Never had food tasted better.

My stomach was as empty as a yawn filled with a growling echo that seemed to threaten that I would eat an oar, had the beef jerky, pork, peas, and hot tea been prepared a breath later than when it was ready.

Benet and McKee sat together, on a fallen log, watching the *voyageurs* and me snap at our meal. For we had been oarsmen, not they.

"They really do eat," marveled the Coldstreamer.

"Like sled dogs," said Benet.

I listened for contempt in my master's voice, but no contempt was there. No snarl of disdain. His voice was merely truthful. We oarsmen *did* eat like sled dogs. Three times I filled my bowl with Brochet's plain and plentiful food. The tea scalded my throat. There is something about having wet feet, I thought, as my burning tonsils nearly screamed, that allows one to tolerate a boiling beverage. The tea was sweet with sugar. Both our food and our drink tasted better, I imagined, than whatever is served in any fine eatery in London. No king ever feasted richer than a hungry oarsman who has pulled a full upriver day.

"Eat." Brochet smiled. *"Mangez."*

I nodded, not stopping until my chin was adrip with pork and peas and porridge. With my bare feet poked nearly into the orange coals of our fire, I ate, stuffing each crack of my empty and aching body until I could swallow no more.

Before retiring, Benet stripped off his clothing and bathed in the cold water, rubbing his white body with handfuls of coarse sand.

For twenty men we had brought eight gallons of spirits. "Rum." I overheard Benet's comment to Ensign McKee. "Rum is what whips the dogs of humanity. Whether they seek coal or whale oil, or fur, a slave of black skin or a bondsman white cannot be asked to chop timber or cotton ere he drains his dram."

"Aye," said McKee.

"Oft do I wonder what doth fuse the British Empire together, and I conclude," said Benet, "that rum is its flux. Our wheels turn more on rum than grease. And our boats would drift aimlessly downstream without each man being mete his measure."

Benet popped a piece of dried and pounded *caribou* into his mouth.

"What is that?" asked McKee.

"Pemmican. Here, have a corner."

"Thank you." McKee chewed. "It's quite dry."

"Dear lad," said Benet patiently, "I dare to say that you shall be so dang *wet* before this voyage is concluded, that you will soon welcome even a dry whore."

McKee laughed. "This rum is a welcome burning."

"Chilly, are you?" asked Benet.

"Nay, not quite. Yet the fire in a man's throat is a cozy comfort that only worthy spirits can kindle."

McKee slapped a bug.

"Are you bitten, Ensign McKee?"

"Aye. I see nothing."

"And you'll not for a spell. Then in a day or so, soon as we leave behind the breezes of Hudson's Bay, *then* you shall meet insects that you'll long remember."

"Bad, are they?" asked McKee.

"You will learn, Guardsman."

My head spun with rum. Thus I decided to partake of the stuff no more. Not even an added swallow. Little was left of the eight gallons, yet a fisting ensued betwixt Renfrew and Grosjean as to which *voyageur* would have the last few gulps. Benet did nothing to stop the fight. Both men were more than drunk and could do little to harm each other. Their battle was more a comic ballet than a besting. There was no winner and no loser, the pair of them finally falling into the shallows of the Albany River, much to the amusement of us who were not much drier.

"Hot rum," said Skinner Benet.

"I beg your pardon, sir."

"Upon our return to Fort Albany, I personally will batch up some hot rum, with cow's butter, or goat's which is far richer, and we shall all celebrate. And if, my young lad, think you that cool rum packs a kick, taste you a tankard or two of my buttery hot."

Several of the Frenchmen were either drunk or asleep or dead. I did not care, as the rum plus my fatigue seemed to overtake me. The scratch of even a damp blanket under my chin was an inviting sensation.

My first voyage!

I could not sleep. Bedded down betwixt La Fleur and Brochet, I was no longer chilled by night air. My intestines were awash with molten rum, and hot tea, and my belly was near to sloshing. Beneath us lay sand and pebbles, a bed of little or no comfort, unless one is a nesting gull. Never before had I slept on rocks, be they puny or mighty in size, and I do not recommend stones for retirement.

La Fleur snored.

Several times Brochet gave the man a kick below his waist to relieve the buzzing. To no avail. I wondered what the cause. Tea? Nay, I would guess not.

I did finally fall asleep, but was awakened by raindrops spitting upon my face. The men were up, overturning the two boats to provide us with shelter. We slept again, as two litters of kittens, our persons entangled in sleep. Somewhere below my bowels, someone's foot slept. Oft a hand or arm of an errant sleeper would flop into my face with a stinging slap. Few of the *voyageurs* were fragrant, and none, my guess was, was too familiar with soap. A cow barn would have provided a far more pleasant smell.

Yet they were warm. So was I.

"Fee fee," mumbled La Fleur.

I wondered what *fee fee* was.

Whether or not the rain continued throughout the night was a mystery to me, as I slept beneath our boat as though conked upon the noggin with a bludgeon. Truly out cold. We were awakened by excited shouts, and yet by starlight.

"Lève! Lève! Lève!"

All the French *voyageurs* jumped to their feet, preparing our two boats for shove-off, as we all inhaled the inviting smells of Brochet's breakfast. The sky softened from black to gray, and no longer did we have to stumble around in the dark. Our fires had gone out. All except Brochet's.

To relieve my bowels, I thrashed away north of our camp, through the brush in search of privacy. At least to be free of the other squatting Frenchmen. I ran. The joy of morning began to uncoil the chilly kinks of sleeping upon pebbles in a tangle of humanity. My blood was now pumping, as I leaped over a fallen log. Here I sat to dump my waste, enjoying my environs, listening to nearby twitterings of wrens and the distant yelps of *voyageurs* in camp.

'Twas then I saw her.

She sat, her back against a rock, grayer than the stone upon which she rested. Her eyes were open, looking at me. Pulling up my clothing, I wanted to call to the others, but seeing the old woman had struck me mute. She was an indian, a Cree, appearing to be more ancient than Canada herself.

Perhaps a trick?

Turning, I raced toward camp, crashing through thorns and thickets, suddenly able to shout my breathless warning.

"Indians!"

Reporting directly to Benet, I puffed out my alarm in a series of hurried pants, pointing off into the bush in a meaningless gesture.

"Cree?" asked Benet.

I nodded, my chest silently heaving.

"You are sure?" McKee wanted to know.

"How many?"

"One," I said, holding up a finger.

Benet's eyebrows tightened. Once again I noticed the object inside his cheek.

"An old woman," I said.

"Is this some sort of jest?" asked McKee, pistol in hand.

"No," I told them.

"Show me," said Skinner Benet.

As the *voyageurs* all mumbled among themselves, edging our two boats into the Albany River, Benet and McKee and I retraced my path to where my warm excrement still steamed beside the log.

She was gone.

"Where?" asked Benet.

I pointed. "There."

"An old woman, you say."

"Yes. I saw her, sir. Her back was against the rock. Sleeping with her eyes open, if you want my opinion."

"I do not, Coe."

Quickly and lightly, his mocs hardly touching the muskeg moss and dried grass, Benet moved to where the old

Cree woman had been sitting. Feeling the ground, he said, "The boy's right. Here is where she sat."

"She can't have gone far," said McKee.

"Stay," ordered Benet to Owen and me, as though commanding two faithful hounds to remain at heel.

Benet found her.

She was too old to have gone far enough to hide from us, and Benet knew it. This time, it was he who pointed, and our eyes that followed the line of his arm. There she was, once again leaning with her back to a rock, without motion.

"What is our old mother about?" McKee asked.

"She is dying," said Benet.

"Alone?"

Benet nodded. "It is the Cree way."

"Barbaric," snorted Owen McKee.

"Perhaps to you. Yet not to her."

"Sir," I said, "may we please bring her some food?"

"No! Give her no food."

"Why not, man, in the name of God?"

Benet turned to face McKee, speaking softly. "Because feeding the old woman would serve only one purpose."

"And what might that be?"

"Food would only prolong her death."

Commenting no more, Benet returned to our riverside camp, McKee and I following like two whipped dogs. Somehow, in the far reaches of my reason, I concluded that Benet was right. Damn his eyes! The man was always right, in every instance where life or death was the issue. A strange feeling took hold of my spirit as I watched Skinner Benet order the *voyageurs* about to hurry their meal and break camp. Whether in the civil confines of Fort Albany or in an upriver wilderness, Benet was definitely the *bourgeois*, the boss.

He ate nothing. His eyes hovered over our packing and loading like a pair of circling hawks, scanning the terrain, prepared to pounce upon the prey of error.

Suddenly I liked him. More than that, as my sentiments bordered on worship. The reason had naught to do with the old Cree squaw. Its base was another indian woman, Doe. I hated Benet most when he spent his nights with her. But here, upriver on the Albany, he was no longer the object of my envy, not a target for revenge. Here, even though he was always our master, he was far more. Benet was a Canada god.

Yes, a god.

More than the Cree or the Huron or the Innuit, my master was the flower of this northern domain. His empire. For 'twas Benet who ruled, and it was surely he who had become king. Just as Elizabeth had ruled her England, Benet's kingdom was far more than just Fort Albany or the Hudson's Bay Company. I mused to myself, wondering if the ladies of London could ever hope to imagine the kingdom of Skinner Benet. Hah! England, in area, is but a speck of lint in Canada's pocket.

Our bellies full of Brochet's boiled oats, sugar, hot tea, our heads still thumping a bit from last evening's rum, we pushed our Yorkboats away from the pebbles of our camp, each prow pointing upriver. I splashed aboard.

My feet were already wet. And cold.

Although my hands were stiff, my fingers forced themselves around the oar's handle, and I pulled. Several times the hull of our Yorkboat scraped along the grainy riverbed. We thumped and bumped over rocks. These were not pebbles. Some weighed more, I guessed, than a full-grown ox. I saw why we took Yorkboats for the early leg of our voyage. Rocks this size would have torn any bark canoe apart, and snapped the ribs of such a light craft as easily as if they were mere twigs.

Yorkboats were sturdy.

In design they lacked grace as well as beauty, and yet there was a substance to their structure as beefy and as bully as all things British. And had John Bull been a vessel, he would have been a Yorkboat.

Out of the boat we splashed, into icy water, in order to maneuver our craft around giant boulders that lay in the riverbed, half wet and half dry, huge hunks of pale pink rock worn nearly round by their long tumble downstream, no doubt pushed farther each season by masses of ice that no human could imagine. Again I noticed the ice scars high up the tree trunks.

Each day the trees grew taller as we worked our way upriver. Usually the current was so slight that the river seemed almost a placid lake. At night we camped ashore, drank hot tea, swapped stories, sang songs, and ate as sled dogs.

No more rum.

Only the first night, Benet had ordered. So no one disobeyed the *bourgeois*. Besides, the rum was gone, except for a medicinal keglet, which Benet called a dogshead.

On either shore, left or right, the banks became steeper. Deposits of silt. So high they were in places that we seemed to be rowing in a man-made canal, unable to see the muskeg swamps that flanked us on either bank. All the elements of growth grew larger, as though fed to monstrosity by some wilderness spoon from Mother Nature's hand. Trees were taller. Even the weeds were over my head. Distance was tricky. A point of land upriver that seemed to be an hour away proved to be half a day's rowing, or more.

My back ached.

Each night I slept, dreaming how I would gladly trade my soul for one day with dry feet. Or fresh stockings, warm from hanging near a cozy kitchen hearth. With each nightly breath, I inhaled the smell of men who had pulled oars, which alone is killing work. But these Frenchmen and I had pulled oars for Skinner Benet. Surprisingly, there were few complaints. A whine or two, punctuated often as not by the thud of a moc against a backside. We became a crew, stroke by stroke, each sore sinew serving as a bond to bind us together. Our rowing became smoother, our strokes longer and less choppy. But the water, when we would jump over the side to haul our boat by a boulder, was just as icy. I had known hot pain, and now cold.

I ate more than ever had I eaten before. Like the trees above us, my body grew. My neck was filling my iron ring.

Chapter 12

"HOW MUCH FARTHER TO HENLEY HOUSE?"

It was Ensign Owen McKee's casual question to Benet, a question I had asked several times, and had received no answer to.

"Fort Albany," said Benet, "is three days downriver from Henley House."

"In miles, sir?"

"My estimate is one hundred fifty."

"We have been boating for a week," said McKee.

"A rule I use," Benet answered, "is that upstream distance is twice-and-a-half the downstream in time."

The two men sat near a fire. Although I pretended to be asleep beneath my damp blanket, I listened to their discourse with interest, hearing also the crackle of Ensign McKee's ever-present maps that he unrolled and rolled at each bend of the Albany River.

"Are we here?" asked McKee. As he spoke, his lean finger tapped a spot on his chart.

"By your map, McKee, we are nowhere."

"Incorrect, is it?"

"Quite, to my eye."

"Then, my dear sir, 'tis your eye I value, and not the eye of Major Graham, who is the territory's cartographer, yet only a Londoner."

"Wisely said, Guardsman."

"A pity."

"What be a pity now?"

"A shame then, that my friend in Virginia is not here, as he knows already more of the craft of surveying than my transit shall ever master."

"Tell me again his name."

"George Washington."

"The fellow who gave you the mare."

"Someday I shall even the tally and bear a gift to him that be worthy of his nature."

"A fitting exchange."

"Monsieur Benet, have you a suggestion?"

"Aye. Take your Washington an indian girl."

McKee laughed politely. "Nay, not that."

"He lusts not for the ladies?"

"Well, as I was so bold when in Virginia to show Washington the picture I carry of the lass back home to whom I am betrothed, he was most appreciative."

"Then haul him home a red Cree woman."

"A most unfitting gift, sir. Washington is a man of lofty ideals, and I presume him to be quite straight of lace, to use a term. When we attended a party, among a host of attractive ladies, not once did my friend George utter even one suggestive word."

"A man perhaps like yourself."

"Alas! Were I only half as virtuous as my Virginian friend."

"A Virginian virgin?"

"Good jest, Benet. You are not without wit."

"Nor would I guess you, nor Washington, are without male desires."

"Aye, quite so. Hopefully my associations in army life have not fettered me unfit to wed my beloved Heatherlee."

"Owen, my lad, if ye be unfit now, I hate to imagine how unfit you be upon your return from a journey upriver with a pack of *voyageurs*."

"They seem lusty enough, sir."

"Lusty is hardly the word, Guardsman. There are few French women at Fort Albany. None at Henley. No British woman would spit on a peaporker. And chasing a Huron woman through the tall timber can be a reckless recreation. Especially if her husband or father lurks behind a nearby tree."

"You are telling me . . ."

"Aye," said Benet. "Do not be distressed at what you see before we trade with Stick Bear and glean the eagle fur."

"I am no prude, Benet."

"Permit me to warn you, sir, that our lusty *voyageurs* are not particular where they sow their seeds."

"Cree or Huron, I imagine."

"Can you imagine a dying Eskimo woman or, worse, even a sled bitch? So prepare yourself, Guardsman, to turn silently away when you discover Le Brun enjoying Osier . . . who is in turn enjoying Mercier."

"No!" McKee laughed heartily.

Beneath my blanket, I held my own breath. And to think that I sleep among such . . . I could think of no proper term. Then I remembered the many lectures we orphans had received from dear Sister Elizabeth. Again and again she had said that once we leave the shelter of our walls and enter the real world, "be not dismayed at strange practices."

I smiled. Recalling how Sister Elizabeth had concluded, in her gentle manner, that "perhaps the most vile immorality of all is to concern ourselves with the morality of others."

"Tomorrow," said Benet to McKee.

"I beg pardon, sir."

"We arrive at Henley House."

"Excellent. I look forward to it."

"Expect you not much," said Benet. "You will find the post occupied by dull people. No sense of humor. Worse yet, these few English who house there have no *rapport* with the Cree or the Huron. Even less than I."

"Come now, Monsieur Benet. I have heard it said that you converse with even the great white bear."

"My dear McKee, if all that is said about me be truth, then surely I would have precious little time remaining to attend the Hudson's Bay Company."

"Well said, sir."

"Unroll your map a bit on the left side."

"Here?"

"Aye," said Benet. "We have traveled now for one week, in a west-by-southwest direction, and tomorrow we reach the forks. We will turn south from Henley House, up the Kenogami River and close to the land divide. Note here, the watershed. These puny rivers here flow south into the great mother of the five lakes."

"Let me guess how much of this territory flies the British flag."

"Guess then." There was a coldness in Benet's voice, a sudden edge whetted and ready to bite.

"To the watershed. Am I correct?"

"Of course."

"The waters that feed Lake Superior are controlled by France and their fur tradesmen."

"Obviously," said Benet. "As all maps in Canada are drawn not by flags, nor by feathers dipped in butternut, but by the stemrod of a birch canoe."

"Never did I realize this," commented McKee.

"Few people do."

"General Braddock would be fascinated to be here, to meet you and ask you questions, sir. And I am sure how charmed you would be to meet our commandant, and my father, Brigadier McKee."

Benet spat into the fire.

"Curse you all," he said very softly.

"Do I offend you, sir?"

"Flags offend me. Flags and soldiers and the stink of gunpowder offend me. That's all you blasted British think upon. Pistols, politics, and Puritanism."

"And what think *you*, Monsieur Benet?"

"Whiskey, women, and wolf hides. Commerce is what I think upon. My father was killed in France. He was Huguenot, and he was clubbed to death by Catholics, in the name of religion."

"Have you no church, sir?"

"Back in Fort Albany I know a man named La Tour who visited a chapel in Rome. With great ravings and gestures of his hands he told me about its ceiling."

McKee said nothing.

"Above us." I saw Benet suddenly point at the sky. "Look you, sir, if you please, for up yonder is the ceiling of my church. Created by God, and not a paint brush."

"Pilgrims say the Roman ceiling is a masterpiece."

"Hah!" Benet snorted. "Grander than the stars, the sunset, or a rainbow?"

"Were they caught, sir? The men who slew your father?"

"One was, some years later."

"By the *gendarmes?*"

108

"No, by me. I am wanted for murder in France."

"Perhaps you may someday return, in honor."

"Return? Benet go back to France? Never. My friend, do you know who designed Hell? A French jailer. Assisted by French judges and French lawyers."

"Are you sure the man whom you undid was one of the guilty three?"

"I wagered my life on it."

"Why, may I ask, are you also bitter against the British flag?"

"Because, young sir, here we be . . . an ocean apart from England and France." Using a scraping stick, Benet drew in the sand between their feet. "And were we to set down one Englishman and one Frenchman here in this wild, in less than a day, they would duel to death, to determine whose flag flies over all of Canada."

" 'Tis truth, sir, and I reluctantly agree. France and England will do battle to see who owns a beaver. Or a moon."

For some hidden reason, both Benet and McKee looked upward, firelight flickering on their chins. Extending a buckskin sleeve, Benet pointed at the moon.

"Is it not enough," he said, "to see the moon, without one's guts burning to own her?"

"Aye," agreed McKee.

"And likewise Canada?"

McKee smiled. "Monsieur Benet, you have me cornered. I am checkmate."

Benet sighed. "Still you fail to understand. I have no wish to wage a war. Perhaps this is why I play chess so poorly. To command a board of checks is more than I can hope for. But to own Canada. Reach you not for Venus or Mars."

"You shame me, sir."

"Nay, I do not. You are a soldier, Owen McKee. You are a Coldstreamer. Your fine brain has been smithed until you now be mindless as an attacking locust."

"And you, my senior sir, are an angel with no ambitions?"

Benet smiled softly. "Fie upon that, for I am about as angelic as Satan. All I wish is to harvest furs, and I grant that practice be bloody enough. But upon my death I will leave Canada as I found her, with no flagpole stabbing her navel, and no gunpowder choking away her sweet breezes."

"Benet the bard."

"Ha! Benet the fool. South of here, miles south, your friend Braddock may be far more daft than I."

"How so?"

"General Braddock, you tell me, marches against the French fortress at the Ohio fork. Does your commandant actually think that a wilderness war against the French and their indians will be liken to an English meadow for close-order drill?"

"Braddock is able, sir."

"I do not doubt he is. The test of his brilliance is that he trusts you to map the Hudson's Bay territory, prior to a strike west by your father's forthcoming detachment."

"And what you are saying, Monsieur Benet, is that General Braddock has no Benet to correct his cartographer."

"Yes, I say that."

"He has Washington."

"A maker of maps, your Washington?"

"Among other things. All our plan calls for is to squeeze the French betwixt two jaws. My father in the northland, and General Braddock into Ohio. They shall meet at the western tip of Lake Superior and exchange trophies."

"Have you, my lad, any idea how far it is from Virginia to the west tip of that greatest of lakes?"

"Quite far, I suppose."

"May I also ask your age, Ensign McKee?"

"Sir, I am twenty-two."

"And you are a freshly minted officer in the Coldstream Guards, able and ready to follow willy-nilly in your father's marching steps, and General Braddock's."

"If I prove worthy, sir."

"Your first campaign?"

"Aye."

"A pity they give you no assignment that is worthy of you."

"Thank you, sir. You honor me."

"Ensign Green-Ears, it is nary my wish to honor you, to salute you, or to drape a British flag over your bier."

"What be your aim, sir, if I may please ask?"

"To keep you alive. You, and our frisky young Coe, and

a score of French *voyageurs* and maybe a few Cree and Huron. It is sorry enough that I slaughter so many beaver, fox, mink, bear, and stoat. Is there not enough blood on my blade?"

As though he were thinking, even questioning, Ensign Owen McKee's hand stretched out to lift up a handful of sandy soil. "It be not my wish, sir, to bloody Canada."

"No? Since when do Coldstreamers come in peace? Please reassure me once again, young man, how King George's redcoats march around our planet spreading the gospels of serenity."

"Speak not against our king, sir. I beg you."

"This be Canada. And we have no king."

"Canada will soon be New England."

"So say you." Benet relit his pipe, the orange of a flaming twig flickering upon his face, turning his eyes into crimson coals.

"Do you believe in destiny, Monsieur Benet?"

"I suppose you do."

"Sir, I trust in England and the Crown."

"And the Coldstream Guards," said Benet.

"Yes, and the Guards."

"Looks to me, Ensign, that your loyal protection of King George is a mile or two farther from the throne room than necessary."

McKee laughed. "You are hard to hate, Skinner."

"And you, my young fellow, are hard to teach."

My spine froze. The cry of a hungry throat was unmistakable. Wolves! And never do they hunt alone, or so John Howland had warned. Wolves come in packs, oft a hundred at a time, and they can hunt down entire herds of *caribou*.

"Soft," said Benet.

"It's a wolf," McKee said with drawn pistol.

The howl came again, closer.

" 'Twas a loon." Benet laughed.

With a deep sigh, I closed my eyes, remembering the loon I had seen yesterday on a widening of the stream. Slowly the loon had been swimming along, eyes beneath the surface, water rippling over his head as though it were a pebble in a spirited brook. Larger than a duck. Black back with white dots, vertical white neck stripes, and red eyes.

"They float asleep in the water," said Benet, "and oft cry out, perhaps in their slumber."

"The osprey we ate was a horror," said McKee.

Benet laughed. "Never roast a bird that eats fish. Osprey and loon are not ducks, and not to be man's prey. 'Twas a joke Brochet played upon you. As did the loon."

"I still think it a wolf," said McKee.

"Put away your pistol. Save your aim for Sick Bear."

"Monsieur Benet, in this wilderness, were I to suddenly confront the King of France along with a retinue of full guard and declared for war, and you said King Louis were a loon . . . I daresay I would believe you."

"How comforting that you take my word in such matters as weighty as waterfowl."

"And how recklessly General Braddock and George Washington and I spurn your counsel with regard to the conquest of French Canada."

"Fools learn slowly," said Benet.

"Ah! Fools and soldiers you mean?"

"Wrong," said Benet, "because soldiers never learn."

Chapter 13

"AHOY! HENLEY HOUSE!"

Benet hollered, although I saw nothing. No sign of life. My back was toward our destination, but I had craned my neck in order to see what lay ahead of the first boat. Ensign McKee and I still rode the second.

My oar suddenly stubbed its tip on a submerged rock; the handle smote my belly a blow, nearly pitching me headlong over the side. A wetting would matter little, as we had waded much that morning, waist-deep in the icy water. Several times we had almost carried our Yorkboat over a shoal of boulders. The physical strength of the *voyageurs* astounded me. They were not tall men, yet overly thick of arms and shoulders. Legs not as beefy. No fat on even one of them. Benet oft referred to them as "ox-men" and they truly were. La Porte could near have hugged and uprooted a tree.

"Hello, the Henley House!"

Benet continued his hailing. I wondered why and wished to ask him. Continuing to row, after my oar had "caught a crab," I received a few dark looks from the faces of my fellow oarsmen. Rowing hard, eager to see Henley House, I thought of all the questions with which I had pestered Benet. So now I kept mum, worked my oar, and decided that the reason Skinner Benet yelled was that the place was managed by Englishmen in a wild who might well use muskets upon us prior to inquiry.

"Hello!"

Besting my curiosity to twist about once more on my seat to look, I pulled steadily, apace with LaFleur.

"Ah!" I heard McKee remark. "At last."

113

Our prow nosed her way into the grainy beach, and we splashed ashore. The *voyageurs*, I told myself, never seemed fully content unless they were all soaking wet, for one reason or another. My feet ached from cold. All I wanted at Henley House was a spell to dry out my stockings, footwear, and breeches.

Benet, I noticed, always remained dry.

Just once, I told myself, I would seize an opportunity to splash water on him, or perhaps overturn his craft and spill him into the drink. One time, I wanted to see Skinner Benet cold and sopping as the rest of us. Even our British ensign wetted his boots on more than a single necessity, heaving and tugging with the best of us. But never Benet. Only when our lead boat was beached safely ashore did he arise from his backrest seat astern, step gingerly forward, and place his dry mocs upon dry land. Oh, I wanted him wet! To push his face under the current, allowing him no air until at last he would emerge, surprised and sputtering for breath.

Sneaking off my garments, I hung them in sunlight, where the midday warmth would soon come to dry them out. I was wringing out my breeches as a familiar moc struck me from behind, flinging me forward onto my face.

"Busy yourself, Coe."

"I will, sir."

As I looked about me, no French oarsman had bothered to tend his own sopping misery, but instead, all the *voyageurs* were at work unloading our two Yorkboats. Others were examining a row of paddles that leaned against what appeared to be some sort of shed.

Henley House itself was little more than a chicken coop. I didn't really know quite what I expected; perhaps some hospitable inn which might serve us pewter tankards of bubbling ale, hot biscuits, and victuals other than peas, pork, and beef jerky. I saw Benet talking to a man in English clothes. Behind the man I thought I saw a woman's face in the shadows of the main building, which was a cabin of logs.

We all hurried.

Voyageurs shouted and yelled, carrying our packets of trinkets for trade from the Yorkboats, piling the brown bales of cargo in neat piles and rows along the stony shore.

Several of the oarsmen seemed to watch Skinner Benet with sideward glances, as though trying to overhear the conversation betwixt my master and the keepers of Henley House. Generally, our *voyageurs* would admit to having no command of our language. Yet they more than understood Benet's sharp barking of orders. La Fleur, on occasion, spoke to me in a short English phrase, or brace of words; to themselves, they spoke only French.

"*Vite! Vite!*"

Working quickly, we completed the unloading of the Yorkboats, hauling our empty crafts up the banking. For some reason, we hid our two vessels among clumps of evergreen. Boughs were bent, not broken, to cover the boats. By error, I broke a branch. Contois discarded it, and then pointed at Le Brun. For a moment I was confused, wondering what Le Brun and a broken evergreen branch had in common.

"The snapped bough turns brown," said Owen McKee. "A bent bough remains green and masks our boats beyond detection."

"Aye," I said.

"Do you know who mentioned such lore to me?"

"General Braddock?" I asked him.

"No, it was my Virginian friend George Washington."

"And now you'll soon wonder," I said, "how well your friend can conceal General Braddock from the French along the Ohio."

"You are perceptive, Abbott, for that was my precise thought."

A warm feeling, to be called Abbott, instead of "Coe, do this" or, "Coe, do that." I had often silently asked if Benet would ever call me by my Christian name. Dare I call him Skinner? I chuckled, remembering the night of the chess game, when Owen had called him Skinny. Luckily, both of them were in cups and less than normally perceptive, or keenly sensed.

My backside smarted.

One day, Monsieur S. Benet, a moc will toe you in the rump hard enough to lift you from the ground. Aye, old sir. And 'twill be the departing boot of Abbott Coe, your bondservant.

From a distance, I heard strong words being used. Not

by Benet, but in an accent far more salty than his. I heard
the word "canoe" several times. The hollering boomed out
from a Canadian body, a voice much like the blacksmith
downriver at Fort Albany, the one who had collared my
neck. But 'twas not the voice of John Howland.

Benet returned.

"Who is the old grandfather?" asked McKee.

"I don't know his name. We all call him Old Hunch, as
his back was once broken in a brawl over a Huron woman."

"An interesting chap."

"But a slow one. On our last voyage he promised me a
new canoe, and now he claims it is not yet ready. He says
one canoe takes a year to construct."

"Then why keep him in your employ?"

"Because," sighed Benet, "that old hunchback is the best
damn canoebuilder north of the great lakes. Red or white."

Owen McKee smiled. "Reason enough."

"Coe!"

"Here I am, Mister Benet."

"Drop whatever you are doing, and tramp your butt up-
trail and help the old man. Do whatever he bids you do.
Do not ask him a score of questions or his temper will
snap meaner than Eskimo Elky's lead dog."

"Right away, sir."

Grabbing my wet clothing, I scampered through the
bush in the direction that Benet had pointed. Building a
canoe would be dull work, and I had no hanker for such
a chore. All I was doing was trading one crusty old
curmudgeon for another; Benet, in exchange for Old
Hunch.

I found the old man.

From the rear he looked like a Cree. His deerskins
were old, ragged, soiled with stains of assorted sources.
I guessed them to be food.

Although bent, he was stout of arm and chest, which
prohibited my asking had he once been a *voyageur*. As
he turned, the look of eagles in his eyes told me that he
was far more than a pack mule. His face was lined and
snow-capped with an unbrushed thicket of very white hair.

"Sir, my name is Abbott Coe."

Squinting, he eyed the iron that encircled my neck. As

his back seemed forever bent, his face was lower than mine. Walking slowly, he approached. I tried not to tremble as his old claw of a hand reached up to examine my collar.

"Benet," he growled. His voice was hoarse and husky, a tired winter wind that whistled through broken rafters.

"Yes, I am his bondservant, sir, and he has ordered me to help you build a canoe."

"Help *me*?"

I nodded my head, and sighed, as though to inform Old Hunch that I sought his company no more avidly than he wished for mine.

"Benet beats you?"

"No, sir, but he boots me around a bit." Usually, I wanted to add, when such treatment is owed to me because of my own sloth.

Bending low, the old man picked up a twig of hardwood, fallen from what I recognized as an ash. With both hands he held the stick, slowly commencing to bend it. Snap! The twig was suddenly in two parts, a half-length in each of his knotty hands.

"One day," he said in his husky old voice, "one day soon you will try to break Monsieur Benet."

"How know you this, sir?"

"Your eyes. I read it."

"My eyes?"

"Your face fights your collar, Abbott Coe."

The iron around my neck grew tighter, until I forced my hand to keep hanging at my side, not to reach up and tug at my bondage.

"You have work for me, sir?"

"Are you a maker of canoes, boy?"

"Never, sir."

"You are English."

"Aye, sir, I am."

"Do you know how old I am?"

"Nay, sir, I do not."

"Neither do I. A lad like you I was, tall and straight as a Huron arrow, when we cut through the ice and come to Hudson's Bay. We walked the last hundred mile, as the bay was solid froze. Whiter than a woman's cakeboard. I been in Canada most my life."

117

"I am fond of Canada, sir."

"So be I. Fond of fur and the trade. Fond of the western empire and her sunset waters."

"Have you been west, sir?"

"Aye. Beyond the hunting ground of Sick Bear. Clear to the high points, clear to the secret portage where two rivers near pass, one to the far ocean, and the other our way. Easterly."

His lungs panted, as though the talk tired him. Or was it the remembering of a journey westward that few white men would ever survive? Old Hunch had paddled there, and returned. His back had been straight then, and his bowels stuffed with pepper. I almost knelt before him, as if he were royalty, for he had been knighted by his own adventure. I felt the envy to do likewise, to paddle west, and to fill my heart.

"I will help, sir."

Old Hunch nodded, gazing at me is if he knew things about myself I had yet to discover. I wanted to say one more word to him, to speak one more name, and see if his squinting eyes would widen: Doe.

"Let us work," he said.

Together we walked through weeds taller than my head. Big, big Canada. Hobbling ahead of me, head to one side, he shuffled through the bush to a patch of thick shade beneath a stand of what Benet had said were spruces.

"Shade," he said, "always in shade."

"Why?" I asked.

"Sun dries out the birch."

Walking farther, deep into a cloud of shadows, upon a carpet of needles from the pines, we came to his great canoe. A year to build for one pair of hands? More like a decade. For me, half a century.

A monster!

My height I knew to be over five feet, and this canoe was a warship of a craft. My eye quickly told me that the canoe would be near to eight times my standing. Forty feet? I saw no extensive collection of tools. Only an axe, a froe, an awl, and a knife with a crook blade.

"Birch," the old man said, lifting up a chunk, his hand caressing the two shades of trunk, dark at the core, lighter outside it. "Heart and flesh," he said, touching the wood as though it were his companion. "Before we begin," he said, "come."

I followed the wave of his hand, beyond the wall of thornbush until I could see where the old hand was pointing. There on the ground, bleached white, lay a human skeleton. The teeth grinned at me as if they knew the jest of death.

"Ever see a dead man's bones?"

I swallowed, unable to answer. In truth, I had not, as I had been taught by Sister Elizabeth the torments of those who sport in the moonlight and the desecration of graves.

"Look well, boy. For these bones are a small canoe."

Silently I stared. He talked.

"Note the ribs, the spine. All that is amiss is the meat and hide. The first canoemaker, whoever the red devil was, first beheld a dead man's bones."

Old Hunch laughed hoarsely, perhaps aware of the crawling horror that my own flesh was experiencing. Reading my face, he continued his brittle laughter until finally his humor dispersed itself into a spasm of coughing.

"Now we work," he could finally say.

"Good," I said, wondering why I was suddenly interested in this exciting craft. Never had I expected to discover an artist of a shipbuilder, a Jason, here in a Canada wild.

"Winters back," he said, "I was a *hivernant*. One who hibernates in the back country, with the Innuit. I had gone there in summer, on a horse. And then winter came."

"You are fond of horses, sir?"

"Mine was delicious."

Breakfast bubbled in my stomach, as if to rise up and into my throat. I wanted to puke. Had he also eaten the dead man's flesh? Would he suck hot marrow from human bones?

Hour upon hour, we worked, wrapping sheets of white birch around his giant skeleton, in which I saw no ribs. The stem, the frontspiece for the bow, he had carved by hand from cedar. His crooked knife, one which was as crooked as his body, had created a series of slits to allow the cedar to warp into a four-foot curve. I took note of the stern piece, also cedar, but of less substance than the stem.

"Bones," said the old man, "and the *voyageur* adds the muscle and the gut."

The white of the birch faced inward, so that the smoother red bark would offer less drag through the water. The two of us chewed beads of spruce gum, and boiled it for bonding. Before I could apply the hot gum to a newly sewn seam, the old man stopped me, rather gruffly.

"Strain it."

"I will, sir. But why?"

"That's why I had you chew the spruce gum. Not to pleasure your mouth. What do you do when your tongue finds a fleck of bark in the gum?"

"I spit it our, sir."

"Aye. Same for the canoe. Because a fleck of bark will puny the bind."

"Ah! I understand, sir."

"Good," he grunted, pulling a sheet of birch with both hands and his jaws. "Add the animal fat to the pitch."

"Why?"

"The tallow'll keep her from cracking in chilly weather. And it gets cold here-parts. Colder than Billy-be-damned."

Atop the white bark, inside the hull, we placed long strips of cedar, bow to stern, of varying width. Then his hands and my hands pressed in the ribs, one by one. The last rib was under the center thwart. I liked working with Old Hunch, and I told him so, receiving one of his many grunts as an answer. Yet I knew he was pleased by the way his hands shared their work with me.

"Stuff her nose with shavings," he ordered me, "to puff out her cheeks, and then we'll paint her face white. Add some scrap for patching."

"Why do we stuff the cheeks?"

"So she won't buckle when her nose punches a rock. We'll add headers to hold in the stuffer. And then rim the gunwales to bury the lashing."

We finished her. And as we did so, the old man wept.

"She's beautiful," I told him.

"Much too pretty," he said, "for Benet."

120

Chapter 14

"Don't move, lad."

Old Hunch's hand was on my shoulder, to restrain me, and the tremble in his voice was a warning. Two days ago, I had heard the bark of a she-bear, sensing danger, a sharp command that had driven her two cubs up a hemlock. His tone was similar.

Raising my face, I first saw only one of them. Then, as my eyes adjusted from the close work of a canoe-painting to a distant probe for trouble, I saw the second man standing between two trees as silently as if he had grown there.

"Who . . . ?"

"Be still," hissed Old Hunch.

The man closest to us forced his face into a smile. Mirthless, as there was nothing to laugh at, yet the man smiled as he gibbered away in what I recognized as Cree. This, according to Benet, was Cree hunting land.

"Corn Brother," said the man. He was fat and short, younger than the man behind him. He pointed to himself.

Corn Brother was dressed in a varied costume composed of articles formerly worn by white backs. One shoe. The other foot was bare, with dirty toes, I saw, as he walked a few steps closer. He wore a pair of black Puritan breeches, a yellow shirt, a green *voyageur* sash, along with bracelets, cuffs, beads, earrings. On his round head, a Scottish tam-o'-shanter that had seen cleaner years. Stuck in the tam was one black crow's feather. From the front of his belt thong dangled a saber, with no sheath. Its blade was red with rust.

Corn Brother pointed back into the trees at his com-

panion. "Seecoya," he said, seeming to be impressed with
the name and expecting Old Hunch and me to be likewise
in awe.

Seecoya never moved.

On Seecoya's head I noticed the furry scalp of a buffalo,
with two black horns protruding. His chest was bare, a
dry red compared to Corn Brother's shiny sweat. At
Seecoya's waist was a long knife which rode his right
hip as though it were an extension of his hipbone. Over
his shoulder was slung a bow. I could see only one arrow
tip, as though Seecoya's claim were that his single arrow
was enough to slay any enemy. His right hand was
shoulder high, thumb hooked through the bow-string, in
the same manner that a white man might rest his hand
on the butt of his belt pistol.

"Seecoya," repeated Corn Brother.

"We have no whiskey," said Old Hunch.

"Whiskey?"

"Nay, I say no whiskey."

"Rum," said Corn Brother. Placing a hand at his waist,
he rubbed his own fat stomach, smiling broadly. I saw no
weapon, but I could not see beneath his yellow shirt. The
more he smiled, the more I disliked the man.

"Benet is here," the old man said. He pointed through
the trees in the direction of Henley House.

Corn Brother nodded his fat head, waving the lone
crow's feather as though it were a black wand to warn us
of its power to commit sorcery upon our souls. The silly
grin still widened his round face. I was sure the two Cree
knew that Benet and the rest of us had arrived. I wondered what else they knew.

"Soldier," said Corn Brother.

"He is friend of Benet," said Old Hunch, "and very
brave."

"Soldier? Who soldier?

Corn Brother asked the question again and again, demanding to learn McKee's identity. His smiling face darkened into an unpleasant frown.

Once, twice, he stamped his foot . . . the one that was
shod. Seecoya, meanwhile, never varied his expressionless
face. He was obviously older than Corn Brother, and his
superior. Possibly his chief.

"I want to run," I whispered to Old Hunch.

"Before you reached the thicket," the old man wheezed, "you'd be a dead English."

"Soldier?"

"Tell him," said Old Hunch to me.

"His name is Ensign Owen McKee," I said, not looking at Corn Brother, but staring as directly as I could force myself at Seecoya. "He is McKee of His Majesty's Coldstream Guards."

"Soldier . . . McKee?"

"Yes," I answered Corn Brother.

"Ha, ha, ha," laughed Corn Brother, then holding up one soiled finger. "One soldier."

Looking at Seecoya's face, eager to see if he also found Owen's coming to Henley House without his platoon as humorous, I saw no emotion, no hint that the man understood our limited conversation. Corn Brother continued to hold up one finger. My loyalty to Owen increased my disliking of the man.

"What do you want?" asked Old Hunch.

"One whiskey. Two."

"No whiskey."

"Seecoya kill."

"Carry Back say . . . no rum, no whiskey. So you tell Seecoya to look somewhere else. Tell him to ask Benet."

I wondered who Carry Back was. Of course. The name was no doubt given Hunch by the Cree, as the old man was so bent that he appeared to carry his own back. A mound of bent spine could often bulge up higher than his head.

"You tell Seecoya," said the old man, "that I am honored to see him. Tell him that he is handsome and should own much looking glass."

"Carry Back give no rum?"

Old Hunch shook his head. "No rum."

Corn Brother scowled. His ruse for a handout had failed. Apparently it had worked on other days. Give me rum or my tall brother puts an arrow into you. A simple message.

"Carry Back . . . bad."

"No. Carry Back is good to his friend," said Old Hunch. "Because when Corn Brother had the pox, who steamed

his face? Who poured boiling water into bottles to help
Corn Brother pull the pus?"

Corn Brother was sullenly silent.

With care, Old Hunch walked forward, gently placing
a gnarled hand on the shoulder of the yellow shirt. "And
if Corn Brother buries a fishhook in his hand, as he did
many summers ago, it will be Carry Back who cuts away
the hook."

"Bad hook."

"Yes, and bad Corn Brother to kill for rum. When I
again have rum, the fire will run down the throats of
Seecoya and Corn Brother to melt their winter."

Corn Brother suddenly looked contrite, as though
ashamed that he had threatened to harm an old man who
had healed his hurts and mended his mistakes. He looked
at his hand, perhaps remembering the pain of the fishhook.

Seecoya grunted.

The grunt was perhaps a throaty command, not meant
to be comprehended by a white ear, and the fat Cree
turned away from us, kicking the long canoe as he departed. He joined Seecoya, and the two Cree muttered to
each other. Seecoya now looked very unhappy.

"And," said Old Hunch, "when the canoe of Seecoya
and Corn Brother is no longer swift, when water fills her
belly, who will patch her? And when the chills of snow
bring you the cough, who will mash the cherries and
steep you?"

"Carry Back," said Corn Brother.

"Aye, it will be."

The two Cree vanished into the high junipers as though
they had been wisps of smoke. I thought I heard a whining grunt, a thud of a moc upon a backside, and a painful yelp from Corn Brother. I guessed that Seecoya was
less than pleased with his brother's appeal for spirits.

My breeches were damp, and not from the waters of the
Albany River, for this time I was at least *warm* and wet.
My hands were shaking. And my old shaggy shipbuilder
had himself a bent laugh at my expense.

"Relief," he said, "flies on many wings."

I will say this for Benet, not once did he visit our working area until Old Hunch allowed me to report that the
canoe was at last worthy. Hurried as he was, Benet trotted

ahead of me to where the canoe awaited his particular
eye. Old Hunch had gone. With him had vanished his axe,
awl, froe, and crook knife. I watched as Benet went over
every inch of the canoe, touching it as it should have been
touched, with rapturous appreciation.

"What does *canoe* mean, sir?"

"From the French is my guess. *Le canot*, the rowboat.
Only the French are in error."

"In what way?"

"A boat is not masculine. Aye, perhaps a clumsy Yorkboat, but not this great giant of a girl. No, not a girl. A
goddess. Queen of the Kenogami. I tell you, Coe, this
canoe is the finest he's ever made. Not a Cree in Canada
can equal him. Look at that seam."

I smiled. "That, sir, is *my* seam."

"Bullroar! I would know the work of Old Hunch any-
where."

"And, sir, the work of Young Hunch."

Benet's fist shot out and caught me off my guard. Not
a hard slap, but one of his usual backhanded stingers, oft
an indication of his pleasure. I felt surprise but no pain.
My ribs smarted.

"And I suppose you will tell me now that *you* will build
the next canoe for the Hudson's Bay Company?"

"No, sir, I do not. But I can repair her if need be."

"So can every *voyageur* who canoes for me. But to design a craft such as this . . ." Again his hand lightly
touched the gunwale as though he were about to strum a
lute. His fingers were delicate, feeling every stitch, every
bead of spruce gum. Benet was the best, I thought as I
watched him; and more, he would tolerate about him only
the most able. Men, canoes, fur . . . and Doe. I found myself suddenly scowling at the back of his gray head.

"Seecoya was here, sir. He and Corn Brother."

"I hate Seecoya, truly be. He hates me even more. And
yet I prefer him to Corn Brother. I tell you this to remember, so mark me well. Seecoya may be an arrow in
your chest, but Corn Brother is a knife in your back."

"Old Hunch stood his ground, sir."

"Yes, as Old Hunch always will. Oft there lies a thin
line 'twixt bravery and tomfool. And it takes wisdom to
know when to rampage and when to run."

"Sir, what would you have done?"

Benet smiled. "I would have done exactly what you did, Coe. I would have pissed in my pants."

"You *knew?*"

He nodded. "I was watching."

I sighed, wondering if what he told me was true, and realizing that with Benet one is tested with each task, each boat, each journey.

"Behind you. With the bead of my musket on Seecoya's belly."

"Why did you not kill him?"

"Bravo, my boy. Spoken like a true Englishman. One day will come when all you British will have your fill of killing. A day that I perhaps shall never see dawn. Until then, must I listen to McKee's desire to kill a moose, and yours to slay a Cree?"

I swallowed, unable to answer.

"Coe, I read your thoughts. There stands Benet, my heartless master, a skinner of animals and kicker of lazy butts, who has nerve enough to measure another man's mercy. Ironic, eh?"

"Aye, sir, it is."

"No one soul is all things, Coe. A lad of your age, with lofty ideals, is always a boundless expecter. If you love a woman, Coe, allow her a frailty. If you work with men, indulge their shortcomings."

"Just as you do, sir?"

Benet's eyes narrowed, his black brows inching closer, almost to touch each other. "Exactly as I do not. I am a hypocrite, Coe. Do you know that word?"

"No, sir."

"I preach one thing but practice another. Yet I will now present you with a kernel of honesty that may again spill your bladder. You can be more to . . . the Hudson's Bay Company than a mere bondservant."

"How so, sir?"

"I allowed you to row, and you will work a paddle with the *voyageurs,* but only on this trip. You are not in Canada to be a peaporker, yet I think it best you learn how to pack and portage and pole a canoe for a thousand miles. And then face Sick Bear. I will show you how to skin a fox. And if you have no knife, I will show you how it can still be done with your bare hands. And by damn, I will teach *you*, even if it be too late to teach Ensign McKee, that a man does not have to slaughter every obstacle that stands in his path."

Benet sighed, lightly lifting a leg to rest a moc on the canoe's bow. "There have been times in my life, Coe, when I truly thought that I would overwork to death every *voyageur* who paddled for me. To be honest, I have ruptured more than one."

"Why do you tell me these things?"

Benet pointed to the spruces. "The wilderness cleanses me, bathes my spirit, and I can hold the truth here from no man." Plucking a small green, he popped the shiny leaf into his mouth, chewing it with rapture.

"What do you eat, sir?"

"I call it wintergreen. You will usually find it under pines and spruce, or near hemlock. Here, have a leaf."

I chewed it. The wintergreen flavor was a cousin of mint, yet the leaves were not furry. A clean taste. The leaves were stiff.

"We must hurry," said Benet.

Together we walked back to Henley House. Not really together, as to walk with Benet usually meant to follow him. He leaped a creek, as would a forkhorn buck, his mocs making little sound upon the forest floor.

"Coe, get seven men along with youreslf, and bring the canoe. You won't have to give the men any orders. Best you don't. Jardin is near as old as I. He has portaged to the Pacific, so he'll not need tutoring on packing it here."

Benet cuffed me. There was no pain; the cuff was given to me as though I were to be his companion.

"You and Old Hunch built a fine canoe. I know, it was near done when we beached here. But the finishing was artful, and I wonder if my arse end is noble enough to sit the dang thing."

The old canoe, equal in size to our new one, was already loaded. The packs and bedrolls were spaced, two by two, yet as staggered as dragon's teeth. The canoe bobbed gently in the eddy water, like Benet, content, yet rather restless.

McKee greeted Benet.

"Why is this Henley House here, Monsieur?"

"We put it away up here to steal fur from the French. That should brighten the tip of your sword, Ensign McKee."

"How soon do we head for the eagle fur?"

"Jolly quick," Benet told him. "Soon as I fetch us a second musket."

Chapter 15

FROM THE DESOLATE POST called Henley House, the Albany River extended westward to the divide.

Our two canoes took the southern fork, the Kenogami. At midday the sun was high, yet in our faces, so I concluded that we were heading almost due south. After a Yorkboat, a canoe of birchbark and cedar is a feathery craft. Rowing with one's back upstream held little charm for me. But in a canoe, sitting on my pack, I could see upstream as we all faced forward. The only disadvantage was that I could no longer look at McKee or accept from him one of his heartfelt smiles. Owen sat in the stern of our craft, the drag canoe, sitting just in front of *le gouvernail.* In the bow stood an *avant,* and both men manned a paddle nine feet long.

"Basswood," Old Hunch had told me a day earlier, when I had asked what kind of tree would be used for new paddles. "Basswood is tougher than pine or spruce, and lighter than hardwoods like birch or maple."

Across the blade my paddle was less than a foot wide. About five inches.

We came to our first portage, Le Moulin (the mill), a white foaming whirlpool of sucking death, with enough rocks hidden below the surface to chew up both body and birch. Six *voyageurs* carried our new canoe, inverted on their shoulders, around the rapids. According to Benet, each canoe weighed six hundred pounds.

"How much," I asked him, "would our cargo weigh when once we load the fur?"

"Five tons. And en route downstream we may not portage Le Moulin."

Above the falls we saw mallards, waterfowl with green heads on the males, pecking away at some sort of wild grain. The ducks were in pairs, devotedly mated. Several strings of ducklings followed along. They all seemed to figure us not as enemies, knowing they all could swim where we could not, or fly.

"Look you," yelled Owen McKee, "a duck hawk."

As if it were fired from the sky as a musket ball, down came the hawk, talons extended, into the flapping and quacking panic of mallards. A female in its claws, it flew off with its meal, up and beyond the trees. McKee and I silently watched.

"Peregrine," said Benet. "A falcon."

All the mallards continued to quack, loudly protesting the presence of the falcon and the taking of one of their flock. Above the portage the water was smooth again, a pond with hardly any current at all. The tips of our paddles tore holes in the water. I watched Benet's canoe ahead of us, seeing the ripples wing out from her bow as though the canoe rode a giant arrowhead.

"*Fee fee*," a *voyageur* commented, causing the others to laugh and even, I noticed, to increase the cadence of our work. I wondered again about the meaning of *fee fee*.

Benet told me, during a pipe rest. I sat with him as he wrote "Fifi" in the sand with a pointed stick of driftwood.

"A girl?" I asked him.

"Hardly a lass." Benet laughed.

"Who then, sir?"

"More woman then you could ever handle, Coe. And the same for me. Aye, 'twould demand at least an ensign in the Coldstream Guards to dominate such a damsel of ample dimensions."

"She is French?" asked Owen.

"A half-breed," Benet answered him. "Goes by the name of Fifi La Fourchette."

"*La fourchette*," said McKee, "if my schooling correctly serves me, is a fork."

"Aye," said Benet. "Fifi the Fork. I cannot tell you what her Cree name is. Her establishment lies ahead of us, at the fork of the Kenogami."

"Fifi," hooted La Porte, waving his pipe in the air as

though directing a piece of music that only his ears were allowed to hear. Allard and Renfrew danced a jig, their mocs stomping the sand, right arms interlocked and then left arms.

"I do believe, Monsieur Benet," said Owen, "that I need not ask the nature of Fifi La Fourchette's field of endeavor."

"Your imagination will serve only to whet your surprise, young sir. An honorable profession," said Benet, "proven by centuries and civilizations to be ever among us."

"Strange," said McKee, "how the business of hookery seems to follow water. Almost like milling."

"Mills of such goddesses grind slowly, but they grind exceedingly fine."

McKee howled. "A superb jest, sir. Capital! As I was saying, I wonder why such establishments seem to flourish so well on waterfronts."

"Must be a reason"—Benet nodded—"having to do with a term now used in the London Exchange."

"And which term, sir?"

"Liquid assets."

McKee roared again, causing most of the *voyageurs* to look in his direction. Owen had a most infectious smile, creating grins among our paddlers, as they somehow appreciated the howling, if not the humor.

Pipes out, we pushed off again, upstream into another portage. There were, I was learning, four degrees of difficulty: paddle, pole, pull, and portage. Unloading our two canoes to carry them was a last resort. Which we did at this particular place called La Gorge du Mort, meaning the throat of death. The water was white, pinched to a raging by twin juts of rock from opposite banks. Peaks of foam floated below.

Above the portage, the water was calm, as if it had no suspicion that the river would be suddenly whipped into froth. And so again our canoes shot forward, as we paddled twenty-four hundred strokes per hour, at the rate of forty per minute. My heart would beat twice for every stroke, and that is how I calculated our paddling rate, with some advice from Benet and Owen McKee.

Moon Portage, I learned as we moved upstream, meant merely a path around the falls that bent like a curving moon. It was an amazement for me to see what one *voyageur* could carry. To call them mules would not be degrading, at least not to my thinking, as each man seemed intent upon outworking all of his fellows.

"A beaver," I suddenly shouted as we stood at the shore of the upper pond.

"Muskrat," shouted Benet.

"Where?" asked Owen.

Benet shifted the object in his mouth from one cheek to the other, eyeing the Coldstreamer with a squint of suspicion. "I suppose you wish to kill her."

"Nay, only to observe."

"You and Braddock," Benet sniffed. "The two observers. All telescopes and no cannon. I am dismayed, Ensign McKee, that you don't wish to skin old Skinner, or mount my head as some trophy for His Majesty's wall."

McKee smiled. "If only, old sir, you had horns."

I laughed. But before my smile was complete, the hand of Skinner Benet whipped from his body, a swift arrow from a ready bow, catching my jaw with force to spin me halfway about. His moc struck in the crotch, from the rear, and I was near to vomiting with pain. Why? The kick hurt so badly that I dared not even turn to face my master to ask what I had done to incite his temper.

"He doesn't know," said McKee.

"The Hell he does not. And when I need your advice, Ensign McKee, I shall seek it, sir. You are a passenger on this trip and no more. Discipline is *my* quarter, not yours, as none of us be soldiers. Understood?"

"I understand, sir."

The ring of iron tightened around my neck; inside my throat, the pain of my private parts had risen to my stomach and above, to near choke me with discomfort. As I helped to load the canoe, I recalled words of Sister Elizabeth at our orphanage, about Canada's being a brutal land. Little do you know, sweet and gentle lady, how brutal. Nor do I yet know myself. Yet if I ever turn on Skinner Benet, or rise up against his will or person, I soon will learn just how cruel this Canada can be.

What had I done to him? Offended him?

Benet was a coiled snake. The man was a walking keg of powder, black and gritty, abrim with charcoal and sulphur and saltpeter, ready to explode. And no crackling torch of a cannoneer was necessary. Aye, even a spark. A red-hot speck from a flint as futile as mine would ignite old Skinner Benet. Nor could anyone predict how, or where his touch-hole, or why.

Paddling, I studied the matter. Every animal has an underbelly soft and white and vulnerable, an area where pain can penetrate. And even death. Yet the slaying of Skinner Benet was not at issue. No threat, no lurking danger. All I did was laugh. But my laugh hit him hard, and it had something to do with his having horns on his head, driving some secret battering ram against some defenseless door.

I will hurt him. God, will I soon hurt him so that he will know the name of Abbott Coe better than his own. My head was pounding, beating twice for every one stroke of my paddle. Only when our canoe drifted from course by a degree or so could I see the lead canoe, and the *bourgeois* who sat in her stern, his back to me. Damn you, Benet! What have I done to put myself in your disfavor, and to receive such punishment before all others?

Think, I commanded myself. Hatred will serve only to cloud your reason, and a wise warrior will be the victor of a foolhardy one, so think, Abbott Coe. Where is Benet's center spot, the bull's-eye of target, the trigger of that mysterious musket that hammers off the unforeseen charge? This man Benet is at full cock, and his temper discharges at the touch of an eyewink. The pan of his trap lies hidden beneath my unwary paw, buried beneath fallen leaves, waiting for my misstep. And then . . . CLANK . . . the toothy jaws snap at me. I am helplessly caught and caged and collared.

Yet my brain wears no iron ring. I am free to think, to parry and to ponder, to be as vigilant as Benet is volatile. I must steel myself with stealth. Be cautious, Coe.

"Fifi!" hollered a *voyageur*.

We sang again. All but me, as there was no music in my spirit. My paddle moved as though I stroked John

Howland's anvil, heavy as heartbreak, so leaden that I could barely manage to lift it from the lake. Sullen in my shame, I had been slapped and kicked by my master as though I were no more than a begging cur that whined once too often at the kitchen entry. My belly ached from the kick, and my cheek felt puffy, but these were small hurts that would pass prior to the pain of my person.

Beneath the tip of my paddle's blade I began to envision Benet's face, laughing at me as it floated in the dark water. I felt my paddle cut at the face, harder than necessary, as all of one's effort at a paddle should be employed to lift it, then relaxing the arms to let it fall into the water and begin its backward task.

My face moistened.

Inside my shirt I felt the rivulets of sweat begin to itch my body, beneath my arms, around my waist, up under the back knot of my hair.

"Fifi!" yelled Renfrew. "Vite! Vite!"

"Allons! Allons!"

Each cry seemed to be urging all ears to hurry, to paddle faster, as Fifi lay ahead, rife with all her charms. Along with the *voyageurs* I felt the excitement along the spine of the canoe. We became a tingling skeleton, anxiously awaiting some forbidding feast around one more bend in the waterway.

"*Mon petit chou,*" yelled Boudreau, "*je n'y puis rien.*"

"*Nous faisons ce qu'il nous plaît, oui?*"

"*Je n'y tiens plus!*"

"*Tenez! Tenez! Tenez moi!*"

"*Comme vous y allez!*"

"*Fifi! Je vous le donne.*"

I spoke few words in French, but I understood far more, along with certain gestures that all males understand. Phrase by phrase, as I heard each *voyageur* shouting his desire for Miss Fifi La Fork, I began to smile. And paddle harder. I had to confess that I was more than curious. Over my shoulder I saw Ensign McKee stretch his neck to catch a glimpse of what lay upriver.

"*Normand,*" said La Fleur to me, "*il va chanter avec l'amour.*"

It was true. Normand was standing up in the canoe, and

he was undressing himself, until Contois pushed him overboard and into the water. We waited for him to hook a
leg over the side and come sloshing aboard so that we
could again move upriver. Normand continued to undress
until all of his clothes were piled in a wet heap inside the
canoe. Naked, he paddled and sang, until a wet fringe of
a sash snapped his bare behind like a whip.

"Fifi!" yelled Contois, *"mon petit jouet."*

Everyone was laughing, even Benet. In spite of his
canoe's turning about in aimless circles. More men stood
up, yelled Fifi's name, pointed at themselves, bragged
about their romantic capacities and preferences, and even
threw their clothes into the water. We made no headway
as the two canoes circled each other aimlessly in a cove,
a bay bathed in the soft orange and pink of sunset.

"J'ai sali mes vêtements."

"C'est bien fait."

"Fifi! Permettez!"

"Fifi! J'ai votre jouet."

Ensign Owen McKee of His Majesty's Coldstream
Guards was laughing. He had drawn his saber in order
to retrieve an article of Renfrew's clothing from the water.
He lifted the sopping trousers up from the river and into
our canoe. Several of the *voyageurs* were jumping up and
down, and it was no small wonder we did not capsize.

"Fifi! Comment vous portez-vous ce soir?"

La Fleur said, *"Elle a mal de tête."*

For some reason, the *voyageurs* thought that Fifi's having a headache was most hilarious. Benet was chuckling,
and so was Owen. Inch by inch, still spinning wildly in
circles, our canoes drifted to shore in the eddy, as if being
sucked there by a strange power, some hidden undertow
against which it was folly to fight.

We saw Fifi.

She could not have outweighed Benet's buffalo, but it
would have been a close balance. Before us, robed in pink
and bedecked in scores of sparkling trinkets and bracelets,
stood the largest woman I have ever seen. Perhaps not the
tallest. Surely the widest. Other women were behind her.

"Chou," she said, pointing to herself, and raising up her
robe to expose a beefy thigh. *"Votre petit chou."*

"What is *chou?*" I asked Brochet. The word she repeated sounded like "shoe."

"Cabbage," said Brochet, blowing kisses to Fifi. "Little cabbage."

Chapter 16

"MERCIER!"

There was no answer to La Fleur's shout, Grosjean and Osier were also calling out Mercier's name. La Porte was yelling loudly, hands to his mouth. Then he ran into the trees to continue his shouting.

"Paul Mercier! *Viens!*"

"Find a pregnant squaw and you will find Mercier," said Benet.

Normand and Allard, a bit unsteady and red-eyed, trotted upstream, their mocs splashing through the water, sending silvery drops into the gold of early morn. Louis and Jardin ran downstream on opposite banks as they alternately called the name of Paul Mercier.

"Go aid them," Benet ordered.

With unchewed bits of Brochet's breakfast bulging in my cheeks, I ran downstream to follow Jardin. He was a short and stocky man, one I could easily catch, and did.

"Mercier!" called Jardin.

Across the river we heard Louis also hollering. Silently we paused to wait for an answer, a response from Mercier, yet all we heard was the rushing of the two rivers which met at the fork, Fifi's fork, two great legs of water.

"Paul Mercier!" I was yelling to the water.

Jardin and I followed the water downstream, sometimes splashing through the river, other times on pebbled shores. All we saw were rocks and trees. No sign of Mercier. He was a member of our drag canoe, and I had gotten to know him somewhat. Mercier smiled often, said little, worked a paddle with dedication. Best of all, he sang. Mercier sang the cheeriest solo of all our *voyageurs*, a leathery baritone that seemed to lift his heart up to the skies of Canada. His song was as natural to this wilderness as the bellow of a bull moose or the cry of a loon.

"Mercier!" yelled Jardin.

I read Jardin's face. The look of genuine concern tightened across his mouth and brow. His eyes were dry, yet behind them I knew that Jardin's eyes were well stocked with unwept tears. *Voyageurs*, I had observed, were men who dared to laugh and to cry.

Again and again, from across the stream, we heard the faint cries of Louis calling, "Mercier! Mercier!"

Easily passing the clumsy Jardin, I ran ahead, wanting to be the first to reach the drunken Mercier, who no doubt had meandered off in the company of a squaw or a measure of rum, or both. Hurrying, I left the riverbank for several yards, running through a stand of pine, kicking the thick carpet of brown needles. Behind me I heard Jardin's scream. Turning, I ran back to his side. Jardin was motionless, his thick arms hung limply at his sides, stocky legs planted as two stumps that could take not even one more step. Following the line of his eyes, I saw the body.

"Non!" whispered Jardin.

We stood upon the riverbank that was as high as a man's head above the gentle swirling eddy, a nest of rocks that had captured a floating log. Around the bark at both ends I saw thongs of root or vine. And a pair of colorless hands. The arms had been tied behind, hands crossed and lashed around the black trunk of the log. Below, a half-clothed body of a man lay in the cold water, under the log. One leg kicked to and fro in the current, which made me realize that the man had not been long dead. The top of his head had been tomahawked.

"Je l'entends chanter," said Jardin softly.

And I also hear him singing, I silently told Jardin. Our friend Mercier would sing no more songs to his canoe and his Canada.

"Cree?" I asked Jardin. He shrugged.

Louis came across the river, recklessly wet, splashing through the water. The three of us cut Mercier free from the black log and bore the dead body upstream, back to our camp. Allard and Normand had returned breathless from upriver. The rest of the *voyageurs* were busily engaged in reloading our two canoes. Benet smiled from a distance, noticing only that we bore the lost Mercier.

"Sober him up," said Benet.

At this, Jardin burst into tears, wailing loudly, sitting his bull of a body down on the grainy shore, Mercier's torn head in his wet lap. His beefy arms held the lifeless face, whose eyes were still open and milky in their unblinking silence.

"*Il est mort. Mort.*" Jardin wept.

"Dead?" Benet knelt quickly, touching the cold hands, searching for a pulse. Head down, Benet rested his ear to the chest of the dead Paul Mercier to listen for a heartbeat that he knew he could never hear, while Jardin continued to sob. Jardin's oxlike chest shook with cold and grief. Louis and I were equally wet. I felt myself tremble, wondering which one of our expedition would be the next to die. None of us? Some? All of us? Suddenly I wanted to see the sweet face of Sister Elizabeth and feel her hands pulling the edge of a rough woolen blanket up under my chin at bedtime.

I wanted to be back in England.

"Who did this?" asked McKee.

"Our enemies," I expected Benet to reply, but for a moment he was silent. Slowly he lifted his ear from the chest of Paul Mercier. Unhurriedly he stood. Drawing back his foot, Benet kicked the dead body. Once! Twice! And then a third kick! The mouths of the *voyageurs* fell open. Contois and Osier crossed themselves as though they had witnessed Skinner Benet slap the face of God.

"What good is he now?" said Benet.

McKee scowled at Benet, a questioning look on his fair face, as if he wondered how any man could so dishonor the wet body of a drowned companion. 'Twas an act, McKee's face seemed about to state, that no gentleman would lower himself to commit.

Renfrew fell to his knees, crossing himself and kissing the good-luck charm that he had probably purchased from Eskimo Elky. Or from Father Joseph.

"What good?" Skinner Benet repeated. "To his family? His children? To Hell with the Hudson's Bay Company.

What good is Paul Mercier to his babies back at Fort Albany? And his woman?"

No one spoke.

"And for what did our friend die? For a rum-soaked kiss from a fat female. His soul leaves us this day because his brain left us last night. He forsook our camp and its protection. Mercier left us. So now he can never return."

La Brun was sobbing in a very high-pitched and almost childlike voice.

"Dig a hole," said Benet.

As I stood there shaking, looking down at the still form of Paul Mercier, someone threw a blanket around my shoulders. Turning, I saw Owen McKee.

"The icy waters of a Canada river," he said, "could be no colder than Benet's blood."

Benet was beyond earshot as Owen McKee spoke, and our *bourgeois* busied himself with the preparation of breaking camp and packing canoes for a tardy start, a situation that he had not yet allowed. And as Jardin and Louis carried the body of Mercier away into the bush, Benet turned his back to the burial procession, humble as it was.

"Will there be a funeral?" I asked, asking no one in particular, still shaken from the discovery of our murdered friend.

"There should be," said McKee.

But there was no funeral. One by one the *voyageurs* knelt at the mound of wet sand and earth that had been heightened by a cairn of small rocks. Each man waved the sign of the cross at Mercier; some kissed their own religious medals or geegaws of superstition and fortune collected in their travels. Jardin still wept.

Benet's face showed no sign of grief. He busied himself in the chores of commerce, continuing our duties in full for the profit of the Hudson's Bay Company. I wondered how well he had known Paul Mercier. Which made me ask myself if any of us knew Skinner Benet, a man incapable of being known, by a man or a beast or even by God. Had I been scalped and bound to a log by red savages and tossed into a river to die, Benet would no doubt have done even less for me as to last rites.

"That man," said Owen McKee as we boarded our canoe, "even kicks his comrades after they die."

I wanted to spit in Benet's face. Just once, I wished that *he* could be captured by Cree and bound to a floating log, to die in water as he would scream silent bubbles into a breathless current. Can a man live who has been toma-hawked? Old Hunch had said so, for he knew a trapper who was called No Hair by the Cree. Atop his head was stretched skin, and a long row of horsehair stitches where his woman had resewn his pate. And had to cut a patch of skin from his back.

Cold and ill, I vomited up bits of my breakfast into the ferns until Benet's command ordered us to push off. Our drag canoe was less crowded now. No longer could I see Mercier's broad back, and his yellow stocking cap and yellow sash. In the belly of our canoe, his basswood pad-dle lay dry and motionless. I saw Jardin reach out his thick fingers to gently touch its handle.

Two pipes later, we portaged. The place was called Bull-head Rock. An hour or so later we portaged a second time at Thorn Pass, where I helped to carry our giant canoe. As we walked up the steep embankment, I heard a cry from a fellow porter.

"Regardez!"

With his toe, Contois pointed at a bit of torn moc be-side a trail. Benet came to lift it up and inspect it. He raised it to his nose. Then, as he knelt, his eyes searched the ground until they found whatever it was that he sought. Once we set our canoe down above Thorn Pass, I trotted back to help with the bundles and also learn what Benet had discovered. In his hands were thin shavings of what appeared to be the cured hide of a *caribou*. Little more than a few torn shreds.

"Cree?" I asked Benet. "Was it Sick Bear?"

He shook his head. "No, I don't believe so."

"From a Huron?"

"Neither, lad. I think we have white company."

"White men? Aye, the French."

"They are called *coureurs du bois*."

"Wood runners?"

"Aye, and our French friends who fur-trade along the great lakes are as fearful of these men as are we."

141

"What do they do, sir?"

Benet rested his moc on a boulder half-buried betwixt a brace of jack pines. His mouth shifted its secret from one cheek into the other. I heard a hard object rattle against his teeth before it nested.

"They are pirates."

"Highwaymen?"

"Aye, and worse. Free-lance furriers they be, robbing from red man and white, from Huron or Cree or British or French. *Coureurs du bois* care not which enterprise they single out, only that they convert our gain to theirs, and they pay only in pain. We are safe en route upstream."

"But what we found was an indian moc, sir."

"Nay, 'tis not. Smell it."

I smelled it. The scent of human foot was fresh, and the leather was warm. Also dry and not at all damp with the dew which can persist until midday beneath shade.

"See this, Coe. Mark how the moc had been patched. Cree do not do such. When a Cree or a Huron tears a moc, he discards it, tearing from his loin-flaps a fresh sheet of hide, to then sew himself a new moc in a little more time than a deep breath."

"A white foot wore this?"

"Aye. But say nothing of it."

"Sir, was Mercier . . ."

Benet placed his hand over my mouth, to bid my silence. "Only an idiot tells all he knows. So now"—he smiled—"here I be telling you."

"Telling me what?" I sort of mumbled against his lean fingers until his hand increased its pressure, commanding my silence and attention.

"I tell you this, lad, because if you spy white faces in the trees, do not conclude they are allies. Nay to that. And to answer your question, 'tis my guess that Paul Mercier was slain by white hands. Perhaps he discovered them and they slew him."

Then, as Benet slowly withdrew his fingers from my mouth, I raised my own hand to seal my lips, as though afraid to ask more. That was when Benet tossed the moc away into the jack pines, covering his mouth with one hand, while with the other he cupped his ear. Then he relaxed his *vignette* and spoke.

"To survive in a wilderness, Coe, where we harvest the eagle fur, a man must speak little and listen much. The ears of an elephant and the mouth of a bug."

"I understand, sir."

My eyes widened as I suddenly noticed what hung around Benet's neck. Mercier's lucky charm! It was an elk's tooth that dangled chest-high on a strand of braided deergut.

"Yes," said Benet, "it was his."

God! Benet would not only kick a dead man, but also rob him. My open eyes must have then narrowed, for Skinner Benet quickly read my face as easily as he read the news of our enemies upon the forest floor.

"Hatred befuddles reason, lad. You must learn one simple precept. There is usually a reason for what I do. Be it a kick in a dead man's ribs, or a stolen geegaw that I shall personally return to a wailing widow, my performing roots in purpose."

Was he lying? No, I decided, as Benet was far too strong to be a liar. According to Sister Elizabeth, liars were persons who sought excuses. Benet was inexcusable.

"You are along on this trip to *learn*, Coe, and not to question my motives." Benet rolled his eyes up to the sky and back again. "Why must youth appoint itself to tend adult deportment? Get to work."

"I will, sir."

As I started to scamper away, his moc kicked out and neatly tripped me, and over I tumbled onto muskeg moss. I lay on my back. In less than a breath his moc stepped on my chest.

"You are my bondservant, Coe, and not my conscience."

"Aye, I am, sir."

"Your mission is to be not Father Joseph's apprentice, but mine."

Upward along my chest slid his moc until it stood upon my neckring, forcing my chin to jut, my eyes almost to close with the pressure. "I am bored with your constant weighing of the righteousness of this journey, of the Hudson's Bay Company, of Canada, and of your *bourgeois*."

I tried to gulp out my apology, but no words could I speak. The toe of his moc maintained its pressure under my jaw, into the soft spot behind the chinbone.

"Mark me, Coe."

Benet knelt down, his hands opening the collar of his deerskin blouse, so that I could see his throat.

"Look you, Coe, at your master's neck. See beyond the cord of Paul Mercier's trinket and tell me what is on my hide."

I saw the scar from an iron collar.

Chapter 17

"WE WILL RACE," SAID BENET.

Our canoes had been portaged above a place Benet called Mud Slide, and were being reloaded for paddling, when Benet made his offer. The faces of the *voyageurs* were still sullen, as they were no doubt remembering the slaying of Mercier. So was I.

"To the winning canoe, to every manjack aboard her, an extra carrot of tobacco upon our return to Fort Albany, a wool blanket, a tin of tea, and a dogshead of the best British rum for every dry gullet. Only to those who win."

"What for the losers?" asked Owen McKee.

"My moc, sir," said Benet.

The men did not cheer. Their mood was opposite from the revelry of last night's visit to Fifi the Fork. No laughter and no song. Since dawn, not a single *voyageur* had as much as splashed his neighbor with impish paddle.

"Our canoe is short a man, sir," I said to Benet.

"Nay," spoke up Ensign McKee, "it is no longer. For I will paddle if you'll permit, Monsieur Benet."

Benet squinted. "You?"

"Indeed," said Owen, "as I have sculled a bit on Scottish waters, so an oar is no stranger in my hand." McKee held a basswood paddle high in the air, shaking it as a warrior would brandish a lance. "And I shall paddle as though the prize were to pin upon my tunic Her Majesty's scarf."

"British," sighed Benet.

'Twas then that Le Fleur clapped a hand on Owen's shoulder as though to announce that he would be proud to have a Coldstream Guardsman as a fellow paddler. I smiled at Owen, and he smiled back. This sort of clinched it, because when Ensign Owen McKee grinned, no one present could escape such contagion. Many of us then laughed, to crack the grief of earlier circumstances.

"Sir, I am game," said Owen.

"Then," said Benet, "I shall add to the winner's list of awards one free ride aboard the brown back of Billy, my bison."

The *voyageurs* chuckled.

"Done," said McKee.

"Go!" said Benet quickly.

As if all of Canada suddenly exploded into frantic activity, all the *voyageurs* splashed for their canoes, along with Benet, Owen, and myself. Three breaths later, all paddles were wet and working. Our cadence was close, I calculated, to three thousand strokes per hour. From my eye's corner I watched my opposite, McKee, apply his paddle. Awkward at first, he seemed to master the art in less than three lengths of a canoe in travel, digging deeper with every stroke until the cold waters of the Kenogami nearly boiled beside his blade. McKee laughed constantly. Not aloud, but the expression on his face was laughter, as he enjoyed his sporting.

To be a Britisher, said Sister Elizabeth, is to be able to game with the best. Owen McKee was surely game. He paddled as though the reputation of the Coldstream Guards were totally at issue. I could almost hear Ensign McKee shout his thoughts in rhythm with his rowing: We shall win, by Braddock, we shall win!

I felt suddenly confident that the idea of our canoe's losing could never enter Owen's mind. He was a McKee, a Coldstreamer, and an Englishman . . . thus such august qualifications just had to amount to victory. Nothing less would be fitting.

We all paddled, except for Benet.

All of us sweated and ached, the warm afternoon sun burning our faces, mile after mile, our canoes abreast as though Divine Providence had ordained a tie across the finish. I wondered where the finish line was. Knowing my master, I realized he would rule that the victor was possibly the first boat to reach the Pacific. My fingers married the basswood shaft of my paddle so tightly that had I perished, the tool might have to be pried from my grip. Strange, but the first cramp came not to my hands or shoulders or back, but across my belly. A low pain, early on, yet becoming more intense with each stroke until the sear of it nearly destroyed my cadence. But I would not stop.

Owen paddled as if Satan pursued. If our canoe gained as much as an inch on Benet's, I could hear McKee grunt out something like: "Lively now, chaps. Keep her cracking."

For an Owen McKee it was hardly enough to be British. Proper form demanded that one be British in opposition to someone else. Africa, someone had remarked, would one day be divided by England into teams, each black tribe with its own crest and its very own cheering hurrah. It was plain to me that Skinner Benet thought little of the British, yet how could anyone dislike Owen McKee? Even the ducks and squirrels of Canada seemed to approach closer to him than to the rest of us. He was a combination of grace and good nature, poise, dedication, honor, a man who would offer even his life for his king or queen. Perhaps question, yet ever obey. I watched him again as he splashed like some driven fanatic, as though determined not to have the Cree near Lake Superior deprived of his charm or company.

Years from now, I thought, Ensign McKee would be another General Braddock, of the Coldstream Guards. He would be respected, obeyed, adored by all the troops of his commands, perhaps even to the last mule. And all of them would weep bitterly when at last he fell in battle.

"Faster," groaned Owen.

Sweat poured from my face and into my shirt, and the edge of our canoe's rib bit into my kneecap, until the pain was terrifying. Usually I sat on my pack, knees up, but our extreme pace had thrust my position forward with each pull of the paddle until my knees were grinding against one of the many canoe ribs. As to the pain, I would endure it for now, until perhaps other aches and agonies would soon come to serve as a counter-irritant.

"Pipe," hollered Benet, and not even one more stroke was pulled by even one paddle.

Falling forward, I rested my brow on a thwart to gasp

for breath. My arms trembled, shaking my entire person as if in the grip of some foreign fever, fearful that the rest of one pipe duration would end even before I could at least sit upright and rest my paddle. My fingers held it hard.

"Grief," said Owen.

I rolled my head to face him. He easily looked as drained as I. But in a breath or two he had recovered, rested his paddle, and unrolled his precious maps to add landmarks from the tools of his pouch, quill and butternut ink.

"Sir, where are we?" I panted to Owen.

"You don't possibly dream that I know, do you?"

I could hear the *voyageurs* laughing through their smoke. All I wanted was a sudsy tub, and to throw up all that I had ever eaten since coming to Canada. Anytime I closed my eyes I saw the raw crown of Paul Mercier's head. Oh, how my gut flirts with puke.

"Here we are," chirped Owen.

"Where?"

He pointed at his map, as his fingertip rested on a black curve drawn by a pen. "One of the tributaries we scooted by had to have been the Current River, ofttimes called the Little Current, but I beg you not ask me why."

"Sir, I'll not."

"Monsieur Benet, who won the race, sir? Our canoes were at necks when you called for a pipe."

"The race ends tomorrow at noon," said Benet to McKee.

"You're jesting, sir."

Benet did not answer. With a musket tucked in the crook of his arm, he disappeared over a head-high bank of sand and into the bush. The *voyageurs* did not stray. Huddled together as winter hens, they smoked and mumbled in French. They understood English. Every command given them by Benet they comprehended, yet seldom would a *voyageur* speak as much as a simple English phrase. French only; among themselves, to their *bourgeois*, and to the hills and heavens of Canada herself.

"Nifty," said Owen.

"Beg pardon, sir."

McKee stood up in the canoe and stretched his legs, his

hands still holding one of his charts. "When I return here, with our detachment, we cannot possibly lose ourselves in the wild, not if we mark well our waterways."

"Are you sure, sir?"

"Quite. All waters flow into Hudson's Bay or to James Bay if you will. And when we advance southerly to meet the sources of any of these many rivers, then we shall know that our boots step on a French feehold. Simple, eh?"

"Aye, sir."

"Braddock and Father will be pleased."

"Is your father also a general?"

"Sort of. He is a brigadier. Yet high in rank, comparable one might say to even Lord Howe."

"I have heard the name of Lord Howe, sir."

"And truly you shall hear more. A fine gentleman and an able soldier. Yet distressed at the moment."

"Distressed, sir?"

"Aye, he is that. Lord Howe claims that we British should extend the boundaries of New York and New Hampshire in a northerly direction, commanding both the upper and lower lakes of George and Champlain."

"Where are these lakes, sir? Surely not in Canada."

"Correct. The two lakes of which I speak are far south of us. The upper foams into the lower at a portage place called . . . these indian names twist my tongue . . . I believe they call it Ticonderoga."

"Is it on your map, sir?"

"Nay, not on these. Yet I promise you 'tis on a map oft unrolled under the nose of Lord Howe and even His Majesty."

"What happens there?"

"Nothing yet. According to Father, his friend Lord Howe claims that Ticonderoga bears watching."

"Sir, for what reason?"

"The French, lad. Lord Howe insists that he has received word, through our Mohawk allies, that French engineers have scouted a certain point of land that juts into Lake Champlain, and plan to erect a fortification at this Ticonderoga place."

"This excites you, sir. Does it not?"

"Aye, it truly does, Abbott. War stirs my blood like no other conquest, more than gold or girls. This French fort at Ticonderoga could be another Fort Duquesne. A gateway to the north, Ticonderoga, as Duquesne is the entrance westward into the Ohio."

McKee tapped the map with his knuckles.

"To my ear, sir, it sounds as if you wish to be directing three campaigns at once."

"Three?"

"Duquesne, Canada, and Ticonderoga."

"Aye, lad, if only I could. Duquesne is Braddock's meat soon to chew up and digest. And 'twill be my guess that Lord Howe, even in England, advances closer to Ticonderoga with every breath. So best I concentrate on my Kenogami for the nonce."

"Owen . . ."

"Aye, lad."

"Where is Verdmont? Is it part of Canada?"

"Nay. I am told that Verdmont is a wilderness territory betwixt New Hampshire and New York, crosslake from Ticonderoga. And 'tis a well-known assumption that it be a parcel of mountainous land inhabited by English colonists most strange and more uncivil than even the Iroquois. We were told by Intelligence that Verdmonters be a bathless and bawdy tribe of settlers that steep whiskey from corn. A drink that I am told has flavor that would poison rats. They are a thorn to the governors of both York and Hampshire, as both colonists claim the territory to be their own."

"They are savage, sir, these white Verdmonters?"

"Worse than that. 'Twas said that a New Hampshire collector of taxes ventured farther west than prudent and found himself more of a donor than a collector."

"They took his purse?"

"His purse, breeches, and hair."

McKee smiled, and so did I. And then both our faces became sober, the pair of us remembering the scalped Mercier. Each time I closed my eyes, my mind saw that mutilated head and those dead hands lashed behind him and around the log.

A musket fired!

Jumping to their feet, the *voyageurs* ran toward us in the canoes, shouting and looking over their shoulders.

"Cree?"

"*Où est Benet?*"

"Le bourgeois?"

Barely breathing, feeling my own heart pound beneath my blouse, we waited for Skinner Benet to reappear. All was quiet. A black crow circled the sky above our heads but did not bark out its harsh cry. My ears heard only the faint rush of water over pebbles that were as varied in color and hue as rock candy.

Le Brun crossed himself.

Each *voyageur* was touching his canoe, with either a wet moc or a dry hand. Close by, I observed Grosjean as he puffed away on a pipe that had burned out. His lips made a sucking noise that sounded lonely and helpless, a kitten mewing for a departed mother.

"Mercier," someone whispered.

"Benet? Êtes-vous mort?"

"Viens ici, bourgeois."

McKee had quickly rolled his maps, cased them, and cocked the other musket. Lightly he jumped over the side; his black boots splashed ashore. He had removed his red tunic and now except for the boots, was a soldier in white . . . wig, shirt, and breeches. He carried the musket easily, steadfastly; the weapon seemed at home in the hands of our Coldstreamer. At his belt rode a pistol, and his left hip carried his saber.

"Brother," said Owen, "if ill has befallen Benet, we'll *never* finish our race."

Without hesitation, McKee melted into the bush as if to tell us there were only a score of Cree or Huron behind cover and he would mince them in an instant, so that he could casually return to his precious maps without further disruption.

"Race?" I whispered to La Fleur.

The Frenchman shrugged his beefy shoulders as if to admit how difficult it was at times to understand a Britisher.

Farther away, a musket spoke again, in the same voice as the first. The same gun, as my ear (trained by Sister Elizabeth and the melodious strings of lute) told me the pitch of the second report was identical to the first. A second musket fired. McKee's? Then I heard a pistol and a chorus of other pistol fire. I counted the sharp yaps of three pistols discharging in trio. Our two against their three?

"Coureurs du bois," breathed Osier, kissing the trinket that hung about his neck.

My own hand lifted, without prompting, to touch my iron collar. Was I also property to steal and sell?

Men were shouting!

After leaping out of the canoe, splashing through the shallows with a deaf ear to the gasps of alarm from the *voyageurs,* I scrambled up the sandbank and into the thicket. So, if Owen McKee were unafraid to help Benet, I would dare to do likewise. But if my master is killed am I a free man? Ha! No question to consider now, I thought, for a dead Benet might well mean a dead McKee and a dead Abbott Coe. Breathless, I peeked up over a fallen log to look and listen, hoping I knew where to go and what to do when I arrived. Benet had outfitted me with a short-blade knife which affixed to my belt at my right hip. My hand touched its handle. Undoing the stay, I withdrew it, looking at the cloudy gray of its tarnished blade. The knife was not new. Benet had taught me how to keen its edge on a whetstone. Several times a day my thumb tested its bite, so I knew the knife was sharp.

Again I ran forward, seeing nothing, snaking along through tall ferns and weeds that afforded plenty of cover. I was almost knocked senseless when the body of a man in buckskin sprang upon me from nowhere, rode me to the earth . . . and then soundly kicked my behind.

"I almost killed you," said Benet.

Chapter 18

"A BLACK PANTHER!" I YELLED.

We were beaching our two long canoes, for only a quick rest, a pipe. As I splashed through the water, my left hand pulling the canoe's gunwale, I spotted what appeared to be a black cat. The graceful movements of the animal made me think it was a female.

La Porte laughed.

The black cat crouched above us, twenty feet or more, atop a giant gray mass of granite, a big boulder in the shape of a stout potato. Animals in the wild, I had recently learned, stared as curiously at us as we at them. She watched us with interest, the jewels of her eyes shining inner fire. Her fur was thick and rich, not really an ebon black, but a deep and lustrous brown.

"I say," said Owen, "it's a wolverine."

We asked Benet.

"No," said our *bourgeois*. "A wolverine has shaggy hair and a stubby tail. Old Hunch calls that animal a fisher."

"A fisher?"

"Aye," said Benet, "but never have I seen a fisher fish. I would call it a large weasel. This is the second time in my life that I have seen such a beast alive."

"Are they trapped?"

"Yes," Benet answered McKee, "by the Cree."

Moving much like a cat, the fisher trotted across the crest of the high rock, leaping lightly to another. She moved easily, without effort, yet continued to observe us below her.

"I can see," I told Owen, "that she is no panther."

"Her grace would indicate so. And when you hooted

153

that you had spied a panther, I looked at once, truly believing that you had."

All the pipes were lit, the *voyageurs* now puffing away contentedly. Some watched the fisher; others sat to look across the Kenogami to the far bank of dark green spruce.

Turning my head, I spotted a red squirrel scolding in a dead walnut tree. The tree was nearly naked, its gray branches scratching the sunlight, except for a cluster here and there of brown leaves.

The red squirrel ate.

He chattered again, as though complaining that there were few edibles in a dead walnut tree upon which to nibble. Again I heard the squirrel. So did the fisher. Her body flattened at the edge of the rock, hardly breathing. Only the very tip of her dark tail twitched as her snout pointed directly at the red squirrel in the dead walnut. Then I saw a black blur as the fisher left the rock, her sleek form hurling itself over fifteen feet, her paws catching a snarl of twigs at the tip of a main limb that was below the squirrel.

"What a bonnie leap," said McKee, "for an animal of that size."

The red squirrel squeaked in panic, retreating to the main trunk of the dead walnut tree, scurrying upward in hurried spirals. Below him, the fisher pursued. It was uncanny to see an animal the size of the fisher that could scramble about in a tree so swiftly. Whenever the red squirrel hopped to another branch, the fisher was close behind, leaping also and gaining.

"Run, little squirrel," I said.

The red squirrel was not only fast, but also quite wiry and well equipped with aerial tricks of his own. As he leaped, he held out a paw to a twig, reversing his direction with a dizzying loop. Several of the brown leaves were shaken loose and fell softly downward, a flight of brown swallows that had detected insects below. Never before had I any notion that a squirrel could prance about so quickly. Suddenly he jumped to another tree, claws extended outward, a tiny star of red fur suspended against the sky, until his talons touched the tips of twigs.

"Jove!" said McKee.

All of us were watching now, standing below with our

heads cocked, taking nary a step. I could hardly blink, such was my interest in the treetop scene. Whenever the fisher got within almost the reach of a paw, the red squirrel would vary his route, dropping once to a limb below, a fall of near twenty feet. Yet whether the squirrel trod on branches thick or thin, the fisher followed.

I saw a spot of black, a hole in the tree trunk, close to where the squirrel scampered. He headed for it, squealing loudly as if calling for help. But the fisher was faster. As if she had known about the hole, she darted toward it, cutting off the red squirrel's escape. Her jaws found his neck, and with one bite the chase ended.

The *voyageurs* manifested little or no reaction, merely accepting the pursuit and capture as a rightful act in the order of things. Hunters hunted and prey was pounced upon. One more hunk of red fur to be trapped.

"Damn," said McKee, "but I found myself rooting for the squirrel."

"So did I."

Benet joined us. "In all my years in Canada," he said, "never have I witnessed a gamer squirrel, or a more resolute hunter."

"Aye," agreed McKee.

"How could the mind of man ever dream so worthy a law as that which we just marked? Nay, gentlemen, no mortal mind could unfold such a treasure, nor could any of us dare to devise such a raw and rightful regulation of life," said Benet.

Never had I seen Benet bow or kneel in prayer. Not even once. But now he was praying. His way, in his words and with thoughts most personal, which he was strongly compelled to share. Standing still, we all looked at Benet as if we wanted him to continue his prayer, or his poetry.

"*Bourgeois,*" said Contois in a whisper, as though to tell himself and all of us that Skinner Benet was ours, to be bossed by and believe in. I had never heard Contois speak a word of English, yet this riverman understood Benet's every word, in full meaning. Contois spoke his one word to say that Benet was our leader because Benet was the best, the strongest, in body and soul and spirit. For without Benet, all of us in this wilderness might start to scream in panic, not unlike the cries of a cornered and captured squirrel.

Darting from the treetop, retreating from the shoreline with her meal, the fisher disappeared. For some reason we all continued to look at the tree, staring at the precise spot on a certain limb, near the trunk, where fangs had sunk into the red fur and where the brown leaves again were still.

"We go," said Skinner Benet.

"Vite! Avec vitesse. Allons!"

All of us hopped to our work, splashing into the icy Kenogami, leaping aboard to man our paddles. Each day my basswood seemed lighter, easier to work. Owen McKee and I were regulars now, even though our oaring probably produced less distance per stroke compared to those of the French *voyageurs*. Still, we paddled in cadence, apace with all our fellows, stroke for stroke.

La Fleur began to sing. One of my favorites, *La Claire Fontaine*, and the words were beginning to make sense to me, even though La Fleur sang them in French.

The lyrics of the song said that he had found a fountain where he bathed (quite unlike the La Fleur we all knew, who did not smell like the flower of his name) and remembered his sweetheart, dried himself beneath an oak tree, listening to the warble of a nightingale. But as roses in a *bouquet* ceased to bloom, so had he lost his love.

La Claire Fontaine was typical of a *voyageur* song, an empty heart and a lost love, much in tune with the rhymes of the lyric poets of England. Lonely, and heartsick, a soft white candle of love blown out by a harsh gust of fate.

Sounding equally heartbroken (not to mention as falsely bathed) as La Fleur, the other *voyageurs* chimed in with chorus after chorus. Osier even wept. I chuckled at his tears, remembering how Osier, stripped of clothing down to nearly his aching heart, had chased Fifi La Fork into the bushes, in search of perhaps more substantial joys than inhaling a *bouquet* of roses.

The song stopped, but our paddles sang on to the Kenogami, stabbing the cold water again as though we attempted to slay it, or mate with it with deep thrusts of basswood.

Renfrew then sang.

His song confessed how afraid he was of wolves: *J'ai*

trop grand'peur des loups. After two lines, a couplet, we all would chorus on "You make me laugh, you do. And never shall I leave home, my sweet, for I am so scared of wolves." More or less, that was the meaning of the chorus that we sang in French, to echo Renfrew's apprehensive tenor.

Paddling, I tried not to remember Paul Mercier, his scalping and his death by being bound to a log to drown. My eyes could still see that hairless crown. And his hands tied behind him around the log, his dead keg kicking to and fro in the eddy current. How his body had stiffened soon after.

"A race," yelled Skinner Benet. "We shall complete our race now."

"Maintenant?"

"Yes, right now. And from here to the Maiden's Crotch."

Benet's canoe slowed until ours pulled up even with his. "There are no portages between here and there. Just open water, almost level. We'll not need to pole or pull. Only to paddle. Ready?"

"Oui," said La Fleur, speaking for our canoe.

"Benet," yelled McKee, "our canoe shall wait for you at Maiden's Crotch. But how shall we know the place?"

"It will be," said Benet, "the spot where our canoe has been awaiting yours for an hour."

"Hah!" snorted McKee.

"And," added Benet, "all you need to do is ask La Fleur, who well knows every crotch on the Kenogami."

All the *voyageurs* roared, the paddles of each canoe splashing the members of the other. I had long ago given up all hope of staying dry. Life as a riverman added up to wet days and cold nights.

"Go!" hollered Benet.

Trees, points of land, hours flew by us as our paddles pulled with no more than a one-pipe respite. I wondered if Benet would now paddle, but he did not, preferring to sit in comfort at the canoe's stern, ruddering with a *gouvernail's* paddle which was a man and a half in length. And he smiled, as if to say, Mark how easily our canoe floats by the wreckless splashing of yours. Most of the splashes were created, I had to confess, by McKee's paddle and by mine. The *voyageurs* reached forward their blades with far more aptitude, tips biting into the water with gentle slaps, spurring our bark crafts with an agile speed.

"Faster," hooted Owen between strokes.

Finally, at Maiden's Crotch, we overtook Benet's canoe, our stern leading theirs by less than a paddle length. I nearly went berserk with victory, as did all our canoe's *voyageurs*. The only man who showed no surprise at our triumph was Ensign Owen McKee.

"We won!" I loudly announced.

"Naturally," said the Coldstreamer. "You did not imagine for even one wink of an eye that I would allow us to *lose*, did you?"

"British," sighed Benet.

Somewhere, in the back of my mind, I slightly suspected that our *bourgeois* had designed the finish of our race to his liking, to serve some subtle purpose of his, to further the prospering of the Hudson's Bay Company and all concerned. Benet, I had discovered, usually acted with a definite plan that would benefit every manjack of us. We were ducklings under his wing. Each *voyageur* was a chick because of his almost childlike simplicity, while Ensign McKee and Abbott Coe were strangers to Canada, to a canoe, and to the eagle's fur.

"Well done, lads," said Benet. Even though I saw little malice on his face, his black eyebrows inched closer, as the lump in his cheek shifted its position.

Maiden's Crotch appeared to suit its name. Two giant hunks of gray granite blocked the heart of the Kenogami River, the twin buttocks of rock divided by a shaft of water at the base of which a basin of rock cradled soil. Up from the wet earth a small patch of green shrubs completed the picture of the backside of some gigantic Eve who lay belly-down in her bath.

"*Manger*," said Jardin. Rubbing his stomach, he looked hungrily at Brochet's bubbling kettle, stealing a close sniff, until driven off by Monsieur Brochet's ladle. Renfrew arrived with a muddy handful of fresh-water mussels, which were added, with little ceremony, to the boiling supper. Without being asked, or threatened by Benet's ever-active moc, I foraged for firewood, bringing a load for Brochet's fire in my aching arms. Our cook smiled.

Silently we ate our meal, and hurriedly.

Little was said, because so many of us finished ourselves as we finished our race. I was not, however, too tired to down my heaping bowl of pork, peas, and one mussel that Brochet's generous spoon had provided. I returned to dip into another thick helping. Ensign McKee and I ate side by side, sitting on the dry sand, but in the company of all the *voyageurs* who manned our canoe.

Benet ate alone. Owen unrolled his maps, to mark his nightly corrections at each bend of his inked rivers.

While the Coldstreamer worked on his cartography, I worked on my feet. No longer did I wear boots, for at Henley House I had switched to a light pair of mocs that would hold less water and dry much quicker. Pulling off my mocs and stockings, I examined the pale whiteness of my water-soaked feet.

"My toenails," I said aloud.

McKee looked at my feet. "What about them?"

"The nails are so soft that they are about to fall off my toes." Pushing my feet closer to the fire, I held the position until my soles were near to roasting.

"I wonder," I said softly.

"And pray tell us, lad, your wonderings."

"If my feet will ever again be dry and warm."

Chapter 19

EVERYONE SLEPT, EXCEPT FOR BENET.

I had been asleep, but then a foot or a knee of a fellow sleeper had poked me awake. Opening my eyes, I saw Skinner Benet. With a musket across his lap, knees up, he sat staring into the fire. Being on watch during the late hours, I had noticed, was not an uncommon practice for our *bourgeois*. Apparently he needed less sleep than all of us who had paddled all day. More than paddled, raced! So he positioned himself as our self-appointed sentry. When we had been closer to Hudson's Bay, he had slept when the rest of us did. Now that we had pushed well into the interior of the wilderness, nearing French-controlled territory, the musket was always with him.

Suddenly he got to his feet. Walking without a sound, he disappeared into the forest, and did not return.

Exhausted, my eyelids again dropped. Until I heard conversation. The talking was not among the *voyageurs*, not in French, nor was it English. The mutterings seemed to be coming along the shoreline, from upriver, and whoever was talking was moving closer to our camp. I heard voices but no words.

Then I saw two indians.

I sat up, quietly, so as not to disturb my fellow paddlers. The two indians were not trying to hide, nor were they attempting to creep up on our sleeping camp. Betwixt them, they were dragging an object. As they came closer into the circle of light made by our fire, I saw that they were dragging a man, each indian tugging on a foot. Then I saw Benet. He reappeared, still toting his musket, but not holding it at the ready.

160

Quietly I rose to my feet, leaving my snarl of sound sleepers, and walked over to where Benet and the two indians bent over a soldier in a white uniform and blue cape. I saw a twisted vine around his neck and concluded that the soldier had been strangled. One of the indians pointed at me and growled some sort of grunt to his companion. Both of the indians drew their knives.

I stopped.

"Who is it?" I asked Benet. "Is he dead?"

Benet nodded. The two indians scowled darkly at me, as though I intended to rob them of their dead soldier. Benet spoke two or three words to them, in Cree, and one of the indians sheathed his blade. The other leaned down, his fingers locking into the fallen man's hair, and with a quick slash of his knife took the soldier's scalp.

I wanted to vomit. Peas and pork rushed up from my stomach, forcing me to spit out undigested bits of a soured supper.

"Keep your distance, Coe," came Benet's warning to me.

A needless warning, as I could barely move my feet, feeling as though my shanks had been pegged into the sand. I just stood, mouth open, tasting my own sour puke and staring at the bloody piece of scalp that hung from the hand of one Cree. The faces of the indians were painted with streaks of yellow and white. Both were naked from the belly up. Around their loins, layers of cured deerhide. From their knees down, the same, bound tightly to their legs by rawhide thongs. No bows, no guns; only their knives. The scalper's blade was edged with blood, which he wiped on his loincloth, and he continued to handle his knife.

Benet walked to my side.

"Coe, you must show them that you are not afraid."

"But I am, sir."

"As well you should be. Yet you must not let them read fear upon your face. I will tell them that you are merely ill, so place your hand over your stomach. Now! Pretend you are ill."

My hand went to my belly, while Benet spoke to the two in Cree. *Pretend* I am ill? Lord, I thought, I truly have little or no pretending in my task. With my other hand I pointed at the scalpless man.

"A French officer," said Benet.

"What do these men want?"

"They bring him here to sell him to us, Coe. They are merchants like you and I."

"To *sell* him?"

"Aye. The Cree have seen McKee in our midst, and they know he's British. These two polecats want to know if McKee wishes to drink the poor soul's blood. Or roast him for a feast."

Again I puked. Nothing remained in my stomach. Brochet's cookery shot from my mouth in a waterfall of waste. Torrent after torrent I heaved up until at last I could spit, and breathe. As I threw up, Benet held my head, leaning me against a tree.

The Cree muttered a question, pointing at me with his knife.

"No, he does not have smallpox," said Benet, who then repeated the answer in their tongue, or so I presumed.

Down on his knees beside the hairless French soldier, Benet began a thorough search, finding little that he wanted. But then from inside the officer's blouse he withdrew a packet of folded paper, which he at once unfolded.

"Maps," he said.

"You mean like Ensign McKee's, sir?"

"Exactly. Maps for a French army, lad, that will guide them north of Lake Superior, down the Kenogami to Henley House and perhaps even northeast to Fort Albany."

Both the Cree glowered at Benet for helping himself to what they obviously claimed as their property. Just as I was Benet's. One of the warriors grunted, the taller of the two that my mind had named Scalper. The other I would call Helper.

"What do they want, sir?" I asked.

"Rum, food, a mirror to look into and see their ugly snouts. Please ask no more questions or I'll let them eat the French soldier and make you watch."

Turning quickly, Benet walked to our pile of packets that were always piled on the riverbank between our two sleeping canoes. In a breath, he selected a pair of trinkets and one small mirror. Returning, he handed a trinket, a medallion on a small loop of twine, to Scalper and Helper. Benet kept the mirror, and began to use it in order to behold his own face. In two quick steps, Scalper approached Benet, and his hand attempted to take the mirror.

Benet yanked it away. Scalper growled. Perhaps his throat formed words to a Cree ear, but to me his voice was the snarl of a vicious dog when a bone is snatched from his jaws by an imprudent hand. He brandished his knife at Benet.

Skinner ignored him, continuing to admire his own face in a mirror no larger in circumference than a ripe apple. Benet moved the mirror, holding it so Scalper could see his own hideously painted face. Benet said words in Cree, and finally handed Scalper the mirror.

"I told the ugly turd he's handsome."

Helper came closer, also wanting to look into the mirror, but Scalper pushed him away with the tip of his knife. Helper scowled at all of us, convinced that he would not get a turn at the looking glass. Helper drew back his leg and kicked the face of the dead French soldier.

Scalper growled at Helper, as though commanding him to be still, beating his own chest to convince us that *he*, Scalper, would make all decisions regarding the fate of dead soldiers and faces in mirrors. Helper was still not convinced. Coming closer, whining in protest, he stood behind Scalper as if hoping to catch a glimpse of his own sullen visage. Scalper handed the mirror to his companion. Helper smiled broadly, laughing at his own face as he held the shiny circle in his hand.

Scalper suddenly spat at the mirror, spitting upon the image Helper was admiring of his face. This witty prank pleased Scalper so greatly that his mocs danced and his knife blade waved in the air. Helper threw the mirror against a rock, smashing it to fragments. Little shiny triangles of moonlight lay upon the dark sand.

"They are children, Coe. Remember this always when you deal with them. A Cree warrior has about as much balance to his temper as a hungry babe at midnight who yelps for a milky breast."

In a rage, Scalper began to beat and kick Helper without mercy, his fists and feet thudding upon his partner until the smaller indian sunk to his knees and elbows, covering his head with arms and hands. Using a hunk of broken mirror, Scalper ripped a long gash across Helper's back. A row of bloody beads appeared; each bead grew to form its own trickle of blood.

Helper let out a shrill cry.

Behind me, I heard the voices of a few of the *voyageurs*, while others slept in their near-undisturbed state. Returning my attention to the Cree, I saw Benet pick up the maps that had belonged to the French officer.

"Come," he told me. Benet leaned his musket against a canoe hull, away from the Cree who stayed by the dead soldier. I followed him. Benet walked to where McKee slept soundly with a white handkerchief wrapped around his palm that had been blistered by the day's canoe race. Bending low, Benet took McKee's maps from the black case. Then he walked slowly to the fire, kicked it until a flurry of sparks snaked upward, and fed both sets to the flames. British and French maps burned with the fury of their own little orange war.

"Canada," said Benet, "I do this for you, my sweet."

Helper screamed once again, louder. I saw Scalper kick him once more, and then kick the hairless head of the dead French officer. This latest barrage of bellowing awakened almost everyone, including Owen.

Ensign McKee sat up from his blanket, rubbing his face. "What is it?"

Benet's blue eyes never left the fire. He just stood, arms folded, enjoying the burning of the Frenchman's maps and McKee's as well.

"Indians?" asked McKee.

Benet did not reply. But he smiled as he watched McKee mark the empty map case, and bounce to his feet with sobering concern. He drew his saber as if by some uncanny instinct.

"My maps?" McKee called out.

Bounding to where Benet and I stood by the instantly brighter fire, McKee needed to ask no more questions. As he looked into the coals, his most urgent query was answered. His maps were half burned, blackened, unreadable, charred beyond use. Down on his knees, McKee tried to rescue what little remained.

"I burned yours," said Benet, "and his."

"The two Cree warriors killed a French officer," I told Owen. "He was carrying maps of our territory."

"Benet, you pighead." McKee was still crouched down on all fours to salvage what little he could of the scorched military maps, the French papers as well as his own.

Skinner Benet's moc shot out with intense force, a merciless kick that tumbled Owen McKee forward and across the fire. Luckily, he was not burned, as he continued to roll beyond the black corpses of smoldering branches. In an instant he bounced to his feet, saber still in hand, its curved blade pointing through the smoke and sparks at Benet's chest.

"Sir," said McKee, "defend yourself."

Benet only smiled. "My foolish lad, surely you do not intend to stand up to the *bourgeois*."

"I do, sir. That kick was your last. My belly sickens at watching you kick us all. Our paddlers, young Master Coe, and now me. I will flog you a lesson, old man, that you'll nay forget."

"Try it, sir, and you may well burn atop your maps."

McKee circled the fire. But so did Benet, keeping the flames between them. I thought that Benet would draw his knife, but his hands swung free. His fingers flew about like butterflies as if to grab the blade of McKee's saber.

"Brochet," said Benet softly.

Before I could turn to find Brochet in the half-light, I saw the quick toss of an indian tomahawk, which Benet skillfully snared with his fingers. Before I could even wink, the handle of the loop twisted about his hand, making the hatchet a sturdy extension of Benet's arm. The man and the weapon were as united as an upper leg to a lower, linked solidly, bone to bone.

Betwixt them, the fire spat in a fit of temper. McKee's saber was lifted and alert, in position to cut a quick downward slash. Benet's tomahawk hung limply, dangling, the edge of its head pointing backward and away from the fire, and McKee. I backed up a few paces, wanting to say something, wishing to see no more blood. The scalping of the dead French officer had been quite enough. The taste in my mouth became sour once more. I wanted to beg them to lay down their weaponry, until I saw the look in the eyes of both men. Benet and McKee were no longer the men I knew.

They were now Scalper and Helper.

"Best beware, Guardsman, or my tommy may spill your bowels." Benet spoke very softly.

" 'Twill not, sir. But your witless arrogance may taste the Coldstream steel."

"If you dare."

McKee charged through the fire, saber high, its blade singing a silver arc, but Benet held his ground. Stepping lightly aside at the very final chance, Benet brought up his tomahawk as his leg tripped McKee. The saber tore Benet's sleeve, but the young officer sprawled into the sand, the knuckles of his saber hand cut and bleeding.

"Get up," Benet ordered him.

McKee rose, and again charged. Benet ducked the saber, his left hand clutching the ruffles of Owen's white shirt. Falling backward, his body coiled into a serpentine ball, Benet buried his mocs in McKee's belly, tossing the Guardsman ten feet behind him. This time, before Owen could rise, Benet had straddled his back, much as he had ridden his bison. One blow of his tomahawk could have split open Owen's skull. Or chopped his spine.

Around and under McKee's neck went the hatchet, as Benet gripped the handle at each end, pulling upward, driving the handle into the front of McKee's throat, forcing his chin up from the sand. A quick upward yank would have snapped Owen's neck as easily as a twig.

"Enough?" asked Benet.

"Never," choked out McKee. "You . . . will . . . kill . . . me . . . before . . . I . . . yield."

"At your service, McKee." Benet pulled the handle tighter, and we watched Owen's face cloud to purple. Hunching his back, Owen tossed Benet off, and quickly regained his feet. McKee's saber slashed again. I saw a rip in Benet's buckskin, lined in red. Then I noticed that Benet moved the object in his mouth. His jaws became tense and hard as his teeth bit down upon it. For a breath, Benet sunk down to one knee, then rose up again.

McKee charged again. Benet was ready. But this time Owen only faked with the blade. A butt stroke scored upon Benet's ear, causing him to stagger. Beneath the black eyebrows that now knitted together, the blue eyes coldly studied their young assailant.

"Come on, Scotsman."

Benet never rushed, never charged, always waiting to counter and block and parry each thrust or jab of the saber. McKee leaped forward, his face catching a handful of sand from Benet's toss. Saber and tomahawk met and crossed and locked, high in the air, above the heads of the combatants. Quickly crossing his legs, Benet kicked at Owen's knees, a scissor motion that cut the younger man down. I saw blood on Benet's ear, more blood on his sleeve and leg.

As the saber twisted, it was freed, its metal clattering uselessly against a short rock. Up came the tomahawk.

"Die," said Benet.

Chapter 20

"No," I YELLED.

As I leaped forward, my arms locked around Benet's neck. Riding him down into the sand, I fought him for the tomahawk, my legs knotted with his. His heel whipped into my crotch, and I was ill with pain. Again he kicked, causing my mind to battle to remain conscious. My legs fought to limit his kicking, while my fingers locked into his throat. Benet's body scent was hot and stronger than a freshly skinned bear. I felt I had caught a hornet.

"You whelp," grunted Benet, "you will pay." His words wheezed through my fingers. My ears heard his voice, in my imagination, reading the terms of my bond and its punishment for a bondservant's striking a master.

"Please," I said, loosening my hold on his neck to allow him air. "I did not want . . ."

The butt end of his hatchet shot back, catching me high in the belly and just beneath the cage of my ribs. My breath went. With a quick spin of his body he broke my hold, leaped to his feet faster than a cat, and stood above me.

"Coe, you will now dearly pay. Grosjean . . . Jardin . . . bring him to me."

Turning his back to me, Benet walked toward the black curtain of forest, and stopped. Strong hands seized hold of me. I fought. But the grips of Jardin and Grosjean were too strong, too mature. They held me harder than the tongs of John Howland had taken its purchase of my iron collar. I saw McKee stagger to his feet.

"Drag him here," said Benet, "and if he kicks, beat him until he learns."

They dragged me to Benet, even though I fought Grosjean and Jardin. One of them could have handled me, for compared to them, my might was less than a kitten's.

"Flop him on his back," ordered Benet.

"*Mais pourquoi, Monsieur?*"

"Obey me," said Benet, "or else it will be *your* hand instead of Coe's."

My hand! I lay helpless, Jardin's weight holding me upon a rock bed, while Grosjean stretched my fist against the log until I believed the pain would tear my shoulder from its socket. Benet stood above me, his thumb checking the sharpness of the hatchet blade.

"No!" I screamed.

"*Your* bond, Coe. Not mine. 'Twas your hand that signed it, and your hand that struck your master."

"Please, sir, please . . ."

"And now, 'twill be your hand that gets chopped. And I will let the Cree boil it for their breakfast."

I screamed loudly.

"Hold his arm."

"*Mon Dieu,*" breathed a *voyageur*.

Again and again I cried out. I felt the roughness of the log scrape the outer side of my arm. Jardin, eyes closed, was trembling as he held me down. "*Non! Non!*" he whispered as if praying to an unconcerned God.

Benet's arm raised the hatchet.

It was then I heard La Fleur's voice, crying out in protest as he flung his own body across my arm. On my wrist, where the tomahawk blade would strike, I felt Le Fleur lay his face. His body shook with sobbing. My upturned palm felt his lips as he kissed my hand, also feeling the wetness of his tears.

"*Seul un garçon, Monsieur.*"

Benet kicked his belly, but La Fleur did not lift his head from my hand. Hard upon my wrist he pressed his ear.

"*Non!*" he pleaded with Benet. As a pleading child, La Fleur's arm gently, but with resolution, encircled Benet's leg and hung on, clinging to the knee with clawing fingers.

"Monsieur . . . Monsieur Benet . . ."

'Twas then that Benet struck the man's neck with the hatchet head. La Fleur moaned. His body slumped into darkness, leaving my arm and hand once more undefended.

"Benet! For the love of God, hold off."

"He challenged my authority," said Benet to McKee, "and like all who err so foolishly, he will suffer for it. A bond is a bond. Coe owes me a hand."

As Jardin still straddled my chest, I could not see Ensign McKee. Yet his voice, as he spoke, came closer.

"By Our Lady, sir, I beg you not cripple the lad. Reflect a moment. Had I been about to slay you, the boy would have acted as boldly in your behalf as he did in mine."

" 'Tis not your matter, Guardsman."

"Nay, it be not. But the lad inflicted neither wound nor shame upon you, sir. Should such courage be rewarded by slicing off a fist?"

"Look you, McKee. You were about to slay me over a burning map. If such be the truth, a chop of a hand is a meager penalty for his rebellion."

"No court of English law would condone such . . ."

"Tripe! 'Twas no other than English law that determined the consequence, so you may watch him pay his price."

"My horse, sir."

McKee stood close to Benet. But my master still stared down at me and upon my arm as though anxious for his tomahawk to strike away my hand.

"What about her?"

"Benet, I give her to you. Aye, my milky mare. Virtue, in exchange."

"For a hand?"

"Nay, for his collar. Free the lad and my mare is yours."

I saw Benet relax. "So this strip of a boy means that much to you?"

"Aye, he does. And to us all, if you heed the pleadings of your voyageurs."

"I may still cut him, at my pleasure."

"Do so, Benet, and you will never sleep easily between here and Fort Albany. Best your eyes ne'er close, for when they do . . ."

"You threaten me, sir?"

"Aye, most respectfully. Perhaps one day with swords or dueling pistols, if the hand be chopped. I wish you no harm, sir. But what you are about to do offends me."

"Offends you? Ha!"

"It truly does, offending all standards of justice and equity. Besides, we need Coe to work Mercier's paddle."

Benet slowly dropped the tomahawk until the blade rested heavily upon my wrist. Lightly at first, then firmly. "Coe, I demand your apology."

"Sir, you have it. As well as my loyalty."

"Free the cub."

"Bless you, Benet," said McKee.

Benet turned, just as I was allowed up by Jardin and Grosjean to regain my feet. La Fleur sat up, rubbing his neck. Looking at me, he cracked a grateful grin. Benet tossed the tomahawk to Brochet, who caught it.

"Thank you, Owen." My voice was husky, and the words caught weakly in my throat.

"We saved each other, lad. But 'twas your enterprise that acted first with little worry for your personal safety. You'd be a bonnie Coldstreamer."

His hand clapped my shoulder.

Benet had turned away from us, returning to talk to the two Cree warriors, who squatted near their dead French officer. Then he turned and summoned McKee, who joined the group. I followed along.

"What do you know of this soldier?" Benet asked McKee.

Bending down, Owen looked carefully at the officer's insignia. " 'Tis my guess, sir, that he be attached to neither artillery nor foot. And not cavalry, as I see no spur-marks on his boot."

"What then?"

"Intelligence, I believe."

"Like yourself, perhaps."

"Quite possibly my counterpart under a French flag. As to his maps that you so wantonly destroyed, how did they read?"

"Ambitiously," said Benet, "as though his charts and yours were etched by the same bloodthirsty feather."

Then, as Owen continued to search the officer's uniform for hidden pouches, the two Cree warriors jumped to their feet and yelled. Scalper and Helper both talked much to Benet.

"What do they tell us?" asked McKee.

"They are distressed," said Benet.

171

"Why?"

"Because we do not offer them enough for their corpse. They say that they should have killed *you*, McKee, to barter you to the French, who are generous."

"Is that all?"

"And they also speak of what mighty warriors they are. They want to know why you and I fought, and why our young spikehorn joined the fray."

Benet grunted words to the Cree. Scalper pointed his knife at McKee, talking much and causing Benet to laugh. He also pointed at McKee. Helper gestured at me. Benet spoke. Scalper was not pleased, however, as he tore the French scalp from his belt and threw it at McKee's feet.

"Our red friend wants to trade," said Benet.

"And you offered them Coe and myself," said McKee.

"Not quite. I never hold a grudge over a jolly good scrap. The tall one wants to know why an officer as young as you has the white hair of an old man."

"Doesn't he know I wear a wig?"

"No," said Benet, drawing his knife, "and you and I are about to shock these two muleheads out of a year's growth."

Stepping behind McKee, and then drawing his knife, Benet pretended to cut Owen's head. With his left hand, Benet grabbed the tail of Owen's white wig and yanked off the entire hairpiece.

"Scream," whispered Benet.

McKee howled as though his pain were unbearable, falling to his knees. Benet waved the white wig through the air and yelled to the stars in a most bloodcurdling warcry.

"Medicine," said Scalper, his mouth open in absolute surprise. "Medicine . . . medicine."

I was surprised that Scalper knew any English words, but then he had probably met British on this river for years, as well as French. In terror, the two Cree warriors fled, disappearing into the trees and the night. All was silent, except for the swamp bugs and frogs that continued their nocturnal notes. Benet threw back his head and howled like a wolf, allowing his whoop to become laughter.

"They say medicine," he explained, "but what they mean is *magic*. And if we meet them again, Ensign McKee, they will call you Two Hair."

Behind us, the *Voyageurs* had once more settled down. The two tangles of sleepers were knitted together once more, flanking the fire. Benet retrieved his musket, laying it down beside his bedroll, appearing to be prepared for sleep.

"What shall we do with the dead officer?" McKee asked Benet.

"Feed the ants."

I was not about to argue, seeing as I could still count on ten fingers on both of my hands. My palms still sweated in a most profuse manner, and my legs felt quite watery. I was also shocked because Benet seemed so easily to forget our fight. Now I looked at the French soldier's scalp as it lay on the ground. "Never will I again sleep," I said, "until we return to Fort Albany."

"I wish we had some rum," said McKee.

"We do," said Skinner Benet. "But best we wait until the *voyageurs* are snoring or we shall be forced to divide it into unworthy shares."

Benet left us. Kneeling down, he whispered something to La Fleur, who chuckled at the humor. With a friendly kick in La Fleur's backside, Benet partly pulled the blanket off the man and left him smiling.

We drank. Benet and McKee and myself, until all of the rum in the stowed-away dogshead had been drained.

"Tinder," said Benet very softly.

"You say tinder, sir?" asked McKee.

"Aye, because that is the substance to which we wither."

"How so?"

"Tinder is dry," Benet said, "and the least spark can ignite it into a red roar. Up here, where only fools go for the eagle's fur, strangers fear what they cannot know. But, gentlemen, I am more afraid than you, for I know where we are camped. I have seen a dead man who had been skinned, while *alive*, his body stripped to the raw purple flesh. We are an army of sorts, our two canoes. Or a navy. We must be armed, alert, and obedient. Even as I, your leader, must obey certain standards without which we could all crumble into a panic, a leaderless mob that would bolt at the chirp of a chipmunk, and become the ultimate food in a Cree's belly."

Benet sipped rum.

"I am ill at the thought, Coe, of how close I came to whacking off your hand. I fully intended to do it. No servant, no *voyageur* is to ever lay a hand to me or attack me, even in a threat. I must maintain the level of conduct or all of us will lose. Can you please understand?"

I nodded. "I think so, sir."

"Do try. And as for your precious maps, Owen, I'll not apologize for burning them, as every one you have shown me is little more than error. The only true map of Canada is rolled up snugly in your brain. Am I not correct?"

"You are, sir."

"Tell me true, Ensign McKee. Give you thought as to the consequence of your maps in French hands?"

"Why . . . no, sir."

"Think then. In your mind they are beyond stealing, are they not?"

McKee nodded. "Aye."

"We all have much to learn in this brutal wilderness, about our own tinder, and how a strike of nerve against nerve can be flint and steel to spark and inflame our tempers. We have paddled far upriver, close to the five French lakes. Closest now to Superior. And I warn you, Coldstreamer, let the French have their lakes."

"I don't agree, sir."

"No, I suppose not. But do you and your father and your General Braddock have such need of all Canada that you would put the torch to her? Listen."

We heard the choir of insects singing in the dark.

"Ensign, would you willfully exchange this solemn mass of solitude for cannon and bagpipe?"

McKee was silent. "At the moment, sir, nay, I should not."

"Would you see these forests nourished by the rotting of wounded Highlanders and Welsh and Irish lads? I will not, McKee. Not to please you or Braddock or King George. Not even for the Hudson's Bay Company. Were there only a way."

"A way to what, sir?"

"Now that we have taken Canada, torn her open, and trapped her treasure, if only we could reseal her again. Roll a mighty stone to mask the mouth of her crypt. If only we'd all leave and allow Canada to rest and lick her wounds, and return ourselves to Europe."

McKee and I were silent.

"At night," said Benet, "I smell the stench of Fort Albany and a garrison latrine, and I hear Canada scream in torment. For to me she is a maiden fair who is being raped and ravaged. Furs torn from her modesty. And somewhere, a litter of beaver kits cry hungrily for a mother who'll not return from iron jaws."

I wanted to say words, but none would come. So I waited for McKee to speak. He, too, kept the silence.

"You see," said Benet softly, "I have no sons."

He stood up. Before he walked off to his blanket, his hand lightly touched our faces. Owen's, then mine.

Chapter 21

"I smell Cree," said Benet.

A day and a half had passed since the midnight fight between Skinner Benet and Ensign McKee, the hour that tempers had flared and flirted with the tinder of our nerves. A fight forgotten.

"Pipe," said Benet, and our two canoes nosed their stems toward shore. We splashed through the shallow water, carefully beaching our crafts. Some of the *voyageurs* lit pipes; others stared upriver, pointing toward a bend in the stream and muttering. McKee and Benet cocked their muskets.

"I see nothing," I whispered to La Fleur.

"*Rien du tout.*" He shrugged.

"And I hear naught but the ripples in the Kenogami and the drum of my heart."

McKee stood close to me, squinting into the forest in all directions as though his head rode a pivot. "So our boss smells the Cree, eh? I am sure, after our last two days of paddling, that the heathens do so easily smell us."

Pipes were smoked, finished, and the gray ashes were knocked from their clay bowls. I heard pipe after pipe thumping into a *voyageur*'s palm. It was a popping noise that usually would signal us to splash aboard once more, to point our canoes upriver. But not at this pipe.

Skinner Benet sat upon a rock, a musket lying across his knees, his blue eyes watching one spot . . . the river's crook. All other heads turned in furtive gestures, trying to see everywhere in one glance. All the *voyageurs* seemed to be stealing little looks at the *bourgeois*. This respite, they all knew, was not just for a pipe. They began to unload our canoes, on command.

"Smell it," Benet told us.

With heavy sniffs and snuffs of my nostrils, I tested the air of Canada with every breath, smelling little except for my own sweat.

"Pray what do you smell?" McKee asked Benet.

"Osier."

We all tried to laugh, yet without sound, using only our mouths to force unfelt smiles. Osier faked an expression of his being offended; in jest, he pointed at Allard, who pointed at Louis. Overhead, two crows in full flight headed north and downriver, as though they were aware of certain movements that were unseen by us, and unheard. One of the crows barked a farewell.

"How do they know where we are, sir?"

Benet smiled. "They always know."

All of us stared upriver. I saw nothing. Heard nothing. Then I smelled an odor that had hit my nose before, an unpleasant, yet slightly familiar stench. A smell of death.

"Is he buffooning us?" McKee whispered to me.

"No, sir, he is not."

"How do you know?"

"Sir, I smell it also."

"Ah! So do I. Yet I do not recognize what I am smelling."

"Fur," I said. "The smell of hides and dead beaver. Like the stink of a tannery."

"And," added McKee, "perhaps a dead Frenchman or two." He spoke as if a fallen Britisher would be fragrant.

"Sir, did you really want to kill Benet?"

"No, my lad, I truly did not. But when he burned my maps and booted me in the bargain, I did intend my saber to whack him a jolly smarting."

Just as Benet pointed his musket upriver, a gesture to indicate direction as opposed to one of battle, Le Brun asked him a question: *"Sauve qui peut?"*

"Then save yourself, Le Brun. Dive into the Kenogami and swim to Fort Albany and your fat squaw."

"I see them," said McKee.

Into view they came, a dozen canoes and then more. Closer to a score, with each canoe paddled by two braves.

Shirtless, their coppery chests shiny in the noon sun, the Cree floated downriver in our direction, slowly, knowing they needed to paddle no more. Perhaps they had sensed for hours our position on the river. Or even for days. I looked for Scalper and Helper, two faces that I would always recognize and long remember. Closer, closer, the armada of Cree canoes floated toward us, their paddles trailing lazily in the almost currentless expanse of river pond above our camp.

Normand crossed himself.

Nearer they came, until I could detect the lines of orange paint on their faces. The Cree canoes swung their bows toward us, even though I saw little or no indication of ruddering, as if each canoe possessed its own compass and saw us as we saw them. Between each pair of warriors lay a pile of furs, causing all of the canoes to glide low in the water. These were not indians who begged at the door of a fort kitchen. These were the upriver Cree, the slayers. They were lean, and they appeared to be both muscular and quick.

"Coe," said Benet, "I want you to contain yourself. Do not move at all, and if you must, do so silently and slowly as possible. If a Cree stares at you, stare back, making sure you see right through him as if he were no more than a wisp of useless fog. Do you comprehend?"

"I do, sir."

"McKee . . ."

"Aye?"

"Direct your musket as I manage my own, yet make sure your piece is unfouled and ready to discharge. If one of the Cree suddenly shrieks loudly, in an earcrack scream, kill him on the spot . . . while the warcry is still in his treacherous throat."

"Kill the beggar, sir?"

"Deader than a winter hog."

The prow of the lead canoe scraped into the grit of the shoreline. Yet the two occupants did not splash over the side. Instead, they sat more still than statuary, eyeing us coldly, watching Benet most of all. I was not breathing. My heart pounded. As I had no other duties to perform, and had been warned by our *bourgeois* to hold myself stocked, I counted the canoes. Twenty-one, which meant we and our two muskets now faced forty-two Cree warriors.

In each canoe, tips of lances emerged like hostile quills, the throat of each lance festooned with white feathers. Hunting bows were slung across red shoulders. I saw the feathery tailwings of arrows. Benet raised his hand, issuing some sort of a welcoming sign to the longest, and most decorated, of the twenty-one canoes.

One of the Cree stood up, very slowly.

"Benet," he grunted.

"Benet welcomes Sick Bear, a strong warrior, father of the Cree who sleeps in snow with no blanket, and who brings more pelts than the Huron or the Algonquin." Benet then spoke words in Cree. Strangely, he used the French word for fur, *fourrure;* and *métier*, meaning to trade.

Two braves held the canoe while Sick Bear stepped from stern to bow, over a fur pile, and then leaped lightly to the shore, wetting only his left foot.

"Benet," he said again.

Sick Bear's right hand clasped Benet's inner right wrist, and all fingers grasped, held, then released. The Cree chief muttered private words that seemed to be intended for only one pair of ears. Benet's.

"Sick Bear friend," the Cree said.

"Benet friend."

The chief nodded. I saw a smile on his lips, a wide grin that unmasked rotten teeth. Sick Bear was tall, less red than many of his trbe. He was heavy. Around his neck he wore a ring of claws, while five feathers from a redtail hawk adorned the topknot of his gray hair. Bracelets of copper and brass encircled both forearms. Around his thick waist was a belt at least half a foot in width, composed of shiny white beads, below which were leggings of deerhide. He was barefoot. Both of his feet were stained with grime. Much of his exposed chest and shoulders appeared bitten by insects. His left eye was badly swollen with a stye, and he rubbed it with a cautious finger.

Sick Bear patted his stomach and said "Flour."

Benet nodded, indicating to the chief that first he wanted to look at the piles of pelts in the Cree canoes. Sick Bear shook his head, then smiled. I did not like his smile, as I read no heart in the gesture. Sick Bear smiled as Corn Brother had smiled.

"Come," said Benet, "and we will smoke. La Porte, bring our guest a pipe and tobacco, so that we may sit, and our ears may drink from the mouth of Sick Bear."

"*Too-bak*," said the chief.

"Tobacco," said Benet, "and only the best for Sick Bear, and the hottest tea."

Sick Bear nodded. "Tea good."

Benet smiled as they sat on the sand.

"Rum good good good."

"No rum."

Sick Bear scowled, looking at our canoes and supplies, as if trying to spy out a keg of rum and make out Benet as a liar.

"Three Dog want."

Benet smiled. "I hope Sick Bear tells his wife, Three Dog, that Benet will bring rum to cure her consumption on his next trip."

"*Prochain?*"

"*Oui, le voyage prochain.* My next trip."

"Gun."

"No," said Benet. "No guns for Sick Bear."

"No trade. Bad."

"Aye! Guns are bad, and Sick Bear could shoot off his foot. Boom!" Benet jumped to his feet and limped.

Sick Bear laughed. "Sugar?"

Benet nodded. "Sugar, flour, tea, and seed to plant corn and peas."

"Work." Sick Bear spat in disgust.

"Benet knows that Sick Bear is a war chief, not a farmer. Ah, but Three Dog is a woman to plant and hoe for Sick Bear."

"Woman work."

Benet nodded.

"Sick Bear sleep, drink rum. Head fly. Laugh good. Walk no good." Sick Bear launched into a long sentence in Cree which only Benet seemed to understand. The substance of the speech was dedicated to how little Sick Bear cared for farm work and how empty his belly was for spirits, mainly rum. Luckily for me, Sick Bear used many signs and gestures, his hands expressing much.

"Sick Bear is wise." As he spoke, Benet touched his temple with the tip of his finger. "A wise chief to bring home flour and tea and sugar to Three Dog so that the hungry Cree do not chop into icy ground to find sleeping toads."

"Ha!" Sick Bear pointed the stem of the pipe at Benet's chest. "Cree call him Eats-His-Horse."

"Aye," said Benet, "because when I was a *hivernant*, I ate my horse, but I shared the meat with my Cree woman. Sick Bear knows that Benet speaks true."

"French pay much for fur."

Benet did not respond. He only waited.

"French good."

"No," said Benet, shaking his head. "Sick Bear knows that it is the British who are friends to the Cree."

Sick Bear scowled and was silent.

"I will ask Sick Bear about the Cree women, his people. It is not the English who rob the Cree. No, it is the French who steal your maidens with promises." Picking up a twig, Benet snapped it with his hands, holding up the divided halves to show the chief. "This is a Frenchman's promise. Broken."

"Kapeeka?"

"Kapeeka is well and cooks much. Very fat."

"Doe?"

"She is well and grows more beautiful with each sun."

"Baby?"

"No, not yet. *J'espère.* I hope."

"Benet is sad?"

"Aye, I am sad. Sick Bear is not sad because Three Dog gave him two daughters."

"No son."

"But is Sick Bear now a grandfather?"

The Cree chief smiled, holding up three wrinkled fingers, and nodded his head three times, followed by a deep-throated grunt.

Our packs were opened for Sick Bear to inspect. Blankets, bolts of red and yellow cloth, cooking pots, mirrors and trinkets, bracelets, earrings, necklaces . . . flour, salt, sugar, tea, plus a store of apothecary tinctures and herbs. Mirrors were popular. Several disputes erupted among the Cree as to whose turn it was to admire his reflection. Sick

Bear kept the largest mirror, which had a polished walnut frame and handle, for himself. Groaning, he studied his face and the reflection of the troublesome stye. Purple and inflamed, his eye was sorely swollen by the carbuncle. Several times, Sick Bear stamped his foot in anxiety over his malady.

"Hurt," he told Benet.

Skinner nodded.

"You fix," said Sick Bear.

"I am not a doctor. Your friend Benet is only a trader and not a medicine man."

"Fix!" yelled Sick Bear.

Benet turned to McKee. "Ensign, as well as being a cartographer, are you also, I hope, a surgeon?"

McKee smiled. "No man is commissioned into the Coldstream without a basic battlefield acumen in the area of physiology."

"Can you lance his eye?"

"I have never lanced an eye before."

"Look, I don't want your history. Only your ability. Your sight is keener than mine. No doubt your hand is steadier. Lance his eye."

McKee stepped forward to approach Sick Bear, who pointed at the Coldstreamer and commented to Benet, "That soldier."

"Yes," said Benet. "Ensign Owen McKee is the chief surgeon of . . ."

"Chief surgeon of His Majesty's Coldstream Guards." With his hands, Benet made a cutting gesture to display McKee's ability to lop off a leg.

"We have no surgical equipment, sir," said McKee to Benet.

With a snort, Benet drew his hunting knife, tossing it to a surprised McKee, who caught it. "Heat the blade," said Benet.

McKee handed me his musket. Into the flames went the blade, then out again. Moving slowly, McKee approached Sick Bear and raised the tip of the knife to the chief's swollen eye.

"Cut him. Now," said Benet.

"It will hurt him some," McKee said.

"Lad, you're now committed. And if you falter, some

of these fine sons of the Kenogami are going to hurt you. They'll lop off more than your eye."

As the tip of the knife touched the stye, the throats of the Cree (all forty-one) began to chant a sullenly two-note theme that repeated itself in a slow cadence. The knife tip punctured the skin. A wee stream of yellowish-green fluid ran down the knife as far as its hilt. The chanting grew louder.

"What are they singing?" asked McKee as the knife executed a second incision.

Benet smiled. "Your death song."

Sick Bear howled in pain. One of the Cree warriors hopped forward, an arrow clutched in his hand. As he was about to thrust his arrow into Owen's throat, Benet fired his musket. The Cree warrior fell screaming, his shoulder bloodied by Benet's shot. Before the brave hit the sand, Benet had poured powder to his musket. From his mouth he released a small gray object into the muzzle, ramming it home.

Sick Bear moaned once more.

Benet's musket was now recharged, near faster than breath itself. No more Cree warriors attacked McKee. My hands were wet as I hefted the weight of the musket. My mouth was very dry. So, I thought, I finally discover what Benet has been biting on.

A musket ball.

Chapter 22

"BAD," SAID SICK BEAR.

He pointed at the knife smeared with blood and pus that McKee still held in his hand. With his other hand he held his eye, then pointed at the warrior Benet had wounded. Sick Bear appeared slightly confused.

"Eye is good," Benet told him.

"Hurt bad," said Sick Bear.

Benet nodded. "Yes, but soon the eye of Sick Bear will again see better than the white-head eagle."

Sick Bear looked rather unconvinced. As he carefully touched his eye, he kicked sand at McKee. All the Cree braves stood as if waiting for the signal from their chief to thumb out the eyes of the British soldier and feed them to the Kenogami salmon. I knew not where to aim my musket.

On the ground, the injured Cree whined and rolled, until Benet knelt over him and examined the man's wound. "He'll live. The flesh of his shoulder is torn, but there is no ball in him. I should have put the lead in his brain, but I doubt the miserable cur has one."

The wounded Cree continued to yelp until Sick Bear put an abrupt end to his yelping by hitting him with a stone. Grunting, the old chief pointed at his own eye, as if to tell the brave that it was Sick Bear's turn to wail because of intolerable pain. As the chief turned his back on the fallen man, the warrior beat the sand with his fist.

Sick Bear grunted a command to his braves. Hurriedly, they loaded all of the trade goods received from the Hudson's Bay Company into their canoes, while the *voyageurs* carefully centered pelt upon pelt into our vessels. Mink, beaver, marten, fisher, wolverine, fox, bear, wolf, and ermine. Animals by the hundreds. Benet supervised the balancing of our cargo.

Sick Bear snorted. Benet raised his right arm as the Cree chief stepped into a near-empty canoe that now floated much higher in the water.

"Farewell to my friend Sick Bear," said Benet.

"Eye hurt," said Sick Bear. "No damn rum."

One by one, each Cree canoe backed away from the shore, swinging its prow upstream. Paddling briskly, they soon were out of sight around the river bend, yet their smell stayed with us. A strong stench of poorly scraped skins coupled with the pungent body odor of forty-two Cree.

"Never," said McKee to Benet, "shall I endeavor to work the arts of surgery on a Cree chief while his nation looks nervously on. Never again, Benet. Do you hear me?"

"Aye, I hear you. Fortunately for the Coldstream Guards, the Cree did not practice a bit of surgery on you."

We pushed off.

Our two canoes nearly sunk with fur. Time came for the evening meal. The *voyageurs* grumbled almost louder than their empty stomachs, yet Benet gave no order to halt. Our paddles continued to bite the Kenogami. Hungry though I was, I wondered if I could eat or retain a meal. Please, not pork. I wanted no meat, as the stink of dead game hung about us, in our hair and clothing, a smell of death that oozed up from bundles upon which we sat. My nostrils wished to puke out the smell. I felt as if I had played a part in the slaughter of all Canada.

As I paddled, I stared at one particular pelt. A small ermine; absolute white was its fur, except for the black tip of its tail. Benet had referred to the animal earlier as a stoat, telling me that the beast was brown in late spring, summer, and fall. But the coming of winter frosted him snowy for his own protection.

"The stoat," Benet had told me, "is a brown little commoner who is knighted by the queen of winter and becomes a lord."

As my paddle continued to push the upper Kenogami behind us, I recalled how Benet had so skillfully handled his bartering with the Cree. Often he would agree, and then disagree, standing upon his ground, offering, yet allowing little to be taken from him. I wondered if the owners of the Hudson's Bay Company realized how puny our cargo would be without our boss.

So loaded, so deeply laden were our two canoes that they reminded me of a mated pair of giant otters, their furry spines nearly submerged behind their heads as they swam down the Kenogami.

"Will we," asked McKee as he paddled, "ever get this awesome cargo home to Fort Albany?"

I looked at him, for such a question was not at all typical of his nature, as he was a master and not a spoil. In his military vocabulary I was sure he had no term for "retreat." His command knew one direction. "Forward. Charge! At a gallop. Hop to it, lads. What would the Queen say, Private Coe, if *she* were to catch that speck of rust on your bayonet?"

Ensign McKee's paddle turned a more modest puddle. His scrap with Benet had dulled his edges. Not fully. Yet the difference in him was apparent to me. Benet looked upon the two of us as mere boys, and perhaps was correct. Quite possibly Owen McKee and Abbott Coe both had much to learn about indians, fur, and the wilderness called Canada.

"Supper!" called out Benet.

Our *voyageurs* groaned in relief, as did I. Ensign McKee's paddle now dragged limply in the river as though Owen lacked the gumption for yet one more hearty stroke.

"Praise the Almighty," he sighed.

Brochet busied me in the task of gathering wood for his fire, although he no longer had to ask me in words, or in gestures. An imploring lift of his brows sent me scampering along the pebbles and sand, or climbing up the bank of the deposited silt and into the bush, then staggering back to our cook with an ample armload of kindling, all dry and eager for his flint and tinder.

"*Bon,*" he said with a nod.

"*Rein du tout,*" I answered, pretending to fall down dead with fatigue.

As he built his little cooking fire, nesting the gray sticks into a star, Brochet pointed a twig at me and winked.

"Abbott . . . you *voyageur.*"

Right then, had His Majesty King George decorated my

stinking shirt with a medal, I could not have felt prouder,
nor would my heart have swelled more. I tossed Brochet a
tired salute and hoped he knew how much his calling me a
voyageur had pleased me. Far more than my ever dreaming that one day, for the Hudson's Bay Company, I might
become the *bourgeois*.

Silently we ate.

Pork! And peas and brown gravy thickened by Brochet's
hand dipping into a flour sack, his white fingers reappear-
ing in a fist, then to release the flurries of flour to help
produce what he called *la sauce*. In minutes the pot was
empty. Contois even scooped out the dregs with his hand
in order to lick his hungry thumb.

"I am grateful," said Owen as he put down his empty
bowl, "that we feast this eve on neither hides nor hair . . .
nor Cree."

"Sir, I be thankful that the Cree of Sick Bear do not
feast upon us."

"Aye. I say, what was the name of that old chief's
woman?"

"Three Dog."

Owen sighed at my answer. "Well, I presume Sick Bear
would hear the fair name of Miss Heatherlee Doon Mac-
Donald and think it equally absurd." He unwrapped the
picture of his beloved, talking to her likeness as he continued his talk to me. "Abbott, we are a precious long way
from Scotland and England, you and I."

"Aye, sir, indeed we be."

"Farther than my weary arms could ever reach, and perhaps even farther than the wren of hope can fly. Hope is a
little bird, you know. A bonnie white wren. Tiny and
tough. Resilient enough to span continents and oceans. Lo,
how I do wish my wren were a homing pigeon."

"To whisk you back to Scotland."

McKee nodded. "Aye, back home. For a touch, a kiss, a
flirting skip of her hand that dances in my hair for a turn
or two, only to flee the floor. Take me home, little wren."

"You shall make me weep, Owen."

"Then weep, lad. And be thankful for fervent feelings.
Ne'er be hangdog about an honest emotion. Many's the
midnight moment that my blue eye glistens to an unseen

silver. And I weep because God made me born a soldier, a tiny tin soldier, a wee tick in the name of Mars."

"Ah, I know you, Ensign McKee. And you could hardly be other."

"Right, my lad. Yet even a soldier packs a soul, down under his powder and ball and the polish for his saber. Buried in his kit for no officer and no foe to discover. And when he falls, they'll not even paw over it, for his soul will dodge harm on delicate and feathery wings."

McKee pulled off his boots, then placed them beneath his head as he lay back to study the stars.

"Pins," he whispered.

"Sir?"

"Somewhere in England, lad, British officers of the Coldstream gather in a war room. They stand before a map upon a wall and move a wee red pin across Canada."

"A pin, sir?"

"Aye, and that pin is Owen McKee, a star in their limitless Heaven, a distant dot. Perhaps my father's hand now moves the pin, up or down the Albany River at his will. And at this moment, I promise you that he thinks the pin as more of a cartographer than a son. Furthermore, were one of the other officers to point to the pin and ask such a highly unlikely question as who is in Canada, my pa would reply . . . 'our mapsman.' "

"Would he not say 'my son Owen'?"

"His heart would perhaps answer thus. But you do not know a Coldstreamer, laddie. He will be first a warrior and then a father."

"Which star is Mars?"

Owen pointed. "There, I believe. The planet with a crimson cast. A redcoat, according to General Braddock. There was once some gossip about changing the color of the tunic from red to blue."

"Will it soon be blue?"

"Nay, not so. Red's a proud color."

"Honestly, I doubt I would ever be a valiant soldier. Nor was it my dream. I don't think that even my enlisting in the Coldstream Guards would transform me into a soldier. Do you?"

"Soldiers are made, lad. Officers are born."

"Yes, I have heard it said, sir."

"An arrogant phrase. Yet it may not always be so. There is some talk of an academy." Owen shook his head, slowly scratching one foot with the toe of the other. "No. The talk is that we may tap America for our infantry. Continued war with France could bleed bonnie Scotland of all her sons."

"Will there be a war here in Canada?"

"Methinks yes. New France is a boil on New England's butt. We can take the Saint Lawrence away from the Frenchies, and take the great lakes as well. Father and I shall advance up the Albany River, while General Braddock goes down the Ohio, to meet somewhere at the western tip of Superior."

"Aye. You said that before."

"When we traded with Sick Bear and his two-score Cree, my lad, I calculated how close we had come to that very *rendezvous* . . . where Brigadier McKee and General Braddock will reunite at Superior."

Behind us, I heard the *voyageurs* mumbling quietly in French, a sudden swell of their voices that was spurred by some petty difference of viewpoint. Then their voices softened again, as though their discourse were about to roll up on a blanket and snore. Owen was even more still.

"What are your thoughts, sir?"

"My thoughts, lad? Well, I lie here thinking about how badly my boots stink."

Looking about for Benet, I saw him along the shoreline, squatting before his private fire. His eyes squinted into the orange and the gray. Musket crossways betwixt the thighs and chest, knees up, mocs braced into the sand. Not once had he spoken to McKee or to myself since we had grunted our burdened canoes ashore.

Owen closed his eyes.

Trying to sleep, I smelled nothing but the hounding odor of dead animals and the decaying meat that so often would cling to the inside of a pelt. Some of the skins traded to us by Sick Bear had been dry and stiffer than a stack of flat leaves. Others, however, were freshly trapped, soft and still limber with life.

"After a while," Benet had once told me, "you tell yourself that you no longer smell the death."

"But you do, sir?" I had asked him.

"Aye. My bowels are ill with the stench of slaughter. Both of my nostrils drown in it. I sink into the mire of that smell as though it is some boundless swamp from which there is no egress. Do I kill for food, Coe? Nay, I do not. Benet kills for profit, so that some pompous jackass can strut about a European court and sport his beaver or fox or mink as though he himself played the hunter."

Eyes closed, I still heard Benet's lament, his deploring of his life and trade. Was he as unwilling a servant to the Hudson's Bay Company as I am to him?

And then I dreamed of the Cree.

Chapter 23

OUR CANOES RACED.

There was no order from Skinner Benet to sprint, no prize dangled before us, no kicks or punches or harsh words from our *bourgeois*. Yet we hurried. Ensign Owen McKee apparently drew the same conclusion.

"Abbott," he said, "do you observe?"

"Sir?"

"That we all so urgently man our paddles. How well I recall Monsieur Benet's driving his reluctant oarsman *up* this very water. As though any moment they all would bolt and scream their way back to James Bay and Fort Albany."

"I was thinking the same, sir."

"Mark you how we all hustle without his bidding or his bite. Once the stem of a *voyageur*'s laden canoe is pointed downstream, he will not stop. Not even if Satan were ahead of us and astraddle of the stream."

"Aye, it's true."

"Could we travel faster even if Death pursued?"

"Worse," I said.

"Who then?"

"Sick Bear," I said, "with another stye."

McKee twitched, pretending to look wide-eyed over his shoulder to escape a following tribe of outraged Cree. He so enjoyed playing the confused clown.

Landmarks shot by us, sometimes at thrice the speed that we had slowly passed by them the first time, en route upstream. I saw logs I had seen days ago, logs like fallen soldiers, dead sentinels in the sand that seemed to be members of some strange defeated army of wood in a wilderness.

Backs like bulls, I thought as I watched Normand, Jardin, Allard, La Porte, Grosjean, and Renfrew work their paddles. Benet, I presumed, would again sit in the aft. But instead, he now stood forward of his crewsmen as the *avant*, and manned a paddle near twice my height. Benet sat only when the water was blue and still, and then always in the bow, looking for the white water that he knew lay ahead.

No stream could be more placid and then more ornery than the upper Kenogami. For miles the river would run silently as if no current existed. Then, like a sudden and unseen whip of force, the tow would suck at our hull. As we worked our way upstream, the problem was to keep inching ahead, to move. Downstream, our problem was to halt tons of cargo that rapidly was increasing its speed, urged by unmeasured tons of waterpower.

"What waits ahead, sir?" I asked Owen.

"Mud Slide is my guess. What's yours?"

"The same."

As it was our last portage upstream, Mud Slide would now become our first. It would be more than a trial to carry these bundles of hides from the upper pond to the lower. I dreaded the task.

"Maintenant, le jeu," said Osier.

The game?

"Bonne chance!" yelled Louis to Jardin.

"Aussi." Jardin pointed his paddle.

Our canoe gained speed. But ahead of us, I saw Benet's lead canoe shoot forward, becoming much like a little boy's toy boat filled with a little girl's dolls. Their canoe was caught in the current, and not even Skinner Benet could halt it. Boss of the Hudson's Bay Company he may be, I thought, but he is not the *bourgeois* of this thundering wet serpent upon whose back we now ride. The roar of the rapids ahead grew louder.

"J'espère," shouted Contois.

"God," said McKee, "that lunatic Benet can't stop!"

"Sir, can *we?*" I asked, hoping that a Coldstream Guardsman had secret sources of information.

From both shores, rocky walls pressed in upon us, forcing the narrowed river to run faster. The belly of our canoe rubbed upon a rock. The heavy cargo would help prevent the craft from buckling. Osier stood behind us, a long paddle in hand, ruddering our canoe toward the white water that hissed beneath our bow. Ahead, I saw Benet's canoe dance between big rocks in the river that were black and wet. Twin boulders cradled tufts of yellow foam where current had whipped the frenzied river into suds. And little nests of wet twigs.

Strange, but I did not remember this part of the Kenogami. As if I had never before seen it. Ah! We had by-passed it, on land, carrying our light upriver loads that I had so foolishly thought to be dreary. I realized that on our way upstream our canoes, by comparison to now, were near empty.

Thump!

Another rock rammed our hull, lifting the aft of our canoe upward, as though we rode a bucking bison, or a great whale. The water beneath boiled its anger at us, soaking us with its rage. As I tried to drag my paddle in the current to slow us down, the wood hit bottom, a solid shock that nearly tore the tool from my hands. My right thumb mashed against the gunwale, and I felt the careful stitches of Old Hunch rip at my flesh.

"We will drown," I said.

"Be steadfast, lad."

Before us, the first canoe plunged from our sight, as if some giant's hand had snatched it, to dunk it downward into a dark death. Icy water slapped my face harder than any bully. Face wet, I opened my eyes. Their canoe was gone. Gone!

"They sunk!" I hollered to Owen.

Or had they dived over the falls? I wanted to jump out and try to swim. But I am no swimmer, I thought, and could barely paddle about on the surface slower than a wet hound. So I did not jump overboard. Yet to stay in this canoe had to be suicide. As we quickly swerved, cold water poured over the side, wetting all of us and every bundle of fur.

Eagle fur. Oh, I prayed to be a golden eagle and fly to the Cree and then back to Fort Albany with a beaver in my beak. To soar over rapids lighter than a redtail hawk.

To be dry. Nay, to be soaking and cold, yet wade ashore,
my mocs splashing over pebbles that bruised the bottoms
of my feet.

Gunk!

"We are breaking," said Owen.

"No," I said. "I built her, and she is sound and strong."
Yet as I spoke, I heard the ripping of birchbark and the
splintering of ribs and thwarts.

The *voyageurs* shouted in French. I heard an oath from
Brochet that could have been as honest and fervent as any
prayer ever gasped from the lips of a terrified man. We
were in the throat of the rapids, gray rocks blurring by us.
Foam smarted my eyes. My basswood paddle lay in my
fingers, useless, trembling in my grip as though it were also
in terror.

"Gauche! Gauche!"

Osier was yelling and the other oarsmen were cursing or
praying, the canoe was cracking, and then the icy water
engulfed us, pulling at my clothes. The river roared into
my ears even though I was beneath its surface. As my
body twisted, the blade of my basswood paddle caught a
rock, causing the handle to whack my chin a healthy clout.
I was choking.

A fist had gripped my iron collar, cutting off my air.
Kicking, I struggled toward the light above the churning
surface. I heard a Frenchman scream. The cruel hand
tightened into my iron; knuckles gouged my throat. Rocks
all around me were hard and wet, too slime-covered to
offer my wet mocs any sound footing. Rope was thrown
above my head, and more rope; a length of it burned my
neck as the cords were yanked taut. Yelling, hollering, all
in French. My hand felt the canoe's edge, so I grabbed
and hung, while the swift current sucked my legs beneath
the torn hull. Loose flaps of birch cuffed my face. Splinters
from a snapped rib cut into my cheek. Full of water, my
nose burned with pain, and my lungs swallowed the misty
air, only to cough it out quickly. As my head hit a rock,
I was confused enough to see stars, and I also imagined
the horrid faces of the Cree.

"Fifi!" I heard a French voice say. *"Je voudrais y être
maintenant."*

I heard laughter.

Why, I wondered, would any of these French fools be laughing? Is to drown so amusing to these people? Are they sane? Or am I in the company of lunatics who tempt rocks and rivers and rapids, then trade jests about a fat indian woman while they are crushed in the current? With a sharp yank that nearly pulled the iron through my neck, I was jerked ashore, into a hard nest of wet rocks.

Benet released his grip on my collar.

"Coe, you are safe." His hand slapped my face very hard, the pain made me stop sputtering and breathe more slowly.

We patched her.

A fire heated our pot of pitch, and my fingers crept along each seam of our canoe while Contois did likewise for Benet's. Where needed, I carved new thwarts, new ribs, some fresh planking. We had capsized, and our leaden bales of fur now seemed almost to balance a dead ox.

"You'll do, Coe."

As I turned, my eyes met Benet's. Above me stood the man who owned me, and had been ready to cut off my hand with a tomahawk.

"Thank you, sir."

"You are now a real *voyageur*. That dive over the falls was merely your baptism. You too, Guardsman."

Ensign McKee snorted. "Nay to that, Benet. 'Twas more like our last rites."

Benet clouted his wet shoulder. We were all sopping, except for Skinner, who looked surprisingly dry. Fist around its barrel, he held his musket over his shoulder as easily as a stroller would carry a cane through a park on a sunlit Sunday afternoon. Looking at him more closely, I saw that he was actually as wet as his crew. Yet his spirit was hardly damp. Beads of water clung to the walnut stock of Benet's musket. These he wiped clear with the flat of his hand, his lean fingers caressing the polished wood, rubbing it dry. Yet only his exterior had been dunked by the white water of the Kenogami.

Instead of ourselves, and to our comfort, we looked to our bales and boats.

"Vite! Vite!"

The Frenchmen urged each other to hurry, as though

Sick Bear had changed his mind and perhaps regretted his trade with us, so that he wished to retake his fur. With *our* hair to sweeten the bargain.

Benet also worked.

Never had I seen him load or unload the cargo of our canoes. Not one bale. Yet he lifted and tugged, looking upriver as though he wondered whether or not Sick Bear pursued.

"Our *bourgeois*," Owen McKee whispered to me as he poured water from his British boot, "wears the frown of worry upon his face."

"Aye," I agreed.

"He is troubled, our old boss, and fears we may fall into the hands of highwaymen or the like."

"The Huron or the wood runners."

McKee nodded.

Together we lifted a wet bale of beaver pelts into the amidship of our canoe, making sure its weight commanded the spine of the craft's belly, so that she'd be less likely to roll and tip.

"*Manger?*"

I heard Allard inquire as to how soon we would eat. Without bothering to look at our boss, Brochet shook his head to tell Allard that hunger for survival surmounted his pains for pork and peas.

"*Maintenant? Non, non.*"

"*C'est dommage.*"

Benet gave Allard a solid kick as if to tell him that our expedition would best be served by work as opposed to whining for a supping.

"Hop to," Skinner told Allard, "or I'll send you upriver and let the Cree slice you up for Sick Bear's breakfast."

No one laughed.

"We are all hungry," said McKee.

"Aye," said Benet, his blue eyes narrowing as he stared at the Coldstreamer, "so we are. Even myself. Once I tried to catch a blacksnake."

Owen shot me a look as if to ask the relation of snake-hunting to our empty bellies.

"This old blacksnake," said Benet, "had just swallowed a mouse. And while I chased her through an open meadow where there was little shelter to abet her escape, she puked out the mouse. He squeaked once, and off he scampered. She was hungry. Yet she willfully disgorged the mouse to increase her swiftness and to insure her escape from danger."

McKee and I waited.

"She chose life before food," said Benet.

Chapter 24

"Thorn Pass," said Owen McKee.

We unloaded, reloaded, and continued our reckless race down the Kenogami. Again and again we bolted head-long over falls of white water that I was certain would smash our canoes and ourselves.

Then we patched the canoes, and ourselves, to continue. Bullhead Rock and Moon Portage and through La Gorge de la Mort, the throat of death. Our worst dunking was presented to us at Le Moulin, the mill, where the mad whirlpool whipped us in circles, sucking mocs from feet. Somehow we clung to our canoes, hanging onto paddles and to one another, screaming with cold, and thankfully laughing that we were yet alive.

"Fifi!" hollered Louis and Jardin placed his hammy hand over his heart to express his sentiment for her, or perhaps to indicate his desire for activity other than plunging into cold water.

But, as we floated past the place where Fifi La Fork's establishment had been, we saw no sign of that enormous woman, no eager smile from her wide face. The woods were quiet. Fifi and her little family of females had departed.

"Mon amour!" yelled Osier.

"Viens ici," echoed Brochet, calling to both banks of the Kenogami, getting no answer from what now appeared to be an unpopulated wilderness.

"Nulle part," muttered another of our crew, which I translated to mean nowhere.

"Our fair Fifi is gone," Owen said to me, as though

198

personally concerned about the hostess, with whom he had enjoyed no contact whatsoever.

"Why?" I asked.

"Ah, a question that we all ask, even though to pose it begs little reason here in the wilds of Canada."

I wanted to ask Skinner Benet why we saw no signs of Fifi and her friendly clan of giggling squaws. What was Benet now thinking? Were he I, I would be concerned. I smelled trouble. As if we had already returned to our home outpost on James Bay to see no Fort Albany. A smithy with no bellows, no red coals, and hearing no sharp clink of John Howland's mighty hammer. And no Doe.

The skies gradually turned gray. Rain poured down on us, making wet men and wet fur not wetter, yet the raindrops stung our faces. Many miles ago I had concluded for myself that being a *voyageur* in quest of the eagle fur was not unlike the life of a fish.

We stopped after sundown in a dark night of rain. Try as we could, we could not start a fire for Brochet. The stew we ate was thick and cold, while my bones ached for just one gulp of hot tea, so scalding that my lips and tongue would burn and my gullet would hiss with its swallowing.

"Rum?" asked McKee.

We knew there was no rum, and his question sprang more from hope than truth. Nothing was dry, so we slept beneath the two overturned canoes, our shivering bodies woven to a tangled snarl of arms, legs, snoring, and a damp odor of dirty men and dead animals that wanted to gag my throat with each breath I drew.

Benet slept alone.

Before I crept beneath our canoe, I saw him roll into his cocoon of soaking blankets, using a beaver pelt for a pillow. He lay under a low and prickly clump of juniper, his back to us, alone with his own thoughts and smelling only his own stench.

Allard coughed through the night. In the gray of morning, the mist was too thick to allow sunlight. Benet was up, heard the hacking of Allard's lungs, and prepared a potion. He mashed dried berries, a sort of wild black cherry that was very small, added sugar and honey, and forced Allard to drink. Allard shook his head and refused

the medicine until Benet beat the man with his fists.
Allard drank it. And then, for extra measure, Benet kicked
his reluctant patient more than once. Then to the surprise
of all of us, he jumped on Allard and tickled the man's ribs
until his *voyageur* begged for mercy.

Benet got up laughing. "That will rush your blood, you
stupid mule, so that perhaps you'll die of old age in the
hallowed ground of Fort Albany, with Father Joseph to
fumble his beads over your body, and to wait for your
stinking soul."

Removing his moc, Allard threw it at his *bourgeois*,
who caught it, smelled it, made a wry face, and tossed it
back. Wet as I was, I laughed. Allard, despite his maul-
ing and his medicine, also smiled.

"Today," said Benet, "we can reach the Albany Forks,
and the shelter of Henley House. So hop to it, you miserable jackasses, and we may down ourselves a hot meal
from a cook who has cleaner hands than Brochet."

We laughed. Brochet spat on his hands, wiped them
both by drawing his palms upward against his trouser
legs, showing them to Benet for inspection.

"Soap," ordered Benet.

Brochet shrugged his shoulders to say he had no soap,
but Benet pointed at one of the packs.

"Wash your hands with soap, Brochet," said Benet as
he touched his tomahawk, "or I'll cut them off."

"And that bugger would do it," whispered Owen.

"Well I know," I answered.

Thinking such a thought caused me to finger my own
wrist, the place where Benet had wanted to lop off my
hand. I looked at the *voyageurs*, who had helped cool my
boss in order to save my arm from ending in a bleeding
stump.

Brochet soaped himself.

Jardin also washed, stripping off his blouse to soap his
hairy chest. Jardin had a barrel of a body, closer to being
Billy, the buffalo, than to being a mere man. As I watched
him wash, I wondered if Jardin's bull of a brain held any
notion that he possessed twice or even thrice the strength
of Benet. But only in his back. Not his eyes. It was
Benet's blue eyes that commanded the Hudson's Bay Company at Fort Albany, and upriver, and not the kicks of

his moc. Benet was our boss because he was the best, and there was not one man in either canoe who would dare to argue.

We ate, loaded, and started downriver. In my mind I saw Henley House and Old Hunch. I wanted to talk with old Carry Back, who had taught me so much in so few hours. I missed him.

"Allons!"

Again and again we heard the same cry, from our canoe and from Benet's, which meant . . . let's go!

Benet was correct in his estimate. The landmarks told me how close we now were to Henley House. Only a matter of hours and miles. Where the current was slow we worked our paddles as if headed upstream. And where no current carried us we pulled ourselves. At such times, Benet did not man a paddle, but merely squatted in the bow, holding his musket. On we went.

"Smoke," said McKee.

The smell filled my nose just as Owen spoke, a faint smell of burning, carried to us by a north wind. As my nostrils tasted the smoke, I saw Benet's canoe increase her speed. Skinner Benet was on his feet, standing in the bow of the lead canoe, his musket in both hands held across the front of his body.

I remembered how the river had widened at Henley House, and how the water had been still, and shallow. There was little current beneath our birch hull, and she whispered over a green blanket of lily pads. I saw a wet blossom with white teeth and a yellow throat.

Benet's canoe pulled away from us, no doubt at his urging. As to our own canoe, we drifted more slowly, because we had smelled the burning and wished to approach with care, if at all.

"Avec prudence," said Osier.

"Lentement," said Normand.

Cooking smoke from a chimney can be so inviting in a wilderness. But this smoke was bitter, hostile. The smoke became thicker, blacker, and for the first time I saw its source. Curls of smoke crept out of the forest to hover above the river. Benet's canoe rounded a bend, darting between two small islands and out of sight. 'Twas then we heard their voices, all speaking as one throat, a collective gasp of horror. As we caught up to them, we saw what they saw, allowing our breaths to catch . . . and choke us.

"La Mort Rouge!"

I saw what once had been human, strung between a pair of willow trunks, stretched out tighter than a spider's web. Thongs of what appeared to be deergut pulled the arms and legs into a naked star. Even though the person was unclad, it was impossible to tell whether it had been a man or woman. Naked would not describe the corpse, as this person had no skin. I saw only raw meat, with no hide, no hair, and even no face.

My body shook.

I heard Owen moan, unable to speak his thoughts, unable even to scream. His fists clenched.

La Mort Rouge? I knew it meant the Red Death, for I had heard the *voyageurs* whisper such a phrase about the time we were nearing our meeting with Sick Bear. Whoever took the skin from this tortured soul knew that we would pass this way, en route to Henley House, and the raw body would confront us.

After leaping from his lead canoe, Benet splashed through the shallow water until his knife could hack the deergut. The stiff body fell, a rimless wagon-wheel of red that caused even Benet to turn away. I closed my eyes tightly, yet I still saw the Red Death and the faceless agony of the tortured victim.

"Go," said Benet.

Contois could not move his paddle until Benet swatted both his cheeks with extreme force. Norman hung his chin on the canoe's rim and tried to puke, rewarded only by a series of dry heaves that echoed off into Canada. Somewhere a loon answered with its lonely and foolish cry.

"I am ill," said Owen.

There was no food to gag inside my neck, only the iron ring that tightened upon my throat as if I had been secured by the hangman. Silently we followed Benet's canoe, a calf following its dam, keeping close enough so that the tips of our paddles bumped. The muscles of my throat seemed trapped betwixt internal nausea and external iron. To our left, the smoke was more dense; not quite black, a great gray shroud that was created to be a drapery for death.

EAGLE FUR

We plunged into the smoke.

Where once had been a crude cabin there now was little more than blackened timbers, burning and smoking. A black rafter fell, kicking up a fury of angry red sparks that swarmed upward into the smoke as if to attack the intruding beam. Two of our Yorkboats were burning. Then I saw another raw star of painful death, strung between a pair of spruce saplings. Buried in the scarlet flesh was a white legbone now bereft of meat as though it had been gnawed and chewed on by some heathen's hunger. Or his hatred.

Jardin crossed himself.

Had I been a member of the Catholic faith, I truly believe that my hand would have done the same, to bless myself . . . even though such an action could serve little purpose in an indian war.

"Land," ordered Benet.

We splashed ashore with Owen in the lead. He had his saber drawn and his musket clutched in his left fist. No one spoke. I positioned myself between Skinner Benet of the Hudson's Bay Company and Ensign Owen McKee of His Majesty's Coldstream Guards. The smoke made me cough, and so I fought making any noise because of my discomfort. Eyes watering, I blinked away tears that were caused not by cowardice but only by the stab of smoke. Several of the *voyageurs* also raked sleeves across their faces.

Osier held a knife, and the giant Jardin bent to lift up a melon of a rock in each fist. Crouching low, we ran along the pebbled beach toward the cover of the pines. I heard very little except a dull thump just before La Porte pitched forward. He lay still with just one foot twitching, on his belly; up from his neck I saw a weed of quivering wood. An arrow.

Grosjean screamed, high in pitch, more shrilly than I ever imagined so strong a man could scream, and more the scream of a widow than a warrior. Brochet pulled him down.

"Ahhhh!"

Le Brun also fell, landing on his side, an arrow through his chest. Wide-eyed, he looked at the feathered tail of the arrow, both his hands weakly holding its shaft. It was as though Le Brun could not believe his own dying.

"Non," he whispered.

Again and again I heard the hiss of serpents, or wasps, in the air and passing close by my own ear. Yet I knew that I heard neither snakes nor bees. Only the stingers of death.

Renfrew fell, an arrow piercing the back of his knee. What had once been his kneecap was now growing a red flower that exploded with blood, coloring his trouserleg crimson. I heard the scream of his agony as if it had originated from another planet, in some distant dream of a nightmarish occurrence that could not happen after dawn. Or could take place only in Canada.

Spilling myself to the earth, I waited for Benet to fire, but I heard no sound of gunpowder from his musket, nor from Owen's.

"Yiiiiiiiii!"

An indian screeched. No white throat could ever have squealed out such a rasping roar, enough to sour my blood. I saw Jardin's massive arm draw back and hurl a stone into the trees. Death hissed by my face.

"Keep down," Benet was yelling.

"Where are they?" Owen asked.

"Behind the arrows," Benet answered him, a reply that sounded absurd until I studied its reason. Benet's cold logic that was ever correct and more on target than any savage's arrow could ever aspire. As another hissed and bit a nearby tree trunk, Benet discharged his musket directly at the arrow's source, causing a red throat to scream.

"Kill them," I said to Benet. "Kill them all."

Benet did not answer. Instead, I saw him ram home the powder and then spit a ball into his gun's mouth. But even *his* speed was too slow. The red body hurtled from the shadows, hatchet in hand. I threw a handful of pebbles at the charging warrior, who came at us more swiftly than I thought any man could charge. Benet pushed me down, and as he did so, the warrior's lance passed through the center of my master's body. Benet stared, his mouth open and wordless. A ball of lead rolled from his lower lip as he fell.

McKee's saber sliced off the indian's head as though harvesting an apple.

Chapter 25

"TAKE THIS, ABBOTT."

Ensign McKee pulled the pistol from his belt and tossed it to me. I caught it, even though the weapon was heavier than its appearance.

"Thank you, sir."

"Can you fire it?"

"Yes, I think so."

As I cocked the hammer, I tried not to look at Skinner Benet's face. Yet I did, just as the trembling mouth fought to form a word: "Load." I could barely hear Benet's command. Few men, with a lance through the belly, could say so much.

McKee fired while I loaded. The metal barrels that Owen passed to me were hot, burning hotter with each discharge until I thought my hands would cook. The stink of gunpowder sulphur was a yellow smell that was laced with the acrid odor of saltpeter.

Osier screamed.

As he stood, I saw the red pool on his shirtfront, centered with a deeply buried arrow. Slowly he sunk to his knees.

"Hurry now, lad."

Lowering my eyes to obey McKee's order, I reloaded one of our two muskets just in time to feel Owen grab it from me and fire. Looking up, I again saw Osier. The top of his head was gone, cut off. There, beside Osier, stood a naked savage who held a bloody knife in one hand and Osier's scalp in the other. High in the air he held the scalp and screamed to the sky. Osier slowly raised his hands and covered the top of his head. Then, very slowly, he lowered his hands to stare at his own bloodied fingers. Falling forward onto his face, he lay still, and dead.

Three savages, also totally naked except for their yellow and white warpaint, burst from the scrub pines to our left. An arrow passed by us. The three charged us with tomahawks. Jardin seized one of them, bent him backward over his burly knee until I heard the crack of the indian's spine. The butt of Owen's musket shattered the jawbone of the second warrior. The third leaped on Owen's back, but before he could bury his blade, my belt encircled his neck. Eyes bulging with death, his fingers fought the leather that robbed his air. Down we tumbled. Yet I did naught to retain my balance, my only purpose being to strangle. Darker and darker, his face clouded with death, allowing me to release my belt.

One more savage charged us. Osier's slayer.

But as McKee was firing, he failed to train his aim upon the green and yellow face that screamed at us and raised a tomahawk high above my skull. Dropping the musket that I was hurriedly trying to reload, I heard it fall on a rock in a helpless clatter, leaving me with but a ramrod. As the painted face howled a piercing warcry, I whipped the steel rod with all my force, cutting him, washing the green and yellow paint into a sudden torrent of red. He was sick with pain. So again I lashed his face with the ramrod. Once more, and again, until his features were hacked into a sightless circle of pulp. As he fell, his hands dropped his weapon to cover his tortured face; he landed on his back. Pushing the tip of the steel ramrod down between his ribs, I pegged him to the earth, watching him die.

"Neatly done, my dear Abbott," said McKee.

I could say nothing. All I could do was stare at the face that I had so torn with steel.

"Reload it, lad."

Only a whisper, but I recognized the demanding tone of Skinner Benet. Even with a lance through his body, he tried to reach for the musket. Nearby I heard Owen fire and a heathen scream. Jardin ran toward us, yelling in French and pointing . . . *"Décapitez!"*

Turning, I saw a savage with a very long knife about to swing its rusty blade upon Benet's throat. In a flash of a

207

moment I noticed how Benet's shirt was torn. I could see the dark shadow where the iron of bondservice had stained his white neck. I saw the slash of the long knife, swinging to kill him in the same manner as I had whipped the ramrod. Like the animal he was, Benet ducked. As the warrior staggered forward, his leg tripped the lance through Benet's chest, causing his teeth to grind. In pain, Benet screamed a silent scream.

Owen aimed his musket, pulled the trigger, to hear only an uncharged click. Drawing his blade, Owen cut at the warrior, who was now closer than saber range.

The long knife sunk into McKee's belly.

Owen pounded the man's face with the hammer of his saber, stunning him. The warrior sank to where his throat was then laid open by the Coldstreamer's steel. McKee slew him.

"Comrade," he whispered to me.

Never had I seen a Coldstream Guardsman fall in battle. But I knew from his face that he would die. His mouth continued a gallant effort to speak, to utter out last words, and final prayers. The three of us huddled together. I watched Jardin crush a Cree skull with a musket butt and then drive both his thumbs into the gushing throat of another. Jardin's body was more like a thistle, as so many arrowheads were stuck in him. He staggered and fell.

I saw Jardin die, and then La Fleur.

There were no more screams, no more tomahawks, no arrows. I sat in a stupor, holding Benet in one arm and McKee in the other. And, because I had so little else to do, I wept.

"Owen," I said.

His eyes were open, unblinking and unafraid, more the face of an angel than a soldier, and I knew that perhaps he now heard the call of pipes from a very distant moor, piping him home.

Softly I kissed his cheek.

My hand felt the pumping of Benet's breast, a heart that would not surrender eagle fur until all pelts piled the pier of the Hudson's Bay Company. The handle of the lance pressed against my ribs, seeming to breathe as Benet breathed.

I heard him say, "Help me, Abbott."

"Aye, sir, I will."

"Pull the lance, lad."

"How shall I?"

"No . . . do not back it out."

"Forward?"

Benet nodded. "Taking that head once . . . was aplenty."

In my hands, the neck of the lance was sticky with Benet's blood. He yelled, groaned and screamed, kicked at me with a helpless moc, but I pulled the handle of the lance through him. I tore bits of Owen's white shirt to stuff Benet's wounds. The rags turned red and soggy.

I wanted to throw up.

Try though I did, I could not, producing only a spasm of gas with each dry heave of my stomach. My bowels, I truly felt, had risen into my throat. After I wiped my eyes, my fingers tugged at the iron collar, my throat starving for air.

"Abbott . . ."

"Sir?"

"McKee's dead, eh?"

I couldn't answer. Too afraid to face the stern fact of Owen's death. And now afraid to wonder if Benet would also die. Silently I watched him snake forward his hand to seek Owen's pulse. We waited.

"Dead," said Benet, releasing his fingers.

"No," I said. "Please, dear God . . ."

"Quiet yourself, Abbott, and accept it."

"Sir, I cannot." My body was shaking.

"Be thankful you're alive, boy. I loved him, too. How could any human breast refuse such a lad as Owen? But he's gone, son. God, how I wish 'twas I . . . with a silent heart, so our Coldstreamer could pack himself home and wed his bonnie belle."

Normand crawled toward us.

"*Bourgeois?*"

"Aye, come on."

"*Mon Dieu . . .*"

"How many dead, Normand?"

"La Porte, Osier, Le Brun, Jardin, La Fleur, Louis . . ." Normand's eyes glistened as he looked at Owen's silent face. "*Et notre soldat.*"

We buried them.

The trench was long enough to place them like rats in a sewer, head to toe . . . covering them with earth and pebbles and then larger stones to deny a hungry wolf's claw. The *voyageurs* who still lived were half dead with wounds, little better off than Benet.

"God rest them," said Benet, as we stood in our rags over the fresh mounds of dirt and stone. "Mercier, La Fleur, Louis, Osier, Le Brun, Jardin, La Porte, and Ensign Owen McKee of the Coldstream. We beg thee, Almighty God, take them to Heaven, for they be worthy of thy company."

The *voyageurs* wept, crossing themselves. Benet's body leaned against us, for 'twas I who supported him on one side, and Grosjean at his opposite hip. We rested Benet down on a green carpet of moss as the man was shaken.

"Abbott," he said. "Fetch the iodine from my canoe . . . and wash the wounds of the living."

"Aye, sir."

"If they object . . . kick them."

"I will, sir, if I dare."

"Do it."

I played the role of surgeon, and Grosjean was my nurse. We painted the cuts brown, and then, upon Benet's insistence, emptied the dregs of the iodine bottle into Benet's tortured belly. He cursed me: "Damn you, Coe!"

"Aye, sir, damn us all."

Brochet prepared us a meal of frogs and roots, and in the darkness we ate, and wept. Renfrew was in agony because of his shattered knee, until Contois mercifully sang him into a temporary silence.

Morning came, hot and steaming, choking us with the stench of death. Somehow we dragged away the Cree to toss their bodies into a sump hole. Henley House still smoldered, causing the heavy air to be even heavier. We still had our weapons. A pair of muskets with powder and shot, one pistol, and Owen's saber, which I retained for a keepsake.

"Abbott," said Benet, "help me up."

He was doubled with pain. Yet with my assistance, Benet limped to where Renfrew sat with his back against a dead treetrunk, grunting in agony.

"Show me your leg," panted Benet.

Bending down, and gasping in the heat with his own discomfort, Benet smelled Renfrew's knee. His face was sober as he turned to me and spoke.

"Bring a knife. Burn the blade."

Renfrew hollered. *"Non!"*

"Yes," said Benet. "I must cut off your leg."

"Pourquoi? Pourquoi?"

"Because it's rotten."

"Non."

Crossing himself, Renfrew begged in French, weeping and cursing Benet and the Cree and all of Canada, along with Fort Albany, England, his mother and father, and the Hudson's Bay Company.

"Sing," Benet told Renfrew.

Sing? I could not believe that Benet would make such an insane request. To my surprise, Renfrew sang, a song of a handsome *voyageur* on his way to Quebec to kiss his sweetheart, to wed her, and sire a score of young lads who would be far too wise to paddle a canoe in quest of fur. He sang as Benet cut.

Benet amputated Renfrew's rotting leg.

Three times he fainted from the pain as Benet had to chop the bone with a tomahawk. We stretched the skin and stitched the bleeding stump closed, using thin strips of deerhide that we tore from a discarded moc, first boiling them in Brochet's cooking pot. I buried Renfrew's leg and threw up nothing.

"Done," said Benet.

His face was ashen, his blue eyes more gray than I had ever seen them. He swore softly, looking up at the sky, and then he smiled aloud.

"Why do you laugh, sir?"

"Irony," he answered. "How the Cree could trap us to sell our hair to the beaver."

"Will we ever be home, sir?"

Benet nodded. "Abbott, we be immortal, thee and me. For I wager, my lad, that if you and I and the rest of us could endure the slaughter of yesterday, we are not yet destined to die. What think you?"

"Aye, we'll make it, sir."

"That we will."

"Was it the Cree, sir? It couldn't have been Sick Bear."

Benet narrowed his black brows. "Nay, not the Cree of Sick Bear. But 'twas Cree renegades that burned this place, and cut us down, and retreated to tongue their own cuts."

"Renegades?"

"Wood runners and scum. A scurvy bunch of cutthroats with little else on their brains except rape and rob and bout with old John Barleycorn. They are in cahoots with the French."

"Let's head for home, sir."

"Aye. Give the order."

"Me?"

"You are the *bourgeois* now. If not today, then you'll be boss dang soon. I truly wish it to be you and McKee heading home, instead of you and me. This is my last trip, Abbott."

"You jest, sir."

"Nay, I do not. 'Twill be you, my lad, who outfits the next expedition to bring back the eagle fur. As for me, I have only one more task."

"And that, sir?"

"To even the score, boy. Not for you or me, and certain not for a few bloody bales of beaver . . . but for Ensign Owen McKee."

"I don't understand."

"No, perhaps you don't. But I promise you that we'll not have to seek our foe, as 'twixt here and Fort Albany, he will scent us out. The French have his ear. He's down-river right now, to feather new arrows, and to greet us as we pass."

"Who do you mean, sir?"

Benet spat. "Seecoya."

Chapter 26

RENFREW DIED.

Less than one day downstream from Henley House, we
dug a pit in the sand of the Albany River to bury our
one-legged friend. As we covered him, his last song echoed
on my ears. All *voyageurs* sing of home, I thought, as we
pushed off in our canoe; and sadly, the one home they
so often find is deep in the wet gravel of Canada's wild.
Alas, they cannot even be dry in their grave.

We were now a force of seven: Normand, Grosjean, Allard, Contois, Brochet, Monsieur Benet, and his bondservant, Abbott Coe.

We hurried down the Albany River, all of us in one
canoe and towing the second. Benet was silent. I gave few
orders, but my *voyageurs* obeyed me. There was little to
command. We paddled in fear, constantly squinting into
the bubbles in search of boulders. We had no sturdy Yorkboats. No timber between us and the craggy current. Only
bark.

There was more room in our lead canoe now, as ghosts
take little space. Benet lay flat, lying on his back, his gray
hair resting on soft brown pelts of mink. I sat in the stern,
where a *bourgeois* should sit, with a loaded musket across
my knees.

"No one robs an empty canoe," Benet had said to us
on our way upriver. But now our two canoes were heavy
with fur. We had gone to where only the eagle could go
and endured what only *voyageurs* could endure. Far more
than soldiers or merchants, each man in our ragged little
platoon was a man of Canada. And now I truly believe

what Ensign McKee had told me about being a comrade, because I trust we would die for our fellows.

As he rode downriver head first, his mocs at my feet, Benet faintly smiled at me as though pleased at my ability to sit in the boss's seat, and rudder us home.

"Good lad," his lips said.

Then I did it to him. Drawing back my moc, I kicked Benet's foot. Not hard. Only firm enough to please him. To let him know that he was more than my master, more than my *bourgeois*.

I saw his pale hand caress a fox pelt, white fingers upon red hair, causing me to conclude ironically how alive and vibrant the fur . . . beneath the lean fingers of death. As he stroked the pelt's softness, gently to and fro, he smiled at me with two words:

"Eagle fur."

At each pipe, I changed the dressing on his wounds, the fore and aft, removing his red rags and rinsing them, to dry in the sun as they clung to the canoe's gunwale. And, once dry to a stiff and starchy pink, I rotated them again. As I knelt at the shoreline, squeezing out his dressings, I watched the purple clouds of his strength ooze from my hand and ebb away.

When we passed the place where we had seen the moose, I recalled his words to Owen, to spare the moose, to let such a beauty of a bull live wild and free, to play a part in a living Canada. Not strangely, I knew that Benet felt the same about Sick Bear, about his buffalo, and even about a certain Cree named Seecoya, his enemy.

It was Seecoya's lance, Benet had said, that I had drawn from his bleeding belly.

I wondered how he had known, as to my eye, one heathen lance or arrow appears much its follower. But then I remembered how much Skinner Benet knew; the rich storehouse of his life was hardly his lofts of eagle fur, but rather his wisdom of Canada. And his constant caring for his chicks. He was a father god and a mother hen and a nursing sister. A brother for a companion. A wise old uncle.

Sitting, with the musket across my knees, I studied his sleeping face. It was all I could do to fight the swaying of the moving canoe as she tried to rock me asleep. Doe had spoken the truth when telling me that Benet's seed was too worthy not to bear him a child.

Doe, please be pregnant.

My eyes nodded. Jerking up my chin, I forced myself awake, dipping my hand in the Albany to bathe my eyes and cheeks with cool water that would, for at least a breath or two, bathe my slumber.

Beyond the sleeping Benet, I saw Allard's broad back work his paddle. Just ahead of him and to the right sat Normand, paddling in concert with the others, with Contois, Brochet, and Grosjean up in the bow as the *avant*. My family. *Non!* My friends, my comrades, and fellow choirmembers. I will get you all home. Or most of you. Even if I must strangle every Cree from the great lakes to Hudson's Bay. You are all my charges now. What do they think of my iron collar? A bondservant for a boss?

Five years! Aye, five years of this, which means I shall *voyage* four more times to the waters of Sick Bear. "Cut him!" I heard Benet's command, ordering Owen to lance the old chief's swollen eye. Again I saw the stream of yellow pus run down McKee's blade. And I heard the hoot of Sick Bear's hurting.

My left hand stretched up to touch the top of my head, as if to reassure myself that my crown still had hair. Ah, my scalp! Still there. The takers of fur do not have the trophy of Abbott Coe's locks to festoon their lodges. Scalper and Helper have not yet sold the beef of my thigh to a hungry Huron. Or to the French for a bounty. I thought of the dead French soldier and his charts, and of Owen's maps. Destroyed. All their charts and both cartographers. Wasted in Canada. Well, my dear General Braddock, you shall march to the Ohio Fork and then westward alone, as there now be no McKee, neither an ensign nor a brigadier, to match your southern conquest with a northern one. So I say to you, General Braddock, sir, give the French their beaver.

And if I become the *bourgeois* at Fort Albany, by damn the mighty Hudson's Bay Company will not endeavor to hold all Canada in fee. How many legbones will shatter in the jaws of our traps, and how many seal pups will get their skulls punished to pulp because of our greed? How many men like Paul Mercier, and Jardin; like La Porte

and Louis and Le Brun and Osier? How many legs does
Renfrew have to give?

How many Owen McKees could sweet Scotland grow?
One, I tell you. Only one.

King George, do not ask for another Owen McKee to
swell your ranks and plant your flags. Send us no more
to cherish and then to bury. For if you have other men
like him, hold them dearly. Squander them not, Your
Majesty. You never knew Ensign Owen McKee, did you?
Somewhere, I thought, in a British war room, a hand in a
red sleeve (with lace ringing its wrist) will reach to a
map of Canada and remove a pin. Well, my lords, I buried
your pin for you. Stuck its cold body into distant dirt.

Somewhere, in my stomach's empty pit, I felt the sap
drain from my soul. I am void of sperm and spirit. Upon
either riverbank Canada blurred by me, unseen, uncon-
quered. Staring straight ahead, I saw nothing but the
smile of Ensign Owen McKee. Water brushed the bark of
our canoe, yet I heard only his laughter, and his poetry.
Closing my eyes, I saw McKee's paddle as he raced, so
determined to defeat Benet's canoe . . . so British, so
Coldstream, and so dead.

Bosh! How I do sit in this canoe, not working a paddle
but steeping myself in the bitter broth of self-pity. So
now Owen laughs no longer, nor does he ship home to
his Heatherlee Doon MacDonald. His journey ends. But
your does not finish, Abbott Coe, so best you be a *bourgeois* to your band.

Be a Benet.

"Pipe!" I barked out.

My voice sounded deeper in pitch, so that even my own
ear alerted to the command. The canoe pointed her stem
toward shore to allow us to splash our mocs over the wet
pebbles, sit in the sand, and smoke. Carrots of tobacco
were near depleted. Capsizing had lost us food and pro-
visions, much of our stores and our one luxury, a puff on
a pipe.

Benet stayed in the canoe, propped upright, to write
upon a paper.

"*Allons,*" said Brochet, deferring to me with a sly wink,
to forgive him for usurping my right to spur us back to
our paddles. I winked back. We all were eager to see the

brown stockade of Fort Albany, and home. The big fellow, Grosjean, was a bit hesitant in getting to his feet. So I gave him a friendly kick, Benet style, which made us all laugh for the first time since our massacre at Henley House.

"Vite," I said to him in French, smiling as I did so after faking a frown as though perturbed at his tardiness. Grosjean sprang at me, his big paws beneath my armpits, and held me high in the air. He scowled, and then grinned.

"Oui, Monsieur Coe le Bourgeois."

I was quite thankful Grosjean acted only in sport.

Splashing, we flopped aboard. Benet had fallen asleep and did not awaken. All paddles worked their eager cadence, and for the first time in days we sang.

"La bas!"

We all looked where Contois pointed his paddle. The high white bow of our canoe swung softly to the right, nearing a fallen log of cedar that stretched to span only a tenth of the wide riverbed. Caught on a greenless twig was a remnant of bright pink, a rag from a woman's clothing, battered and bloodstained. As if the rag had been placed there to stop us. Contois reached for it.

"Fifi," he said.

Yes! I recognized the garment. This was the explanation of why we had had no sign of Fifi La Fork when homeward bound. She and her sisters had perhaps met the same fate we had met ourselves. Contois handed the scrap of cloth to me as though expecting me to work some British miracle to resurrect Miss Fifi and her kith.

We heard a warcry!

Before us, running across a wide shallow flat where the Albany River was, in many places, little more than ankle deep, I saw the three warriors coming at us. Fleet as deer, their mocs hardly touched the water, sending tiny silver showers left and right in very rapid rhythm. The three were naked in the sun, wearing no deerhide about their loins, no bows, no arrows. Each of the trio wore mocs and carried a tomahawk.

Firing, I missed.

The range was too far, but rapidly shortening; I reached for the second musket, aimed, and waited. Allard jumped from the canoe, splashing to the near shore on our right, diving up the bank, clawing at the dirt. As he disappeared, I heard one sharp and terrified cry of alarm, and then stillness.

The three warriors charged us, running strongly through the shallow water, screeching their warcries. I read the paint on their faces before I fired the second musket. The man on the left leaped high, his body grotesquely twisting, falling face-down into the bar of brown sand.

Someone had reloaded, and again I fired. I missed. Neither of the pair slowed or fell. Normand drew his knife. Brochet's hand held a blade that would have been far more useful in a kitchen than on a battleground. I pulled the trigger of a musket that was neither cocked nor loaded. I dropped the powder tin. My fingers searched in panic for a round of lead.

They reached us. One wore horns of a buffalo.

Grosjean hurled his big body at the warrior nearest our bow. The other savage came for Benet, his tomahawk cocking against the blue sky, his open mouth screaming a vicious scream. He was Seecoya.

Swinging the butt of the musket at his face, and missing my mark, I tumbled over the gunwale. Pain shot through my arm as my elbow cracked upon a riverbed stone. My eye's corner saw the chop of the tomahawk as its edge buried into Benet's chest. I heard a sickening sound of granite crunching into human bone. Blood spurted up on Seecoya's legs. Benet's blood.

Up came the reddened tomahawk for one last blow, a final strike. Somehow I regained my feet, leaped, landing upon Seecoya's back with my gun barrel under his chin. I yanked hard. His breath croaked; his panting slowed to a husky wheeze. My arms were strong from days on a paddle, and no throat was a match for my weapon's iron. Against my chest, the bucking back of the Cree warrior was wet and steamy hot from his charge.

Lifting up my feet, I pulled both of us into the water just as I heard Grosjean cry out in pain. Water swallowed me. Seecoya's legs kicked the sand, and he fought with the ferocity of a panther. I could not breathe, my head being under; nor could he. My arms tightened, cramped, locked to the musket barrel as two oak beams. I was killing him and he knew it.

His hatchet whacked at me weakly, impeded by water and sand and death, for its blade could only sting or bruise me. He could draw no blood. But I was trapped beneath his weight.

I slew Seecoya.

Lifting my head from the mud and sand, I watched Grosjean and Normand smashing the other warrior's face, the two *voyageurs* holding rocks in both fists. The rocks were crimson red. Brochet was bleeding. Contois motionless. And then, turning to get up, I looked into a face I had seen before and nearly forgotten. His fingers held a bow as he dived at me, his big body bulling me backward into the river. As the hunting bow encircled my neck, wedging my throat helplessly into a corner to cut my air, I remembered my attacker's name.

Corn Brother.

Fat and heavy, his weight was far more than I could fight off, his mass rendering me defenseless. Stupidly I had left my musket under Seecoya's crushed throat. I had no knife, no tomahawk, no air. Corn Brother's strength was near that of a bison. Beneath his fat, this man commanded twice my might. My arms ached from my struggle to slay Seecoya. Weakly I fought. No breath. My throat cried for air, but Corn Brother's grip on the bow was severing my head from my body. The iron collar was helping him to choke me. My eyes blurred, and I grew weaker.

A loud scream!

Corn Brother's face was all terror, then expressionless, as I felt his grip relax and his bow allow me life. He twisted off me, rolling face-down into the Albany River, to color it with a great growing cloud of red water. Buried in his back was a crooked knife.

Then I saw Old Hunch.

Chapter 27

BENET LAY IN A POND OF BLOOD.

His lung was smashed, his ribs broken from one blow of Seecoya's tomahawk. Yet he was alive. Tiny mists of red drops sprayed from his mouth as he fought for one more breath. To aid his respiration, Old Hunch and I lifted him up to a half-sitting position against a bed of fur. Normand and Contois went to find Allard, and to bury him. I recognized Allard's wet scalp hooked to Corn Brother's belt. We all were battered, but no one, other than Benet, was dying.

"Ball," he said.

As I knew what Benet's request meant, I located a lead ball in the belly of our canoe, where my untrained musketry had spilled them, and gently placed the ball in his mouth. Benet bit on the lead, and smiled a very weak and soft smile, with eyes that were once again blue. With a shaking hand, he pointed to a paper inside his shirt, which Old Hunch carefully withdrew. We unfolded it. The top of the paper was entitled "WILL" and, at Benet's insistent expression, I read it aloud:

WILL

BE IT KNOWN that I, S. Benet, do hereby will, endow, and entrust my entire estate to be equally divided, share and share alike, betwixt my two heirs:

1. Doe Benet, my common-law wife and the former woman of Seecoya, a Cree warrior. She be the daughter of Kapeeka.

220

2. *Abbott Coe Benet, adopted legally as a son by me with this instrument, formerly an orphan and bondservant but now a free man and my successor in the Hudson's Bay Company of Fort Albany in Canada.*

From my estate, the sum of twenty pounds is to be paid to one John Howland, a smith and an employee of HBC, for which he will remove from the neck of my son, Abbott Coe Benet, a ring of iron which is to be then destroyed.

To my friend Father Joseph, my chess set.

At my death, soon after as it be possible to execute, my bison Billy is to be set free to roam as he likes for his evermore days.

To my ornery friend Old Hunch of Henley House, whose craftsmanship I have admired, I do hereby bequeath his latest canoe, sturdily built for the HBC and which bears his initials, poorly disguised, on the starboard gunwale.

To my VOYAGEURS, *my eternal thanks and fervent respect.*

And to Canada, my love.

S. Benet
BOURGEOIS HBC

I finished the reading of his will, my voice husky, and my eyes a blur. All I could do was take his hand, now thin and weak, holding it tenderly in my own. Slowly I yielded to the tug of his fingers, lifting my hand to his mouth. I felt his lips kiss the spot upon the inside of my wrist where his tomahawk had almost struck. Then he closed his eyes.

"Is he dead?"

Old Hunch felt his heart. "Aye."

We buried him, wept, prayed, all of us hanging onto one another for physical support and in some silent and spiritual brotherhood that needed no words to express. And we touched one another, knowing that we were all men too strong to be ashamed of our gentleness, or of sentiment. Before covering his face with dirt, I took the musket shot from his mouth, which I would keep along with Ensign McKee's saber.

Old Hunch patted my shoulder.

The six of us headed for Fort Albany, and by damn we made it, with two canoes abrim with the eagle fur, and not one toenail left on either my left foot or my right.

"Water rot," said John Howland, as he removed the iron from my neck. "They'll grow back."

"But that curse never will," I said.

"Nay," he said, smashing the iron collar with his hammer until we saw the ring's end.

Doe and I were wed, by Father Joseph, and a year later I reported her swollen belly in person to Sick Bear, who smiled a near-toothless smile and clapped me solidly upon the back. And less than a week following my second return with the eagle fur, our child was born, to us and to Canada.

Our little son, Owen Benet.

A Note About the Author

Robert Newton Peck's first novel, *A Day No Pigs Would Die*, tells of a Vermont boyhood on a family farm. Several of his historical novels are about Fort Ticonderoga: *Fawn, Hang for Treason, The King's Iron*. His home is Longwood, Florida, where he serves each February as the Director of the Rollins College Writers Conference. Peck sings in a barbershop quartet, plays ragtime piano, and is an enthusiastic speaker. His hobby is visiting schools "to turn kids on to books."

AVON ◆ THE BEST IN BESTSELLING ENTERTAINMENT